ORCAS
ILLUSION

Books by Laura Gayle

The Chameleon Chronicles:
Orcas Intrigue
Orcas Intruder
Orcas Investigation
Orcas Illusion
Orcas Intermission

Tales from the Berry Farm:
Orcas Afterlife (forthcoming)

ORCAS ILLUSION

Book 4 of
The Chameleon Chronicles

Laura Gayle

BOOK VIEW CAFE

Book View Café Publishing Cooperative

Orcas Illusion, by Laura Gayle

Cover art and design by Mark J. Ferrari
Interior design by Shannon Page

Second Edition

ISBN: 978-1-61138-996-8

BOOKVIEWCAFE

www.bookviewcafe.com
Book View Café Publishing Cooperative

To Orcas Island itself
A place both real and illusory

CHAPTER 1

Seemed like I was always moving house.

Since I'd moved to Orcas Island last November, I'd lived two—well, three—okay, technically four—different places, and now I was packing up to find new digs again.

Two of those places had only been for a night or two: the Brixton main house, my first two nights; and Jen's place, when I was recovering from my kidnapping and gunshot wound.

But now I was leaving the house I'd been in the longest: Lisa Cannon's. Which wasn't as bad as it sounds. In fact, I was actually pretty excited, because of the reason I was moving out: Lisa was coming back!

At long last, nearly four months after she'd left, she was returning to her home on Orcas, where I'd been caretaking.

Today *was* the first of April, so it might just have been an April Fool's joke—but I kind of didn't think so. The "fooling" had already gone on all winter, as Lisa had repeatedly let me know of her impending arrival, then canceled at the last minute due to more vague, unspecified complications back in Bermuda, or Seattle, or South Dakota, or wherever else all her vague, unspecified business had taken her these last few months. "I'll bring you in the loop, Cam, I promise," she'd said any number of times. "If you're going to be my assistant, you'll need to know all these things. But not right now—it's better done in person, and besides, I have to scoot!"

And she'd just kept on scooting while I went on caretaking. Taking care. Taking care of her large, fancy, yet comfortable home perched high over the rocky beach of Massacre Bay.

At first, there had been some actual caretaking to do, as I oversaw the repair of that broken water heater, and the reconstruction of a good deal of floor and part of a wall that had been damaged in the resulting flood. And of course there'd also been the repair of the garage door opener, which had mysteriously broken at the same time—all under the feeble supervision of Marie, Lisa's previous caretaker—who was now caretaking *next door*. For the Brixtons. My *old* employers.

Backstabbing, job snatching; it was a regular little Gossip Girl around here.

Marie, who had not in fact left the island after all (despite having told Lisa that she had), was continuing to suffer—or create—all kinds of dramas and emergencies over there, though things had finally settled down in the last month or so. I had more or less trained her to take over there after JoJo, that dark-hearted traitor, had vanished just as soon as he'd gotten me fired. Well, yes, I'd quit, technically, but only to have the satisfaction of doing it before Diana Brixton could fire me, because she had been *so* going to fire me, if I hadn't.

Since all that dust had settled, I had been living in this nice house, playing with my cat and raising my rabbit...and writing my play—which was done now!

I'd written the final scene a week and a half ago, then reread the whole thing, resisting the urge to tear it apart and reshape it yet again. I had to admit to myself that it was actually pretty good.

At least, I hoped so. The true test would come when Lisa read it.

Lisa, who coincidentally was now actually on a ferry, heading to the island!

Which was why I had to move again. Yes, there were plenty of bedrooms in this house, but I'd learned by now that caretakers don't live in main houses with their employers. Diana Brixton had been fairly opaque about her guesthouse before I arrived, so I'd spent a few nights trying to make myself at home in her huge McMansion before I found the appealingly cozy place Marie was currently occupying. I hadn't known that was a thing, here, the separate quarters, but Lisa had blithely assumed that I would choose one of the several guesthouses on her property. "Just look around and see where you think you might feel most comfortable," she'd told me. "It's entirely up to you."

But I'd put it off, and put it off, and put it off, rationalizing that Lisa's house needed to stay occupied—what if the water heater broke again? Or something else? Now I couldn't put it off any longer. She'd texted me from the ferry line. It was really happening this time.

She'd probably have let me stay in the big house with her, if I begged. But I didn't want to appear pathetic to my newish employer.

"Come on, James," I said to my cat—no longer a kitten, my orange beast had achieved what I at least hoped was his full height, though he was still scrawny as a stray, despite all he ate. I'd even had him tested for worms, though Marliese, the vet, assured me he was just a growing boy.

"All teenage boys are like this," she'd said, "whether human or feline."

My brother had been a relentless eating machine in his teen years, too, so she was probably right. "As long as you're sure I'm not starving him or anything," I'd said to Marliese. But I was relieved to know James was healthy. Healthy, and hyperactive, just a bundle of broomsticks covered in fur, all whiskers and legs and sharp claws, with an inquisitive nose poked into everything I tried to eat, or read, or wear. Yes, he was more and more like my brother as a teenager, though I missed my brother. How did that happen?

"Let's go figure out our new home," I said to James now as I headed to the front door.

He rose from Lisa's white sofa, stretched ostentatiously, and jumped down to follow me.

I'd walked around the property before, of course, when I'd first moved in, and once or twice after that. I'd wanted to get a sense of the scope of my responsibilities, though a crew came in to take care of mowing, edging, pruning, trimming, beating back the growth of greenery in the Pacific Northwest. And, honestly, I'd been sneaking around Lisa's property ever since I'd arrived on Orcas, one way or another. I'd even fled a kidnapper across her lot. It was nicer to explore the entire property in broad daylight, with no fear of being chased, or of accidentally erasing myself by chameleoning. It was nicer still to get *paid* to snoop around.

It took some time to explore it all. I had walked the beach just for fun. Imagine, fifty-plus yards of waterfront, all to yourself. Lisa had something like ten acres—two lots, undivided by a fence of any kind. Some of these structures still gave me the creeps. I'd escaped from one of them in the dark of night, though I still wasn't really sure which one it had been.

I was fairly sure it wasn't the biggest guesthouse. I would start there.

I headed down the path through the woods, heading away from the Brixton estate. Another point in its favor. Neither Diana herself, nor either of her eccentric offspring, had been back to Orcas Island since our falling out. Even so, I wanted to stay as far from my old digs, my old job, and my old employers as possible. Marie was welcome to them all. I still had issues with Marie, I just couldn't help it.

James and I hiked up to the big guesthouse with its own driveway down from Deer Harbor Road, and a newer path from Lisa's house. My boots squelched in the mud; it had been raining for weeks now, only clearing up long enough to gather its breath for another downpour. The Pacific North*wet* indeed.

Cats aren't supposed to like water, but the muck didn't seem to bother my cat. He'd never known anything else, had he? He darted into and out of the woods, returning at one point with a dead leaf on his nose. "James, you're such a goofball," I said, leaning down and flicking it off. He darted away again, this time up to the front steps of the guesthouse.

I should have been checking on these houses more regularly, I supposed, but the few times I had, there'd been nothing broken, or leaking, or damaged; no dangling roof gutters or raccoon break-ins; just empty houses in the woods. This one had the advantage of a nice, dry little attached one-car garage to park in, and of course the privacy of its separate driveway. Not that I really craved more privacy…honestly, I was going sort of crazy, waiting for Lisa to come back.

I pulled the set of keys out of my pocket and opened the door, wiping my boots on the mat as James ran in ahead of me, hopefully not leaving muddy little paw prints all over everything behind him. The air inside the house was clammy and cold, so I checked the thermostat. Hm, it was off. I cranked it up a bit. I could hear the electric baseboard heaters come to life, and smell the strangely comforting smell of heated dust as I explored.

It was about the same size as the Brixtons' guesthouse, though much older. It had a comfy-looking living room with a retro freestanding fireplace, a dining area with a door that led to the attached garage (with a washer and dryer against one wall, that was nice), and a kitchen with avocado green appliances. I opened the fridge, flicked some pushbuttons on the stove. The chill in one and heat from the other let me know that, yes, these relics were still fully functional. I tried to imagine cooking in here.

Hm. Not so sure.

I turned off the stove, and went down a short hallway that led to three tiny identical bedrooms, each with a double bed, and a tiny bathroom decked out in pink ceramic tiles. I walked through the house wondering, *Could I live here?* It was a little boxy, bland (except for that bathroom tile) if efficiently laid out, probably built in the 1950s. It had all the necessary comforts, down to the heavy old Revereware pots in the kitchen and stacks of clean sheets set on the foot of each bed.

But it felt like a vacation house for rent by the week, not like a home.

"Gee, spoiled much?" I muttered at myself. If I'd seen this tidy little house when I'd been fresh off the boat from Seattle, I'd have thought I'd died and gone to mid-century heaven. But I'd just spent the winter in a multi-million-dollar mansion with sweeping bay views and a dozen bedrooms, a professional-grade kitchen, and a wine cellar suitable for any five-star restaurant.

"Well, might as well look at all the options," I told James. I made sure everything was turned off, shut down and locked up, and James and I continued our exploratory mission.

I thought, as I walked, how much I'd have enjoyed looking at these with my mom. Not my birth mother, whom I avoid thinking of, but my foster mom, who'd raised me, and who wanted to fly me home for Easter. I'd made excuses. The play, Lisa's imminent return(s). But the truth was, I felt rooted to Orcas now, and oddly afraid to leave.

I'd call Mom later, though, and tell her all about whichever place I ended up.

The next few buildings were just generous storage sheds, full of yard equipment and water items. Beyond them was a building I'd been avoiding since I'd first taken over. As I said before, I'd never really seen its exterior the night I'd been locked in a room there, in the dark. But I somehow *knew*. "*I understand that one of them will have certain associations for you,*" Lisa had said, and she was right: This was it. This was the place where Sheila had held me, that awful night. The place where sheer terror had forced me to intentionally chameleon for the first time.

Now I stood there, cultivating calm. Yes, I'd been imprisoned here, but this was where I'd freed myself. In forcing myself to chameleon, I had begun to take hold of my power—literally and symbolically—and saved my own life. My friends had come to save me, too, but in the moment of truth, my ability to vanish at will had given me the critical moments I'd needed to get past the gun-wielding Sheila and out of the house.

This house.

I stood at the doorway, keys in hand, unwilling to put them in the doorknob, much less go inside.

It was a plain, unassuming building, painted a dark Pacific Northwest forest green. One of the bedroom windows was covered with plywood. I'd probably been in that one, because not a sliver of light had reached me in there. All I could remember was a dank, sour smell and absolute pitch blackness.

The skin on my arms began to prickle, the telltale sign that I might chameleon. I rubbed them vigorously, and tried to calm my thumping heart.

"No one is here," I said out loud. "This place is empty."

This had been Sheila's house, when she had been Lisa's caretaker. It was probably THE caretaker quarters; the last house had obviously been for guests. Despite the boarded-up window, this place might be nice inside.

But Lisa had told me I could choose. So I chose to leave Sheila's grubby old kidnapper-hovel undisturbed. I turned on my heel and walked away, not toward any destination, just in the direction of the water. The water was a fine place to let my brain finish disposing of that night's events, and all the baggage that came of them.

Sheila had gone from missing to dead to not dead and in custody. She was exposed and incarcerated. She was being charged with who knows what, and I doubted she could ever make the bail they'd set. She couldn't hurt me now. I was free, I was here, and I was safe.

I lifted my chin and watched the sun glint off the water through the trees. The ground was higher here, and I realized that I was still on sort of a trail, though I couldn't really see where it led to through the trees.

James, of course, dashed ahead, losing himself around a corner. I'd pretty much stopped worrying about him in the woods. But exploring was my job this morning, right? So I followed along behind him, turning the corner myself, and stopped, surprised to discover a tiny A-frame cottage I had never known about. Just a boathouse, maybe? But no, boathouses weren't perched at the top of a cliff a hundred feet above the water. And they were not nearly this cute.

I walked closer, wondering how I hadn't known this was here. I was still on Lisa's property, wasn't I? Yes, of course I was; in fact I'd turned a bit closer to her house when I'd started heading for the water. So this was definitely hers.

I walked up to it, keys in hand—and yes, one of the keys I'd never used was labeled "cottage". I tried it in the ornate, clearly hand-carved wooden door, and it worked.

"This is it," I whispered, as the door swung open to the most adorable space I'd ever seen.

It was tiny, but seemed more than sufficient. Just one room, the back wall of which was a kitchen. The front wall was a kaleidoscope of windows of various sizes, even a few stained-glass ones, arranged in no discernible order. Deeper inside, a table and three wooden chairs sat under a sweet little window by the fridge; a loveseat and comfy chair were arranged by a wood-burning stove just inside the door closest to me. A ladder led to a sleeping loft at the back, above the kitchenette.

"Miaow?" James asked, looking up at me.

"You betcha, kid," I told him, and stepped into our new home.

❧

The breakers had been turned off. I switched them on and soon ascertained that everything was in working order—tiny stove, narrow fridge, charming lights. A generous stack of firewood sat on the porch beside the front door, complete with cedar kindling and even a pile of old newspapers, all dry under the deep overhang. I was tempted to light a fire, but thought I probably shouldn't until I was ready to stay here and tend it. Who knew when the stovepipe had last been cleaned? Fortunately, there was also a tiny electric wall heater, which made the small space cozy within a few minutes.

I climbed the ladder to the loft. The triangular roof's apex left just enough room for the bed—a mattress and box spring set directly on the floor. The mattress label said McRoskey. I didn't recognize the brand, but it felt very nice when I sat down on it. Behind me, James sneezed; I hadn't even heard him climb the ladder. Or even realized cats could climb ladders.

"What do you think, dude?" I asked him.

He jumped up onto the bed, turned around three times, then lay down and started purring.

"I guess we're home."

I climbed back down and found a small closet under the ladder. There were folded sheets, down comforters and pillows, plus kitchen towels and—oh, bath towels.

So…where was the bathroom?

I felt my heart sink. This was the most adorable little dwelling I'd ever seen in my entire life, but if I had to use an outhouse…

Then another little door caught my eye, snuck in on the other side of the fridge from the ladder. I opened it and—sure enough! The bathroom was ship-small, an add-on behind the main structure, but it had everything I needed. I breathed a sigh of relief, but before I could check to see if the water was on, my phone chimed with a text. I pulled it out of my pocket, and found a message from Lisa: *Docking now! See you in 15 minutes.*

Yikes, I'd taken longer than I'd thought. I started to close the phone and head back to the main house, then glanced back at the screen in disbelief.

Four bars??

I'd changed service providers after asking my local friends how they always had reception when I didn't, yet mine still hadn't improved that much.

But this sweet little cabin on the point had robust cell service! Yep, this was the place. I took a quick 360-degree view of it with my phone to send to my mom, so she'd know where I was going to be staying—which I'd have to send later.

Lisa was almost home!

"James? You staying?" I called up to him. I could see only a flick of orange tail over the loft rail in reply. "All right," I said. "Don't pee on my new bed." I wondered if I should leave the door ajar for him, but I didn't want to lose all the heat just getting established. He'd be good; he hadn't had an accident in the house since we'd moved to the Cannon estate.

I wrote Lisa a quick reply—*Great!*—as I headed back through the woods to her house. The tiny cottage was even closer than I'd realized; I'd taken a circuitous route to get here. This was just so perfect. I could be right nearby but also completely private. Lisa would never know I was here either, until she needed me.

I would have wondered why Sheila hadn't lived in this sweet little cottage—but of course weird, gruff, spooky Sheila would have chosen the weird, gruff, spooky house.

After rounding the corner of Lisa's house, I paused to punch in the code on the keypad to reassure myself that the garage door still opened and closed as it should, then headed on to her house. Just inside the front door was the neat stack of things I'd gathered up before going house hunting. Everything I owned was in this pile. Except for Master Bun, of course, still ensconced in his hutch on the back deck. I would have to figure out where to put that...soon. Was there time to carry a load of my stuff over to the cottage before Lisa arrived? Probably not, so I set it where Lisa wouldn't trip over it on her way in.

I stood in the entryway, looking left into the kitchen and then down the few steps into the living room, trying to see the place through her eyes. I'd kept it tidy while I'd lived here, of course, and had done a deeper cleaning-and-straightening each time she'd told me she was coming back—it was all in good shape. Still, I bounced on my heels a bit, nervous.

This would be the first time I'd seen Lisa since she'd changed my life so utterly last December. That had all happened so fast. What if she changed her mind? What if she got here and decided I hadn't done the job well enough to merit the ridiculous salary she'd kept sending into my account since then?

Stop it, Cam, I told myself. *Everything's fine, and you like Lisa, and she likes you, and stop making problems where there aren't any.*

It wasn't easy. I was so familiar with problems, it was hard to get used to their absence.

I was still wandering from room to room checking things when I heard the rumble of the garage door. My heart sped up, and my skin began to tingle. *No you don't*, I told myself fiercely, rubbing my arms to soothe them. *This is Lisa, and everything is* fine. I had clearly become too much of a hermit if even Lisa's return alarmed me this badly. I shrugged my shoulders hard, pasted a brave smile on my face, and stepped out the front door to greet her.

I didn't recognize the car pulling into her garage—tiny and blue, with a hard top that looked like it would be removable—but whatever anxiety I'd been feeling vanished as Lisa stepped out of it like a familiar breath of longed-for fresh air. My skin settled right down as Lisa brushed her perfectly tousled hair out of her eyes and gave me her warm smile.

"Cam! Oh, it is so good to see you."

"You too! Do you need, um, help with anything?" If she had luggage or supplies in that wee little car, I had no idea where they were stashed.

She laughed, gentle and tinkling. I had missed that laugh! It gave me a happy pang to hear it. "No, dear, I keep what I need in the house so I never have to pack much." She followed my gaze to the car. "Do you like it? I thought I needed a treat after everything I've been through. It'll be fun when the weather gets warm."

"It's adorable!"

"If you're very good, I might even let you drive it."

Oh yes, I would be very good. My sad little Honda looked even sadder, parked in the wide spot beside the garage. Who had ever thought a car should be beige?

And I'd apparently become a car snob as well as a wine snob and a house snob. Lisa Cannon was ruining me. I followed as she walked into the house with a small bag over one shoulder, not much bigger than a purse: apparently the extent of what she needed to bring with her when *she* moved house. An even smaller pile than mine.

"Oh Cam, it looks marvelous in here," she exclaimed, stepping down into the living room and looking around. "I don't see any water damage, or smell any mold."

I nodded, feeling proud as I followed her down. "That was all your contractor," I assured her. "He said things weren't wet long enough for mold to set in."

"In this climate, that's like a magic trick," she said, smiling. "Especially in mid-winter." She stepped into the hallway, pausing before the closet that held the new water heater. "The carpet matches perfectly."

"Yeah. They had it woven to match." I'd learned so much about carpet while getting this restored; enough to know we walked around here on a fortune of wool.

"Ah, I've missed this room," she said, heading into her bedroom. It was large, and spectacularly furnished; I'd been tempted to sleep there, but, like Marie, had found it too...Lisa. I'd chosen a nondescript guest room, now restored to its former pristine state.

Lisa swept back out again, leaving her shoulder bag. "Well! It's early for a glass of wine, but it's what I like to do whenever I get here. Want to join me?"

I grinned at her. "You're the boss, boss."

CHAPTER 2

Sipping one of her magical vintages and bathed in mid-afternoon sun slanting through her picture windows, I felt at peace. Because hadn't this been the highlight of my early days on this island? Sitting here with her, in this magnificent, modern home, drinking the best wine I'd ever tasted, and having someone so kind, successful, and wise listen to me as if whatever I had to say was worth listening to? Lisa was kind of my hero.

I had other friends here, of course. And I adored them. But I'd been working so diligently on the play that I hadn't seen them much over the winter.

"I am so looking forward to reading your play, Cam," Lisa said, as if reading my mind.

My heart fluttered a little. My deepest fears and highest hopes were all tied up in this play. What if she didn't like it? I'd reluctantly offered to email it to her a few days ago, when I was finally maybe almost pretty sure I was done. But then she'd told me she was really, truly, for real this time, coming back, and that she wouldn't have a moment to read before getting here. She added that she would want me nearby in case she had questions or thoughts while she read.

That part still made me nervous.

I buried my nerves under another sip. She would either like it or she wouldn't; I'd done the best I could, and now it was out of my hands. "So!" I said, desperate for a change of subject. "I think I want to live in that cute tiny house looking over the water."

She looked puzzled for a second. "Oh! The A-frame." She smiled at me over her own glass. "It's one of my favorite places on the property. But Cam, it's *so* tiny. I added on the bathroom, but I've always thought of it more as a creative retreat, not an actual place to live. If you need the bathroom at night, you'll have to climb down that ladder."

"But it's a great ladder," I said. "It's perfect."

She sighed, still smiling. "I had such visions for this place when I first bought it and started the build-out. I'd imagined that A-frame as my painting studio, or a writer's den. I haven't picked up a paintbrush in ages. I haven't ever really used the place for anything."

"I love it," I blurted. "And so does my cat—he's there now, in fact. If it's okay with you, maybe I should get my stuff over there and make sure he doesn't need to go out or anything."

She waved a delicate hand at me. "I'm sure he'll be fine. Cats can walk through walls, if they need to, you know."

My eyes widened. I'd accused James of that very thing, more than once.

Her smile deepened. "You're sure you'll be comfortable in so small a place?"

"It's more space than I had in Seattle." And all mine this time, not shared with Kevin—who *still* hadn't left Orcas Island… though neither Jen nor I were giving him the time of day. "And it's adorable," I added. "I can't believe I didn't know it was there until today." Oops—should a caretaker have admitted that?

She was still smiling. "All right, but feel free to change your mind after you've tried it for a while."

"Okay." I set my empty glass on the coffee table. "So I should take my stuff over there, and let you get settled." And check on my foolish cat, whether he could walk through walls or not.

Lisa raised an elegant eyebrow. "You found how to turn on the power?"

"Yep, all good." I'd just need to get some groceries.

"Shall we have dinner in town together?" Lisa asked. "Maybe New Leaf?"

"Oh, I'd love to."

"Perfect! Come by around six," said Lisa. "I'll drive."

The New Leaf was yet another restaurant that had been beyond my means…before Lisa's generosity had changed things. Now, thanks to my new salary, I'd been able to treat Jen to dinner there several times. Jen Darling, my dearest friend, who seemed to know everyone on this island, including the servers and kitchen staff at New Leaf, so that things we didn't order and which weren't on the menu had arrived anyway, and when the bill came, half the food we did order, and all our drinks, were mysteriously missing from the tally. That Jen.

Of course, that Jen *had* also hooked up with Kevin and vanished on me during those dark days last winter…which only proved she was human, I guess. Nobody could be perfect, but she was pretty darn close. She'd figured out her mistake about a billion times quicker than I did, as far as that went. I could hardly judge. It had taken Jen a few weeks to get up the resolve to come set all that right with me.

I wasn't sure I'd ever seen her so sheepish before—or since—as she was the night she'd come over to Lisa's big house with a bottle of Dry Fly Three-Year and two tumblers. I'll never forget that conversation. It was that night when I'd really known for sure that Jen and I weren't just going to be a passing friendship.

She'd knocked on Lisa's door. She'd looked almost stern, standing there with the Dry-Fly and her tumblers. "There's glasses here," I'd awkwardly blurted as I let her in, unsure what this was all about, exactly.

"Nope, it's gotta be done this way," she'd said, as I pulled the door tightly shut behind her before the freezing blustery wind followed her in and sucked all the heat out of that big ole house. She marched down to the sunken living room and plunked both bottle and glasses onto the coffee table. "Pull up a seat," she said, "and get ready."

I did as she commanded. I'm not completely stupid. This was going to be an excruciating conversation, and I was glad to be directed through it.

"I don't have to explain to you the attractions of the man," she began, bluntly.

"Nope," I said, taking a big swig of the whiskey. It was good, though I was no expert. Even so, that gulp was too big. I felt the heat burn all the way down my gullet and into my stomach.

"Good, that'll save time." But she stopped then, taking a swig of her own amber liquid, then staring into the glass as though it held the keys to every problem she'd come here to fix. Finally, she looked up at me. "How did you stay with him for, two years?"

I started to answer—it had been closer to a year and a half—but she held up a hand.

"Never mind, I don't actually want to know." She took another swallow. "I thought I was ready to do this."

"We don't have to do it now," I said, though I was dying to hear the story. "Or anytime. Jen, I'm just—"

"No, we do have to, and it does have to be now." One more gulp and she set her nearly empty tumbler down. "I just don't know how a man who knows so much about *some* things can be such an idiot about *other* things."

She fell silent again, until I said, "Food and love are very different sets of knowledge."

"Yeah." She laughed, without humor, and glanced at the bottle, then seemed to come to some decision. "He made the same proposal to me that he did to you."

I felt my mouth drop open. "He asked you to *marry* him?"

She snorted. "No, of course not. I mean the rest of it. He wanted me to travel with him in that Intruder, and support his mobile food-truck-Instagram lifestyle or whatever—said with my friendly openness, I could handle all the social media and the customer interface, while he developed the recipes and did the cooking. Scoffed at the idea of letting me cook too—even though I have plenty of my own recipes."

"So all the work of running the business and all *his* social media would be *your* job, while he farted around and did the fun stuff? Typical Kevin."

"Not that I don't have experience working three jobs at once," she said, polishing off the last bit in her tumbler, "but yeah, that was the gist of it. And I don't even do social media," she added, with a grimace. "I live on a freakin' *island*. I know people in person. That's kind of the point. But he was sure I'd pick it up, and that I would, and this is a quote, here, 'handle the customer-facing aspects of the business' better than he would." She eyed the bottle again. "He even suggested that I wear…um, 'more fun' clothes, that we could build our brand better that way…"

I blew out a breath of frustration, outraged on my friend's behalf. "Jerk."

"Right? I said no to all of it, of course. I told him my home is here, that I have no intention of leaving the island, that I thought it was great that he had a dream, but it wasn't my dream, so, let's just enjoy what we had here, and if he needed to leave, I'd be sad to see him go but I would understand."

"Good for you."

"Yeah." She poured a little more whiskey into her glass, taking a smaller sip this time. "He was super cool about that, and said that was fine, and that winter wasn't a great time to drive across the country anyway, so he was happy to stay here."

I nodded, waiting for the other shoe to fall—because with Kevin there had *always* been another shoe.

"Then he…well, never mind that part." She blushed. I didn't ask. "But he just wouldn't let it go. He kept…hinting. Poking.

Talking about other lifestyle bloggers, other Grub Network shows, how much So-and-So had made, new recipes that we could try if we only had access to regional ingredients found nowhere near here..."

I rolled my eyes. "Yeah. I know just what you're talking about."

"Like I was going to somehow not figure out that he was trying to sneak up on me, or—I don't know, half the time it was like he actually pretended I'd agreed. I mean, I'm sure he thought he'd wear me down, talk me into it, but he acted like that had already happened. That the decision had already been made, and I just hadn't realized it yet."

"Very familiar."

"But that wasn't even the worst part. It was the negging."

"Negging?" I'd heard the term, but couldn't relate it to Kevin.

"He just kept, ever-so-subtly, tearing down Orcas Island. And, by extension, me, and everyone I love. It wasn't even overt patronizing—he wouldn't say mean things directly, exactly—just, his attitude, hon. It's insufferable! Nonstop gaslighting; that's what he does."

I nodded again. I'd loved the man, but he'd been very, very good at making me feel very, very small. Of course, I'd been frightened of the world back then, when I imagined I loved him. There'd been security in letting him be bigger and stronger than me. Small had been what I understood. But I had changed since then. I didn't want to be small anymore. And I couldn't imagine Jen Darling had ever wanted to be small in her life.

"It finally all broke for real when he started negging you." She polished off her second glass of whiskey and held the empty glass out to me. I refilled hers and mine as well.

"Me?" I asked, meeting her eye. "It's okay, you can tell me."

She shook her head. "Oh, don't worry, I'm telling you. I just... it still makes my blood boil. To think of you spending so long with that man."

"I...hadn't had much relationship success before him," I said, trying to put it nicely.

"Better alone than with someone who doesn't respect you."

I raised my glass to that.

"Anyway," she went on, "he tried to make out as how he'd done you this giant favor, teaching you so much about how the world works, and taking care of you, and introducing you to all his friends, and—"

"What!" I cried. "I hated his stupid, pretentious hipster friends. I always felt like the outsider around them, even in my own home; and I'm pretty sure that's what Kevin wanted. Not a lot of big favors in that."

Jen nodded. "I know, I know. If anyone was being taken care of in that relationship, it was him."

"Even financially," I muttered. "Half the time, Kevin didn't even have a job." Of course, the other half of the time he had some fancy chef-gig somewhere, but he always managed to lose these jobs—or quit them in a huff—within a few months. I had worked in the salon the entire time we'd been together, bringing in a steady, reliable income and good tips.

"That's what I figured." She was sipping much more slowly by then, which I was glad to see. I'd already figured she wouldn't be driving back across the island when we were done here. "But all that was just the lead-up, hon, not the deal breaker. You ready? He went on from there to whine about how after wasting all that effort trying to *civilize* you, you turned out to be—and I'm quoting here—'*kind of unstable,*' and just ran out on him for no reason one night. Can you *believe* such trash?"

I couldn't answer her. *Kind of unstable.* Those three words had sent a spike of volcanic rage shooting through me. Now I was frozen, trembling, and voiceless, afraid of what might happen if I spoke—or moved—or breathed too deeply.

"I know you, Cam," Jen went on. "I don't know everything about what happened in your life, or what…secrets you might still have, but I *know* you; and if there's one thing you're so definitely not, it's…" Jen finally seemed to notice my condition. "Cam? You okay, hon?"

Kind of unstable. He had… The night we ended it, he'd…

"Cam, honey?" Jen leaned forward, peering at me strangely.

I shoved down hard on all the rage, cramming it back into whatever box it had come from before I did something to make Jen wonder if Kevin had been right after all. "That…*poisonous snake!*" I spat.

"Oh, you said it, girl! I'd had it then. I told him to take me back home and take himself off my damn island."

Hearing her anger on my behalf was like an antidote. My friend knew me, and knew him now, for what he was. I felt the anger begin to drain away again. No one out there was defending Kevin tonight. I felt sure of that. But Jen had *my* back. "Good for you!" I raised my glass again, feeling warm everywhere suddenly, not just my stomach.

She rolled her eyes. "If only that was the end. We had to fight for three more days about it before he finally gave up."

"He didn't, like, not let you leave or anything, did he?" I could feel my anger starting to burn again. So much anger. But Jen tamped it right back down again.

"Ha! Not likely." She shook her head vigorously, red curls bouncing. "I just…maybe I'm too nice, is all. I guess I thought I could talk some sense into him. You know? I just couldn't believe he could have been with you for so long without understanding the first thing about who you are. Without respecting you. I thought if I just explained it better, somehow…"

I exhaled again. Even strong, smart, cheerful, self-confident Jen wasn't immune to his act. She'd still thought she could change Kevin's mind.

"You're not too nice," I assured her. "I mean, you're exactly the right amount of nice; but he's too—too Kevin, I guess. Too convinced of his own talent and gorgeousness to listen to a thing anyone says."

"I mean, that'll serve him well in Hollywood," she said.

We both burst out laughing.

"Anyway," she went on, "by the time I finally got him out of my hair, you'd been calling and texting me for days, and—I just knew I'd screwed everything up, and I wanted to fix it, but I was—overwhelmed."

"But you did text me back," I said, reaching over and putting my hand on hers briefly. "And just at the right moment."

"I should have talked to you sooner."

"It doesn't matter. We're good now."

She smiled at me. "I know, and I'm glad. I never want to do anything like that to our friendship again."

"Thank you. I don't want that either."

We sat for a minute, just smiling at each other. I knew I was pretty tipsy; she was a bartender, for one of her jobs anyway. She could probably hold a whole lot more liquor than I could, but even she was swaying a little in her seat.

"So!" she said, lifting up the bottle once more. "Now you know the whole sad story. What should we do with the rest of this?"

"Let's talk about it over dinner," I said, getting up and holding onto the edge of the couch until I was sure I wasn't going to fall over. "I'm putting a pot of chili on the stove. Chili from a can."

"Canned chili? With beans?"

I gave her a look laden with meaning. "Is there any other kind?"

"Nope," she said quickly. "Just tell me you have shredded cheddar cheese to put on top of it."

I nodded. "*And* chopped onions."

She sighed happily. "You are my favorite person in the whole wide world." She reached up a hand. I pulled her to her feet, and together we staggered to the kitchen, where we made a stunning repast of canned chili in one of Lisa Cannon's extraordinarily expensive gourmet pots, and served it up in two of Lisa's hand-thrown pottery bowls with grated cheese and chopped onions.

Just the way we liked it.

❧

Remembering that night, and reflecting on just how much I and my whole life really had changed here, made me smile as I carried my several armloads of stuff—including James's litter box—down the mossy path to my new cottage. James didn't look like he'd moved since I left; his fuzzy orange head popped over the rail when I opened the door, and he blinked at me, in that *No I'm really awake, no really* way that cats have.

"What a fierce guardian you are," I said to him. "Protecting our new home!"

He rose to his feet, stretched, then went to stand at the top of the ladder, looking down dubiously.

"You climbed up; I'm sure you can climb down," I assured him, waiting to see what he would do.

He looked at me, then down at the ladder, then at me again.

"I'm not lifting you down from there. If you can't get down, you shouldn't have climbed up."

"Miaow."

I shrugged and starting putting things away, wondering where to put the litter box. I couldn't put it in the bathroom; the door would intrude into the room too much if I left it open. Plus, the spare floor space in there wasn't much bigger than the box itself.

"Miaow!"

"I mean it, James." Hmm, there was some space beside the fridge; but litter box and fridge weren't a good combination... Wait, what was this? In the opposite corner of the back wall, I saw a little nook just perfect for the box. It was kind of an open closet; a bar hung across the top, with just enough room for three or four hangers. A broom was the only thing in there now, but the broom could go beside the front door. I pulled it out and set the box in, shaking the clean litter to spread it evenly.

"Miaow!!"

"Here's your litter box," I called up to him. "I'm setting your food and water out now. You must be hungry, hmm?"

He gave one more pathetic wail; then, out of the corner of my eye, I saw him put a tentative paw down on the top step. He withdrew the paw, put it down again, then followed with the second front paw. In moments, he'd scampered down the steps, and stood in the center of the room, calmly licking his back leg as if he'd never cared at all about that silly ladder.

"I knew you could do it, little man," I said, pouring kibble into his food bowl, then filling up his water bowl at the sink. I set the bowls beside the small kitchen table. If I had company, I'd have to scoot them out of the way, but this would do for now.

James tucked into his food with great enthusiasm. The vigorous nap must have really worked up an appetite in him.

It only took me a few minutes to unpack and organize my few things. There weren't very many places to put them. Soon I was sitting at the table, watching James clean his whiskers.

It was truly a perfect little space. I could see why Lisa had thought it would make a great painting studio: the light was amazing. I'd be able to write here—assuming I wanted to continue writing.

Assuming she liked the play…

She will, she will, she will, I told myself. Maybe if I repeated it often enough, it would come true. I texted the view of my new little home to my mom, and smiled at the string of heart-eyed emojis she sent. *You get to live there? When can I visit?*

Soon. I sent back a few hearts, and went to brush my hair.

❧

Lisa and I had a great dinner out that night, though we talked about nothing of much substance. She'd made it clear right away that she wouldn't be going into anything about what she'd been up to these last months while in a restaurant, on a tiny island, surrounded by the ears of people who knew her. I supposed I couldn't really blame her, though curiosity was killing me. She gently coaxed me into doing most of the talking instead.

I told her about Colin's low-wattage pursuit; and about my rekindled friendship with Jen—after her brief hook-up with my ex-boyfriend—and even about the time I'd been spending with Paige Berry, up the hill. I knew all Paige's goats by name, and was more or less able to keep them from chewing my clothes to bits whenever I visited. I said nothing to her about the whole azalea fiasco. I wasn't sure what she'd think of me prying into other people's business like that; and besides, the story was too full of secrets that weren't mine to tell.

Oddly, I didn't mention Kip to her either. But then, I didn't really know what to say about him.

Of course, Lisa hadn't had time to read the play—though she did assure me she had printed it out: "I can't take in the nuances on a computer screen. It's not a real play until it's on paper."

Back at her house afterward, we parted ways at the path, and I walked through the little patch of woods to spend my first night in my new home.

I hoped I would enjoy sleeping in a loft. I tend to like small, confined spaces—until they get *too* small. It was a challenge making up the bed. The sloping ceiling made the sides a little tight, but I managed. Thanks to the high peak of the A-frame, I could even sit up easily in the bed without hitting my head on the ceiling.

The mattress was crazy comfortable. I didn't wake once in the night, which was a treat. Sunrise was coming earlier these days, so it was already getting light when I woke at my usual early hour. I'd have to get some curtains for those big front windows. But had no idea where a person would find curtains for a picturesque triangular wall of random assorted windows?

I looked at my phone, and found a text from Marie sent sometime in the night. Ugh. It was much too early to deal with needy Marie. This could wait.

Ten minutes later, sitting at my table with a cup of coffee and my laptop, I let myself consider what my life would look like now. As much as I'd missed Lisa, I'd gotten used to living alone. Having all day to focus on my writing, or on what little social life I'd managed to preserve...

As if I'd conjured him, my phone lit up with an incoming call from Colin. I smiled. Shortly after Lisa left, he'd reappeared from whatever business had called him away. People seem to come and go kind of randomly here. Anyway, we'd been getting reacquainted, and that made me quietly happy.

"Hey," I said.

"Mornin'," came Colin's warm voice. "Not too early, is it?"

I chuckled. "I've told you again and again it's never too early to call me."

He matched my soft laugh. "I know. Just can't quite fathom it."

"So, what's up?" I took a sip of my coffee and set the cup down.

"Just checkin' in. Heard Miz Cannon returned to the scene yesterday."

I'd long since stopped wondering how news got around so fast here, reaching even a taciturn—though undeniably friendly—guy who lived on his boat in West Sound's harbor. Island life. "She did, so I moved to a little cottage. It looks right out over the water. You should come over for breakfast. I'll scramble you some eggs."

There was the briefest pause. "Oh, the A-frame?"

"The very one. It's supposed to be an art studio, so I guess I'm an artist now."

"Writers are artists," he mused.

"A good point. So, what do you say? Come for breakfast?"

"I could eat some eggs," he allowed.

"Great. I'll put on more coffee."

"Be there in ten."

I smiled as I set the phone back on the table and got up to figure out how this tiny kitchen worked.

CHAPTER 3

Twenty minutes later, the knock on the door surprised me. I hadn't seen Colin walk up. As I went to let him in, I realized why—and why this apparently random arrangement of windows was so genius. They were mostly high and small and jewel-colored on the path side of the door; larger and view-grabbing on the other side. It just *felt* like I was living in a wide-open space. Actually, my privacy was absolute.

In a minute, Colin sat at the table with a steaming cup in front of him, looking as ruggedly attractive as the day I'd first seen him. He was one of the very first people I met on the island, in fact, when he'd pulled his red pickup truck over to make sure I wasn't lost.

I hadn't been, technically—I knew where I was, and why—but in every other sense, I'd been completely at sea. So Colin had become my first friend here, followed very quickly by Lisa.

And of course Jen—who had taken to me at once, when Colin had brought me to the Barnacle Bar for a not-date.

We were still not-dating, Colin and I, though I was pretty sure by now that he'd have been glad to remove that *not* from the equation any time I was ready. I'd have been pretty sure about that even if Jen hadn't told me. He was helpful, present, and very comfortable company, all without feeling intrusive or underfoot.

Just the right amount of here-for-me.

Of course, he had disappeared on me for a few months, but that was for work. And I understood that people did have to work. But overall, he'd proven himself caring and steady. Kind and gentle, capable, and very easy on the eyes. I didn't mind that he lived on his boat; that was charming, in fact, not a strike against him at all. He would, I'm sure, have made a marvelous boyfriend…for someone else.

Because, in spite of his undeniable appeal, I just didn't feel it. Whatever "it" is—the spark, the little germ of something that says *Oh yes, this one, take this one into your heart.*

Or even *your bed.* Though at times, I was tempted. It had been *so long*, and he was *so cute.*

But I didn't let myself go there. And he didn't seem to mind, so if he wasn't going to make a problem of it, I certainly wouldn't.

I stirred the eggs slowly with a wooden spoon, folding up the cooked portion and letting the raw part flow down to the bottom of the pan. "Just about ready," I told him, as the toaster popped up two golden-brown slices.

"Want me to butter those?" he asked, already on his feet.

"Sure."

In a minute, we were both at the table, yummy breakfast before us.

"Good eggs," he said, after a bite. "You find farm fresh after all?"

I rolled my eyes. "No, I got these from the co-op. If anyone's got eggs to sell, I still don't know about it." I took a bite. They were good, it was true, but… "Why all these farm stands if you're never going to open them?"

He laughed gently. "You moved here, what, last November? Farm stands are a summer thing, is all. It's still just April."

I shrugged and took another bite. "Yeah, well. It still seems silly to have a stand there, and not offer anything."

"You want 'em to knock down the stands in winter, then rebuild 'em every spring?"

Well… "I guess not."

He grinned at me over his plate. "They'll be open soon."

My phone buzzed with an incoming text. All this crazy cell service was going to take some getting used to. I glanced at the screen, then reached over to click it off.

Colin raised an inquisitive eyebrow.

"Just Marie. Again," I told him. "She can wait."

"She still…not quite gettin' it right?" he asked.

Well, that was a polite way of putting it. "I don't know how a human being gets to be her age without becoming at least a little bit competent at, you know, *life*."

"She's pretty young," he pointed out.

"She's not *three*. Honestly, dude, she has a pharmacy degree— that's like twice as much college as I had. And yet every couple days it's like, 'Can you help me spread a tarp over this firewood?' 'Can you come over and show me how to defrost a freezer?' 'There's a spider in here and I don't know what to doooo!'"

We both laughed. Another text buzzed in.

Cam pleeeeease pick up!!

"Pick up what?" I said aloud. "You're texting, not calling."

"Calling'll be next," Colin observed.

"You're right." So I typed, *Sorry, eating breakfast—what do you need?*

Are you going to town today? I'm out of kombucha!

Oh, perish the thought. The girl lived on nothing but kombucha and coffee. And protein powder. *Probably*, I answered. *I'll grab you some.*

From the co-op! Not Island mkt.

"Kind of pushy for someone asking a favor," I muttered. *I know*, I replied. *Co-op only.*

Colin was watching the whole exchange with amusement. "You can't say no?"

"Easier to just do it," I told him. "Otherwise, the whole thing just escalates."

"Poor Cam."

I rolled my eyes. "Why am I so nice to everyone?"

"'Cause you're nice." He finished his last bite of toast. "Say, I'm takin' the boat out on Tuesday, wanna come for a sail?"

"I'd love to. What's Tuesday?"

"Second day of next week. Right after Monday."

I resisted the urge to reach across and punch him in the arm. "I know what day it is. I meant, what's the occasion? Any other reason for sailing Tuesday?"

"Should be nice weather. Need to get the cobwebs outa her sails and lines, get oiled up for tourist season."

"Sounds great." Then I smiled. "I love that phrase: 'tourist season,' like, that's when it's legal to hunt them?"

He nodded, but didn't laugh. Maybe I wasn't the first person ever in history to make such a joke. Almost certainly not, now that I thought about it. "Sure is. I don't catch 'em for my boat, the next guy does, and I don't eat."

My phone buzzed yet again. "Now what?" I looked at the screen.

Nevermind! Delivery is here!

Huh? "She's ordering kombucha online?" I wondered aloud.

Colin shrugged. "Those little airplanes gonna put all honest businesses out of business."

I couldn't argue with that. Even if I did love the modern convenience of having things delivered to our remote island—for free—from the bounteous mainland. Far less trouble than going off island to shop myself.

I'd hardly been off island since I'd moved here, in fact. I'd walked onto the ferry and taken a day trip to Friday Harbor, on San Juan Island; that was fun, and way more cosmopolitan than Orcas (though even there they still had no actual stoplights). I kept meaning to go check out Lopez Island, but the town there was miles from the ferry landing, so I'd have to take my car. But there'd been no need at all so far for me to go back to 'America'—as locals called the mainland here.

Those little planes also brought us lots of cardboard, which made great firestarter—something I'd really appreciated back in the Brixton guesthouse. Lisa's main living room had had a gas-log fireplace, but with this woodstove, I was going to need more kindling again. Which made me think of asking a favor of Marie for once.

I picked up my phone and typed, *Marie, can I take some of your cardboard boxes to use in my stove?*

Sure? she replied. *But you'll have to break them down?*

Of course I'd have to break them down. She couldn't be expected to handle a complex task like that—for someone who just handled half her shopping and all of her crisis management.

Colin laughed a little. "I can tell who you're talkin' to by the expression on your face. It's like you're sniffin' sour milk." I looked up and met his eyes, and he looked a little embarrassed. He got up, carried his plate to the sink, and started washing up. That was the deal, after all—one person cooks, the other cleans. Once again, I thought about how comfortable he was to have around; and yet...

I carried my plate over too—all of two steps from the table.

"Nice digs, this," he said, taking the plate and giving it a rinse before turning off the water. He had soaped up the sponge and went to work getting the bits of egg off both plates. "Definitely the sweetest little house she has, but you sure this is gonna be enough room for you?"

"Says the man who lives on his boat!" I laughed.

"I don't have pets. Where's Master Bun?"

I felt a pang of guilt. "Still in his hutch at the main house. I need to figure out where to set it up here—and get over with his breakfast soon."

Colin glanced around the small room. "He gonna miss being able to roam all day?"

I sighed. "Probably. I was going to set him free when he was old enough, but then…"

"Yeah."

Viral rabbit hemorrhagic disease had become rampant on Orcas Island since last winter…right about when James had brought the very young Master Bun to me, in fact. Had the bunny already been orphaned by then? I had no idea, but there'd have been no returning him to his mother—even if she hadn't perished from the virus. He was a wild cottontail, and the disease *supposedly* only infected domestic rabbits…but our feral population was totally interbred with domestics by now. And there was no way I was letting that trusting little creature make his way in the wild at this point anyway, even if the rabbit virus went away again.

And, okay, I really liked him. He wasn't a cat, but he was sweet and soft, and he enjoyed being held, and eating chopped lettuce, and he never made a sound.

Colin opened the front door and stepped out onto the porch. "This overhang is plenty big enough," he pointed out, looking up and down and around. "You could set the hutch right here, wouldn't even block your view. Just move that woodpile a bit."

"Like moving a woodpile is no big thing. Plus, every spider on the island is probably nesting in there."

"Oh, don't go all Marie on me." He chuckled. Before I could protest, he added, "I'll move your wood, little lady, don't you worry 'bout a thing."

I stifled a sigh. As banter went, it didn't quite live up to JoJo Brixton standards…and I was *not* going to conjure up thoughts of that spoiled, rich, back-stabbing, false friend jerk-face again. "Thanks," I told Colin, because now that he'd decided to do it, there was no talking him out of it. And because I wasn't kidding about the spiders.

He made short work of restacking the wood just a bit farther from the door, leaving a hutch-sized space right outside it. "Carry it over for you?" he offered, as he stepped back inside.

"Sure. I'll get Master Bun himself, but I think the hutch is beyond me."

How Paige Berry, in her mid-eighties if she was a day, had gotten it to Lisa's back deck in the first place was something I couldn't quite wrap my brain around. Then again, almost everything about Paige Berry was just slightly outside the realm of credibility.

We hiked the short way through the woods and up to the side of Lisa's house before I remembered it wasn't even eight a.m. Was Lisa an early riser? I didn't know; we hadn't really lived in the same place before. "Maybe we should wait a bit," I said. "Lisa could be sleeping."

"Nah, she's up." Colin pointed to the open garage door. He put a hand on the hood of her little blue roadster. "It's warm. She's already been somewhere."

"Okay." I still hesitated before knocking on her door, but Lisa must already have heard us talking, because she opened it, smiling, fully dressed and groomed and obviously alert.

"Good morning, Cam. I haven't finished reading your play yet." Her smile widened into a mischievous grin.

"Ha, ha. We're just here to fetch Master Bun, and didn't want you to think intruders were on your deck."

Her mouth fell open. "Master Bun?! You seriously named that creature Master Bun?"

"Sure." I shrugged, feeling even more self-conscious and awkward. "Something wrong with that?"

"Well, just that it sounds like—never mind." She shook her head and was clearly fighting the urge to laugh. "Cam, you're so pure. It's one of the things I enjoy most about you. And hello, Colin," she added.

"Mornin'." He pantomimed doffing a hat, though he was bareheaded. "Welcome back."

"Thank you. It's good to be back."

She let us cut through the house to get to the deck rather than looping around, then left us to our task. I eased my rabbit out of his hutch; he snuggled into my arms, though he must have been confused about why we were going straight to cuddle-time without seeing to breakfast-time first. "Don't worry, little dude," I assured him. "Your veggies are waiting for you."

Weirdly, hay made up the bulk of his diet—which hardly looked like food to me, but all the sites agreed, as did Marliese the vet. Like he was a tiny fluffy cow or something. Which was true, in a sense: like cows, rabbits eat all day long, so they need food that's long on busywork and short on calories. But he loved, loved, loved fresh veggies, especially brussels sprouts and—even more weirdly—mint. It was funny to snuggle him after he'd scarfed down a bunch of mint. He smelled like something you'd find on your pillow in a fancy hotel. At least, that was the cliché: mints on your pillows. My life thus far hadn't included any stays in fancy hotels.

"Perfect fit," Colin announced, setting the heavy hutch on the cottage's porch and sliding it into the slot he'd cleared for it. He opened the door. "You wanna feed him here, or in the house?"

I thought about it a moment. He would need to get used to my new place, and food would help imprint it for him, but plopping him down in an unfamiliar house after being carried through the woods might be too jarring for him. "I'll keep him in familiar quarters for now. Let him get used to how it smells around here." I lowered him slowly from where he was nestled against my chest and set him just inside the hutch, giving him a gentle pat on the back. He hopped forward, sniffing around his home as if he'd never been there before.

Colin hung around for another cup of coffee while I fed and watered my little charge, but when I was done with that, he pulled on his jacket. "Thanks for the eggs. I better go get on with things."

"Yeah, me too. Thanks for the help."

I gave him a hug and he headed off down the path, back to his truck. Hmm, yeah, I was always going to be schlepping groceries through the woods now, wasn't I? Well, perfection never came without a cost, I supposed.

❧

The truth of the matter was, I didn't really have any "things" to get on with now. I was just waiting to see what happened next… with the play, with my actual job—whatever that actually was right now. I wasn't sure whether I was still a caretaker, or just a personal assistant in waiting. I was fairly sure I'd done well enough at the first to still be in the running for the second. But I was uncomfortable without any clear duties to fill my time.

Well, even if Marie didn't need her creepy fermented tea-mud-mushroom-stuff, I still needed groceries. I made a list, refilled James's bowl (empty as always), checked on Master Bun (content and calm), and then marched back through the woods to the main driveway, and knocked on Lisa's door again.

"Still not finished reading," she teased, giving me another wicked grin. "I'm liking it so far, though."

"Oh, I, um, that's great," I said, shuffling from one foot to the other as explosions of relief and excitement went off in my stomach. "I was just headed into town for groceries and wondered, did you want me to shop for you too?"

She looked surprised. "No, Cam. Why?"

"Um, doesn't your assistant shop for you?" I remembered seeing Sheila unload bags of groceries into the side door of the big house.

Lisa laughed. "Not generally. Thank you, though. I'll pop into town later, after I decide what I want."

"Okay." I shifted to my other foot again. "I just—I don't really know what I'm supposed to be doing, now that you're here."

"Anything you like. Taking a little time off, perhaps. Don't worry, Cam. I'll have plenty for you to do, and soon. But we have time to work this all out. For now, just take it easy. Read a book.

Spend time with all those friends you told me about last night."

"Okay," I said. "Text or call if you think of something, though; I'm probably going to hit both the grocery store and the co-op."

Lisa's smile was so warm, so gentle. "Thank you. Have a nice drive."

As I was unlocking my car, my phone buzzed. "My goodness," I said, pulling it out. Marie again!

CAM!!! Have you left yet?

Just leaving now, I sent, and stood by my car for a moment, waiting to see what she wanted this time. When she didn't answer right away, I started walking over to the Brixton estate. I'd have driven, but Diana had changed the code for their gate since we'd parted company, and getting poor helpless Marie to open it for me seemed likely to take longer than just walking over.

My shortest route was the little path between estates, and I was already circling the main Brixton house to get to the guesthouse behind it when her next message came through. *Don't go!!!!!!!!! I need to talk to you!!!!!*

I typed, *Already here*, ringing the guesthouse doorbell and pressing "send" at the same time.

Marie yanked the door open and grabbed my hand. "Come in!" she said, already dragging me so hard, I would have fallen onto my face if I hadn't moved my feet. I pulled the door shut behind me as best I could while being hauled forward. I wouldn't have thought such a mousy little creature would have such strength in her.

She led me to the couch and dropped my hand as she sank onto it, allowing me to get a better look at her. "You look awful," I blurted, because I'm suave and subtle that way. Not to mention sensitive.

"Ugh," she sighed, dropping her pale face into her bone-thin hands and resting there for a moment. "I feel awful."

"Was it…something you ate?" *Or didn't eat?* Maybe she'd feel better if she actually ate real food once in a blue moon. "Do you have the flu?" I wiped my hand on my jeans, wondering if I should rush to the bathroom and wash my hands—though of course, any germs on her hands would be all over her bathroom.

"No, well, I don't know," she said. "At least I don't think it's the flu. I just…I got the new kombucha, and it tasted a little weird, but I had a glass anyway, and…I feel even worse now."

"Maybe it's bad?" I asked. "Doesn't it have to stay refrigerated or something—is it safe to mail order it?"

She rolled her bloodshot eyes. "No! Cam, I've explained this to you before." Her voice had no energy in it. "It's *fermented*, that's the whole point. Shelf stable until it's opened." She sighed. "I should just make it myself, but, ugh. So much work."

I would take her word for it. "So, what's up? What do you need?"

Now she was leaning her head against the back of her couch, with her eyes closed. Her hair was even lanker and flatter than usual; how long since she'd taken a shower? I didn't want to get close enough to investigate, for more reasons than just potential flu.

She opened her eyes. "Can you pick me up some kefir?"

I just stared back at her. "Are you serious? Marie, just eat real food."

"Kefir is real food. I like the strawberry kind. From the—"

"From the co-op. I know."

❧

I left her under a blanket, assuring me that she was fine, she just needed a little more rest—and some kefir, and that she really and truly could live on her stupid meager diet of mail-order supplements and yucky fermented things. I took a moment at her back door to grab a bunch of her delivery boxes, flatten them, and carry them back to the car, where I threw them in the trunk. Then I drove up the hill at last and turned toward town, deciding to bring her some apples and cheese and brown bread too. Marie could refuse to eat them if she wanted to, but it wouldn't hurt anything to try to get something solid into the girl.

I meandered up Crow Valley Road, admiring the big, gorgeous open fields to my right. It was really greening up now that springtime was here in full force. I pulled up to the stop sign at Nordstroms Lane, being sure to stop fully, and it was a good thing I did, because pulling up just behind me was a very familiar sheriff's cruiser.

I looked in my rearview mirror, catching the eye of Deputy Larissa Sherman behind the wheel. In her passenger seat was Deputy Kip Rankin. I lifted my hand in a wave, because I was completely certain that Sherman not only knew it was me, but was watching me like a hawk. Then I took my foot off the brake and drove on, careful to keep my speed at a perfect thirty-five miles an hour all the way into town—except when I went even slower around curves.

If there were a medal for passive-aggressive driving, I'd take the gold.

Every now and then, I snuck a peek back in the mirror again. I wasn't close enough to see any facial expressions, but Kip's body language was eloquent enough. He'd been reinstated to the force after his...mysterious little emotional episode, last Thanksgiving weekend...but he still had to share a car with Deputy Sherman, who was still on loan from San Juan Island, and doing the driving nearly every time I'd seen them.

When I turned into town, they continued on up Lover's Lane, toward the substation.

I decided to do the main market first, then the co-op for anything I hadn't found there. But as soon as I turned onto Prune Alley, I was confronted by an Intruder.

"Are you kidding me?" I practically shrieked, drawing gazes from pedestrians even though my windows were rolled up tight. "What is he *thinking?*"

My ex-boyfriend, Kevin, had parked his freaking *absurdity* of a motor home at the edge of the Island Market's parking lot with the sides let down, and was grilling something tasty-smelling. Half a dozen people gathered around his makeshift window, smiling and talking amongst themselves. I saw two teenage girls gazing up at the window longingly. Yearning for the food, or the chef? I didn't want to know.

His pop-up food truck was completely out of scale for tiny little Orcas Island, not to mention illegal, I was certain. I wished the deputies had followed me all the way into town. I had half a mind to pull out my phone and call Kip, and I would have, if I hadn't known Sherman would come with him. Even the temptation of harassing Kevin wasn't worth inviting more of her into my day.

I drove on past the store, parking by the little nursery behind it. I'd just have driven on out the back and done all my shopping at the co-op—but they didn't have cans of chili with beans, which everyone who didn't live with a terrible hipster foodie snob knew was the only way to go. Big bowl of canned chili, sprinkled with shredded cheddar cheese—which you can buy already shredded, did you know that, because Kevin clearly didn't!—and chopped onions, which I managed myself just fine, a concoction that Kevin would loathe but that I would defend to the *death* because it was easy and tasty and gave me terrible breath, but that was just fine because there was no one for me to kiss. Kevin's soft, soft lips wouldn't be settling on mine with tenderness and passion, only to be repelled by my onion breath. So there.

I sighed. Obviously the man still had the power to get under my skin.

I turned off my engine and just sat in my car for a few minutes, leaning my head against the steering wheel, eyes closed, trying to purge the fury from my system. I supposed he was not an awful man even if he had completely failed me. Failed to understand me, to listen to me, to accept me for who I was—who I am. Tried to co-opt me into his own life plan, his own vision—as an

adjunct, an accessory, a convenient (junior, invisible) partner—
and then turned around and done much the same thing to Jen,
stealing my friend in the process. Or at least he'd tried to.

And almost four months later, the man *still* hadn't left the island. No, he was digging in, trying to make a place for himself
here.

As far as I knew, he hadn't lured any other local women into
the Intruder—or his life, or his bed—but would I know if he
had? Yes, I decided, after thinking about it for a minute, I would
absolutely know; Jen was fully tapped into the island's communi-
cation network, and there wasn't a person here who wouldn't tell
her if they'd seen him with someone.

So what was he *doing* here? Why didn't he *leave?*

And why couldn't I just quit caring? I'd moved on; Jen had
moved on; Kevin had to live his own life, whatever that meant.

I unbuckled my seat belt and got out to go do my shopping,
not letting my eyes wander to the other side of the parking lot.

When I was in the checkout line, I could see through the big
front windows that the crowd in front of the Intruder was even
bigger than before. Could that seriously be legal? My finger
itched to pull out my phone and call Kip, but I told myself, *Not
my circus, not my clowns.* Yep. That's what I told myself.

But my finger didn't stop itching.

The checkout clerk—a sweet teenage boy who always acted
delighted to see me—sang out my total. I shoved my credit card
into the chip reader, still thrilling at the fact that I didn't have to
worry about how much this was costing me.

He asked if I wanted a receipt.

"No, thank you, Seth." I grinned back at him, then suddenly
asked, "Has that food truck been out there long?"

"Oh, that." He glanced around behind him, then around to
make sure there wasn't anyone else in line before going on in a
lower voice, "Yeah, a few days now. I asked the manager…" He
bit his lower lip, looking doubtful.

I gave him an encouraging smile. I was learning, slowly learning, that people volunteered more if you didn't rush in with words of your own.

Not that I was any kind of *investigator*, mind you. Just…curious.

"Well," Seth said, "apparently, there's no actual local rule about it. I mean about being parked there. But if he doesn't have a business license and a whole bunch of other official permits and stuff, he could be in big trouble with the county." His hazel eyes lifted to mine. "If someone complains, anyway."

"Oh *really*." I held my smile. A woman with a full shopping cart was approaching his checkout lane. "How does the store feel about it?" I asked, quickly.

The boy shrugged. "Well, I mean, we've got our own deli here…" He glanced over at the very well-appointed deli and bakery counter.

"Got it." I picked up my bag of groceries, making way for the next customer. "Thanks, Seth! I'll see you soon."

"Later, Ms. Tate," he said, already starting to ring up the new customer.

I walked out of the store and stood for a moment, staring across the parking lot. *Kevinz Kookery,* said a big sign over the vending window. *Stupid name*, I thought, and the hand-forged look of the lettering—was it literally burnt into a piece of raw wood?—annoyed me even more.

Shifting my groceries to my hip, I dug out my phone.

"Hey, Kip?" I said when the deputy sheriff answered. "You got a minute?"

❧

After siccing the deputies on my ex-boyfriend after all, I hurried to my car, wanting to be good and gone before things started happening. I really didn't want to walk or drive past Kevin's oversized RV/food truck; with any luck, he'd never even notice

I had been here. So, even though I was going literally across the street to the co-op, I drove out the far side of the lot, down to Main Street, past Prune Alley, and then up North Beach Road, finding parking in one of the slanted spots in front of the health food store.

I got out of my car and went to stand in the pass-through that led back to Prune Alley and the market, hoping to watch from a safe distance. Sure enough, within minutes the sheriff cruiser pulled up, and Deputies Sherman and Rankin got out, hitching their belts in that way cops do, adjusting all that bulky equipment.

Feeling both guilty and satisfied, I ducked into the store and loaded up on healthy groceries for Marie. And a few interesting things for myself.

Then I scurried out of town, back to the safety of West Sound and beyond.

CHAPTER 4

"You did *what*??" Jen breathed into the phone. The mixture of horror and delight in her voice pretty much exactly matched my own.

"Well," I said, grinning as I gazed down at my sweet little view of Massacre Bay through my front window, "I'm *sure* he has all his paperwork in order. Don't you think?"

We both collapsed into laughter.

"Oh hon," she said when she recovered, "good for you."

"I mean, he *could*, right?" I asked. "He's not an idiot. He has to know that parking that thing in the middle of town and selling cooked food is…bound to attract attention? Right?"

"In some senses, he's not an idiot," she said. "But I don't know about the practical end of business matters."

I chuckled.

"Anyway," she went on, "I gotta run. My shift starts in a few minutes."

"Your shift where?" I asked, puzzled. This wasn't one of her days to drive delivery, and the Barnacle Bar, where she mixed drinks and waited tables, didn't open till five p.m.

"Oh!" She laughed. "I forgot to tell you—I'm doing some housekeeping."

"You're what?"

"Hang on." I heard the phone being set down, and then the tinny shift in sound as she put it on speaker. "Yeah, some friends of mine—do you know Craig and Rachel?"

"No."

"They have the Green Goose Inn, and they've lost their long-time housekeeper just before the season starts. So I'm filling in till they get someone else." I heard soft bumps and crashes in the background, and her voice got louder and softer; she was obviously scrambling around her house, getting ready to leave. "Hey, you wanna do some room cleaning? Super easy gig, and they pay twenty-five an hour."

My face flushed as I thought about how much more Lisa Cannon was paying me to do...quite a bit less than stripping beds, hauling laundry, and scrubbing bathrooms.

"I think my time is all spoken for," I told her, as diplomatically as I could.

"I know." She laughed again. "Just checking! Anyway, I should run—"

"You are *too* nice," I told her. "Do you really need more to do, or are you just helping out people you like?"

"Oh Cam," she said. "I like everyone. I want the *money*."

And she was gone.

Still smiling, I tucked my phone back into my jeans pocket. Well, Jen liked *almost* everyone... We'd just laughed together over my calling the sheriff's deputies on Kevin.

But Kevin was a *jerk*, and he'd treated us *both* badly.

Jen wasn't an idiot and she wasn't a pushover. And she still fell for him, at least briefly. So maybe I could let up a little on myself for having fallen for him too.

I really, *really* wanted to call Kip and ask him what had happened when they'd confronted Kevin. Except I knew what he would say: "Well, you know, Ms. Tate, I cannot comment on an active investigation..."

I snorted, shaking my head. What I really needed to do was take little Marie her groceries.

☙

I grabbed the bag off the back seat and skirted Lisa's house on my way to the path between estates. I was going to wear out these boots if I kept marching back and forth like this.

Maybe someday Marie would figure out how to take care of herself. Hm? It could happen.

Meanwhile, it seemed I'd become a person who took care of strays since coming to the island. A leggy kitten. A baby rabbit.

A hapless caretaker.

Was Marie my human version of Master Bun?

No, he was quiet.

I skirted the dark, looming Brixton main house and headed for the guesthouse. It, too, was dark. Okay, it was the middle of the day, but still, houses with people in them generally show some signs of life. You know? Marie's car was here, but was she even inside? Or had she wandered down to the beach or something while I did her grocery shopping in town?

Really?

I knocked anyway, and waited.

No response.

I knocked again, louder. Still nothing.

I was about to leave her dang bag on the porch and go when the door creaked open a few inches, framing the bedraggled Marie in the slit. A stale odor wafted out as she croaked, "Hey," her voice throaty, phlegm-filled.

I took a reflexive step back, not wanting to get any of it on me. Whatever it was. "Oh, you're really sick," I said.

She gave a rheumy cough, deep and low in her tiny chest. "I am. I'm sick."

I held the grocery bag out at arm's length, now really wanting to just set it on the porch and back slowly away, except that would be *so* rude, except…I hadn't had a flu shot, and holy carp, she looked awful.

I took another step back. "I got your kefir and…some other stuff," I said. "In case you got hungrier."

"Aww," she said, and coughed again. She gave me something like a halfhearted smile, except it looked ghastly on her pale face. She made no motion to reach for the bag. "Thanks, Cam."

"No problem." I rocked from foot to foot. "So, um, I really don't want—"

"No. You don't want this, whatever it is," she said, her wan smile kind of frozen but still holding. "Just leave the bag on the porch, I'll pay you later. Go, stay safe."

"You don't have to tell me twice," I said, setting the bag down. I turned and went around behind her house, where I broke down another batch of tattered delivery boxes to carry back to my car, where my own groceries were still waiting to be unloaded. When I got back to my parking spot at Lisa's house, I stuffed the new boxes into my trunk with the others and pulled out my carrier bags full of food. While I was right there anyway, I thought about knocking at Lisa's door. Just a casual, *I happened to be walking by* kind of a visit, and maybe checking in to see how far she'd gotten on my play, and if she saw potential there or maybe was I completely wasting her time and everyone else's by thinking I could write a play, and she didn't have to be polite, she could just be blunt, just break it to me…

Stop it, Cam, I told myself fiercely. Lisa had already teased me twice today about not being done with the play yet. *She will tell you when she's read it. She's excited to read it, and she knows you're waiting to hear. And you actually kind of like what you wrote. In fact, you're proud of it. So calm down.*

I sighed and started back to my fabulous little A-frame, where I put away my groceries, ate some cheese and olives, snuggled on the couch with my bunny, who was very happy to do so, and then with my cat, who tolerated it for a minute before he started batting at my hair.

ᡱ

A knock on the door startled me. Somehow I'd dozed off. James, similarly asleep in my lap, lifted his head when I jerked awake.

The knock came again. "Ms. Tate?"

Kip? "Just a minute!" I called out, and set my cat on the floor. My legs were wobbly under me as I stood up; I'd been sleeping funky on them, the left one was all pins and needles. "Hang on!"

When I finally managed the three steps to the door and opened it, I smiled to see Deputy Kip Rankin in his crisp, clean uniform. His bright blue eyes shone in the afternoon light, and his smile...

Stop it, Cam.

"Come in!" I said, stepping aside to make room.

He gave a polite nod and glanced around the tiny space as he entered. "Forgive the intrusion," he said, "but I stopped by the main house and Ms. Cannon told me where to find you."

"Right," I said, still grinning at Kip. I could never get over his golden voice and careful formality.

And I could never figure out if I was sweet on Kip or not. Or the reverse: if he had designs on me. Colin had designs; he'd made it low-key apparent even if Jen hadn't told me. But Kip? He was so...polite, so proper. This was leaving entirely aside the question of whether I wanted to date a man in law enforcement. Even small-town law enforcement. Because I didn't.

But Kip. Sigh.

He had removed his cap as he'd stepped past me, and now held it properly, politely, behind his back, in his capable-looking hands. He had the loveliest hands. "This is nice," he said, giving the place a slower once-over. "Not...too small, though?"

I laughed. "Big enough. Except when both James and Master Bun are hopping around."

His gaze darted toward the floor, and I could almost read his thoughts: wondering if he had accidentally stepped on a baby rabbit.

"Bun's in his hutch, outside—don't worry," I told him, stepping over to the stove and turning on the kettle. "Can I get you a cup of tea? I…was about to have one." Not completely true, but the adrenaline surge of being startled awake had left me craving a jolt of caffeine, and green tea wouldn't mess with my sleep later as badly as coffee would.

"No, thank you," he said, "I can't stay. I just wanted to give you an update on the matter you reported in to us."

I turned around and stared at him. "What? You…but isn't it an ongoing investigation?"

He had really cute dimples when he smiled. "Nothing to investigate. Mr. Ndoye did have all his paperwork in order, including the Washington State Food Handler's license. We advised him that restroom facilities would need to be arranged for, rather than just sending his customers into the Island Market, but he has thirty days to address that. Otherwise, everything is in order." He was still smiling, but was it looking a little strained? Or was that just my imagination?

"Oh," I said, and sat down in my chair. "Okay, sorry to bother you guys then."

"It was my pleasure," he said. "Our pleasure, I mean."

There was a little awkward silence before the kettle started to whistle. I hopped up to turn it off. "Are you sure you won't stay for tea? Or coffee?"

"Nope, sorry, but I thank you." He was already backing toward the door. "Deputy Sherman is waiting in the vehicle. I just wanted to follow up on your inquiry." He glanced around again, and did his eyes flicker up to the loft? Surely not. "And congratulations on your new digs. It's very…triangular."

"Um, thanks. I'm just…settling into my new geometric lifestyle."

He smiled politely. "I'll just let myself out." He put on his cap, and then he was gone.

Did I have to be so awkward around him? I made myself that cup of tea anyway, feeling absolutely flustered. "James, I don't know what that man wants," I said to my cat. "If he was intending to ask me out, don't you think he would have by now? We worked so closely on that thing about the flowers. I thought we were getting somewhere. Didn't you?"

James did not answer me. Little stinker.

❧

Plays are not long, actually. Not in comparison to a novel. A play might take an hour and a half to watch, but it doesn't take anywhere near that long to read.

What was taking Lisa so long to finish reading my play? Maybe she hated it. Maybe it was like trudging through wet cement. Maybe I should have just spared her the embarrassment, thrown everything in the car, and snuck onto the ferry so she didn't have to face me. Maybe I should spare her the discomfort of letting me down easy.

It's hard to pace in a miniscule A-frame, but I figured out how the following day. I did other things besides pacing. I took care of my animal charges, organized my various tiny closets and cabinets, gave the bathroom a good scrub, and washed the windows I could reach, inside and out. But I also figured out a small but serviceable route for pacing around the cabin in between all these other things.

It was late that day—*two full days* after her return to the island—before Lisa finally sent me a text. *Love the play! I have a few notes. Let me know when is good to go over them.*

I stared at my phone, heart pounding, then gave a little shriek of delight and started hopping up and down, bouncing around the room, annoying James.

I texted my mom, *She loves the play!*

Mom replied with a string of blowing party horn emojis.

Then I stopped jumping, as the rest of Lisa's message sank in, and texted my mom again. *But she has a few notes. What does that mean? Notes. These notes are all about how much she actually hates it. Right?*

This time, Mom sent words. *Nothing is perfect the first time around, sweetie. Have faith.* And of course, she added the praying hands emoji, to illustrate. They should just call them Momojis. Except I sent a few back; some heart eyes, crossed fingers, and then I added a turtle just to confuse Mom a little.

Why did I have to be such a loon? I forced myself to take a few deep breaths. Then I sat down at the table and carefully composed my reply to Lisa. I refrained from emojis entirely.

Yay! I'm free anytime. Want me to come over now?

I stared at the screen again, second-guessing before I hit send. Did that sound too eager? Yes. Yes it did. I erased, rewrote, and settled on: *Yay! I'm free anytime, let me know.*

Then I sent it before I could fret further.

Lisa's answer came a moment later: *Come over now? I've just opened a bottle of Rattlesnake Hills cab franc.*

The wine she'd served me the first night we'd—what? Hung out? One doesn't just *hang out* with Lisa Cannon. The first night we'd started getting to know one another.

I'll be right there, I texted, and grabbed my jacket.

❦

"It's open," she called out from the living room.

I stepped through her slightly ajar front door and pulled it closed behind me to stop the chilly night air from pouring into her large and lovely home. Then I wiped the leaves and mud off my boots before shrugging back out of my jacket and hanging it in the cedar-lined coat closet. My coat always smelled wonderful when I took it out of that closet. And, finally, I sat on the Eames bench and took my boots off because, well, white carpet.

"Hey," I said, heart pounding all over again as I stepped down into the sunken living room.

Lisa already had two large glasses of red poured, sitting on the coffee table. A pile of manuscript pages was stacked neatly between them. I couldn't see any indication of anything on them—no scribbled notes, no post-its, no turned-down page corners. I forced myself to stop trying to read the pile of paper like it was tea leaves, and sat on the couch by what was clearly my wine glass.

Lisa smiled at me and lifted her own; we clinked and sipped. "So!" she said brightly, setting her glass down on the table and turning to me. "Have you been keeping busy?"

"Kind of." I shrugged. "I'm pretty well moved in—that bed is really comfortable."

Her smile widened. "Ah, yes, the McRoskey. I almost stole that mattress for my own bed, but it's a double and I needed a king here. Lucky you."

"I've never heard of the brand," I admitted.

"It's a small company, San Francisco. I discovered it when—well, never mind that, it's not important. But their beds are just the best ever. I've been meaning to order a king for the house here and just haven't gotten around to it."

Is that something a personal assistant should handle? It was on the tip of my tongue to ask, but, well, I wasn't her personal assistant, though the idea had been floated more than once. And why would Lisa, who slept alone as far as I could tell, need a king mattress? But I refrained from asking. I just smiled back at her, took another sip of my wine, and said, "I don't know when I've ever slept so well. James likes it too."

"James?" She raised an eyebrow.

"My cat."

"Ah. Of course. You and your way with the animals. Our own little Doctor Doolittle." I only sort of remembered who Doctor Doolittle was, but I liked the amusement playing over her face. "Oh, it's just lovely to be back on the island. I can already feel all my muscles unclenching."

"I'll bet." I glanced at the coffee table, wondering when we were going to talk about my play. I was so nervous about her reaction, I even felt a little bit of skin-tingling. I'd worked so *hard* on that play, all winter long.

She'd said she loved it!

But notes...I took another sip of wine.

So did Lisa, and then she laughed again. "Oh, Cam, I can just see you're bursting with nerves about the play." She patted my knee, quickly and softly, before leaning back to her side of the couch. "It truly is a good work, very fun and full of life. I can see the staging for it already." She leaned forward again just a bit, holding my gaze with her clear grey eyes. "But I will be honest with you: I also see signs of the beginning writer in the product."

My heart sank, and I dropped my gaze to my lap. I knew it. She hated it.

"Stop it!" she said, not sharply, but...firmly. "Stop that right now, Camille Tate. I know what you're thinking. It's written on your face. But if you want to be a writer—and I think you should want that, I meant every word I said about the life and energy of the work—you are going to have to learn how to take constructive criticism."

I gave her a helpless, embarrassed smile. I *knew* this, I totally understood it, and I'd even prepared myself for this...except also completely not. Obviously. I'd so clearly been clinging really hard to a fantasy wherein she would declare the play a work of unutterable genius, not one word needing to be changed, rehearsals could start immediately, awards and prizes would start pouring in the moment the play opened...

"I know," I told her. "I just...you're right, this is new for me, and I don't really know—well, anything, really."

"That is not true," she said, finishing the wine in her glass and setting it down. "You know a good deal about human beings, how they behave, how they can say one thing and mean another—far more than most people your age. You've obviously spent a great deal of time observing people."

I felt my blush deepen.

"You have a strong ear for dialogue," she went on. "And a good sense of the absurd, although I think that could be pushed even further in a comedy like this." She raised an eyebrow. "This *is* supposed to be a comedy, correct?"

I burst out laughing, but only because she followed the question with a wink. "Yes," I said. "Please tell me you thought it was funny."

"I thought it was very funny," she said, smiling. She reached for the bottle and refilled her glass, then held it out toward me. I extended my glass for her to top up. "I laughed out loud several times, and I think once we have real live bodies speaking the lines, they will be even funnier. Do you see Bella for Felicia, then?"

"I do, but, you know, it's your company—"

"No, no, it's the *community's* company. I'm simply a patron." She waved a hand, dismissively. "Yes, I see Bella for Felicia; I think she can bring something special to the character. We'll have to make some adjustments, of course, but those are details."

"Okay." If I'd had any idea how hard this whole thing was going to be, I'd never have started writing in the first place. But now I totally wanted to know the details, the adjustments; I told myself to be patient.

Lisa was being kind. I could see that, even through the amazing discomfort of this process.

"In fact, I sense that you had members of the troupe in mind for other characters as well," she went on. "How well did you get to know them over the winter?"

"Not very," I admitted. "After...the whole Brixton thing, I didn't run into them again—at least, not all together. I wanted to go see *Murder for Two*, but with all these goings-on about the azaleas..."

Lisa looked confused. "The azaleas?"

Oops. Maybe this second glass had been a mistake. "It's a long story. But the upshot is, *Murder for Two* slipped away before I could go see it." Not to mention that I was so tired of herding those actors in and out of the Brixton house, and the fact that they cost me my job there. All that hadn't left me in the mood to watch them do their thing.

"And that was the end of the season. I have no idea why they chose a murder mystery farce. For the holidays?" She sounded highly skeptical. I nodded, pretending I had the first idea of how to put together a theatrical season.

"Well, what's done is done. The coming season opens in late spring with *Shakespeare in Love*, and I was hoping your play would be the summer show. Although I confess I have no idea how you're going to decide who gets to play Charlotte Winkleton. That's the kind of part people line up to play. She's a wonderful character, but I have no idea who she's modeled on."

I smiled and thought a moment. Should I tell her? Or pretend that I had made her up out of whole cloth? "Actually, she's inspired by Paige Berry." I waved in the general direction of There's No Point Road.

Lisa chuckled. "Oh, that's good, very good. Yes, she's...quite the local character. I do see it." She gazed at me over her wine glass. "Do you think she won't recognize herself when she sees the play? She's a great supporter of the local theater—of many local arts, in fact."

I shrugged, feeling my face flush again. "I don't know; I tried to disguise her—and to make the character sympathetic, likable. But she is pretty perceptive. I don't know if I'd mind seeing someone based on myself if they weren't a bad person. Do you think she will?"

"You'd be surprised." Then, as she saw my expression of dismay, she added, "No, don't worry about it, I'm just always curious where inspiration and ideas come from. As I'm not creative myself—at least, not with words, not like this—I'm fascinated to learn how writers come up with things."

"I don't really know," I admitted. "I mean, I got the idea for the play from working in the salon, obviously, but for the longest time it was just the general concept. 'Crazy things that happen in a hair salon.' It wasn't until I got really into the writing that I figured out what the story was, behind all the anecdotes."

"And as I mentioned," Lisa said, leaning forward and picking up the manuscript, "I think you've got that part down very well. A one-set play is the ideal for regional theater, and everything takes place in the salon. And you've given the actors what they need to succeed: snappy lines, room to ham it up, and each character has his or her little moment to shine, so even the smallest parts have a highlight. You clearly have the knack for this. Understand, this is a regional company and our actors get paid, but we want this play to have community theater legs, Cam. You could make money in royalties. And you've nailed the hardest part of writing a play that works in community theater: knowing that you have to give each actor a reason to show up every night and do all this work for free. You seem to have understood this naturally."

I was almost glowing from her praise. I was certainly blushing. "I think I just love all the characters. And I want the audience to love them, too."

"And they *will*." She continued piling it on. "And it's such a wonderful *story*. I think most people can learn most anything if they really set their minds to it, but I confess, I've never seen a person without a sense of story learn how to become a great storyteller."

I could feel my blush deepening at the compliment. She thought I was a great storyteller?

"Anyway," she went on, "I've made very detailed notes in the first few scenes in Act I, places where I think you can push things a bit further—or a lot further, in some instances—and places where the pace drags, where you might want to trim it up, or cut parts entirely. You'll find that momentum is absolutely key to a play's success. So you can get started on these if you like." She handed me the stack of papers. "And then, after you've digested what I've done there, we can discuss how to tackle the rest of it."

The rest of it. Hm. I took the manuscript from her, wanting desperately to start thumbing through it right now. But that would be rude. Would that be rude?

Lisa laughed again. "Go ahead, take a look." She got up and headed up the three stairs to the kitchen. "I'll get us something to nibble on."

I glanced up at her, making sure she wasn't watching me over the rail, and flipped to the first page of the play—the one after the title page.

It was covered, covered, in handwriting. Tiny, perfectly elegant notes in blue ink, so many that you could hardly see the printed words.

Less physical description, read the first note, right by my first stage direction. *It's fine to write with a particular actor in mind, but remember, if all goes well, many companies will want to stage this play! Leave them room to put their own actors into the roles.*

Okay, good point.

Each director will work out their own blocking, but a few notes help here and there. We can't have actors wandering about the stage.

Okay, that seemed fair. But hadn't she just asked me for *less* stage direction?

Age these young characters. We need to keep our talent pool in mind.

What? Was everyone supposed to be old?

Lisa stepped back down into the living room, carrying a tray and a second bottle of wine. Had we finished the first? Had *I*? My goodness. I dropped the manuscript on the sofa and looked up at her, as if she'd caught me doing something I wasn't supposed to do.

"Here we are." She set the tray on the coffee table and refilled my glass. "So we don't starve."

It was a complete Middle Eastern platter, featuring dolmas, sliced pita bread, huge green olives and smaller black ones, hummus, a sauce that must be tahini, and that minty-bulgur salad that always left green flecks in my front teeth. She picked up a dolma, swirled it around in the hummus, and took a bite. "Mmmm," she said. "Perfect."

I followed suit, and she was right. And it was all incredibly fresh. Where in the world had this come from? "Did you just whip this up now?" I asked.

Lisa grinned, still chewing. "I just put it on the serving dish." At my look, she went on: "I know you've been on the island for months and months now, but trust me, there are resources here not evident to just everyone."

"I hope you'll let me know what they are when I become your—" Whoops, I'd clearly had too much wine.

But she only laughed. "My personal assistant, yes. We are going to talk about that, but you're my captive playwright and my under-utilized caretaker at the moment. As well as my friend." She let her gaze rest on me, entirely comfortably, and I felt a warm answering comfort fill myself, starting at my heart, radiating outward. Oh, oh, *oh*, how I had missed Lisa! I just grinned back at her.

"Okay," I said.

"Besides," she said, reaching for a triangle of pita and spreading tahini on it, "we can't make any important business decisions while drinking. Right?"

"Right," I said, around a mouthful of dolma.

My phone rang in my pocket, startling me. "Go ahead and take that," Lisa said, leaning over the platter and fixing another pita wedge. "I don't mind a chance to eat some of this."

I pulled it out: Jen. "Hey," I said, when I swiped open the call. "What's up?"

"Too bad about the fuzz not haulin' our man in yesterday."

I laughed. "Yeah. Apparently he *was* smart enough to get his paperwork in order after all." I didn't even wonder how she knew. I mean, above and beyond the fact that she could have just driven by and seen the Intruder still parked there.

Across the couch from me, Lisa raised her eyebrow again, in inquisitive amusement. I nodded at her, hoping to convey *I'll tell you later.*

"You busy for dinner?" she asked. "I thought I'd invite myself over to see your new place."

"Um." I was already getting kind of full on the Mediterranean feast. Not to mention all the wine. "I'm at Lisa's right now, and she's—"

"Oh! Gosh, sorry, you shouldn't have picked up! Call me later!" And the line went dead.

I pulled the phone away from my ear and looked at the screen. "Huh."

Lisa cocked her head, polite but clearly curious.

"It was my friend Jen, and as soon as I told her I was here, she hung up."

"Hm," Lisa said. "I think she might be a little afraid of me."

"What?" I stared at her. "Jen's not afraid of anything, and besides, you're not scary." And then I felt my face flush. Of course she wasn't scary. I mean, she was elegant and wealthy and cultured, and kind, and mysterious, and maybe she was mixed up in weird things, maybe unpleasant weird things, but I didn't really want to think about that, or know that…

"You have the most expressive face, Cam," Lisa observed, wryly. Then she picked up an olive and busied herself with it, extracting the pit from her mouth as deftly as I'd ever seen such a thing done. "You should never try to keep secrets."

"I've been told that before," I said, as my brain scrambled to catalog all the secrets I was currently keeping. Most of them, thankfully, belonged to Lisa. "Oh hey," I said, as the memory was triggered. "Your binder—it's still in the safety deposit box in town. I can get you the keys and all that whenever you want."

"Ah, that's fine." She smiled at me. "As I told you before, I just need to know it's safe. But it's not something I need to access regularly—or ever, if things are going as they should. The important thing is that it not fall into the wrong hands."

As it did, at least for a little while, was left unspoken between us.

"Well, um, it should be safe now," I said, suddenly finding my wine glass very interesting. A vault at the bank in town, what could be more safe than that?

A metal box in a tiny small-town bank, on an island where everyone knew everyone…and everyone had definite feelings about year-round people versus part-time people…

I shook my head and grabbed an olive. That looked like a good thing to focus on for now.

"So, are you at liberty to share your friend's bit of gossip?" Lisa asked.

"Oh! That." I smiled. "It's both our gossip, actually."

"Even more interesting."

I leaned back and thought a moment, wondering where to start. "So…remember that ex-boyfriend of mine I told you about?"

CHAPTER 5

I needed my phone's flashlight function to find my way back through the woods to my little cabin. The days were getting significantly longer now that spring was settling in, but apparently I'd stayed even later at Lisa's than I'd realized. It had taken a while to tell her the whole story, which she found hilarious, and she vowed not to patronize Kevin's food truck, no matter how hungry she found herself when she was in town.

Speaking of hungry, James would be wanting his—

He met me on the path, even as I started to have the thought. "Yes, yes," I said to him. "I'm sure you're on death's door, as you always are, every day, because you are so neglected and abused, you poor darling." He darted in and around my ankles, nipping at the hem of my jeans, even batting at me with his sharp little claws.

"Though if you succeed in tripping and killing me in the woods before I can even get home," I pointed out, "you'll go even hungrier. Remember who has the opposable thumbs here."

He didn't listen, because of course he didn't, because he was a cat, but somehow I managed to make it back to the cottage unscathed. I fed him, considered whether I needed anything else to eat beyond eight dolmas and ten pieces of pita bread and twenty-seven olives, plus uncounted gallons of hummus and tahini (not to mention the wine), and decided I was good.

It was too early to go to bed, and too late to get started on writing revisions—even if I didn't already have too much wine in me to be clever or even coherent about them. So I called Jen instead.

Now she was the busy one; she'd only been on a break at the Barnacle when she'd called me earlier, and was serving a late-evening influx of customers now, before the bar closed down, and then she'd have to do cleanup and breakdown before finally getting to go home.

"You shouldn't have picked up!" I told her, happy to be able to hand her line back so soon.

She laughed. "Yes, but I was afraid you'd decide I hated you again, and we can't have that."

"What's your schedule tomorrow?" I asked her. "Maybe we could get lunch or something?"

"Delivery route in the morning, then I clean rooms at the Green Goose, then I'm opening here."

"Hmm. When do you eat, or sleep, or breathe?"

She laughed again, as though I were joking. "Oh, sweetie, don't worry. I'll drop by if I've got a delivery out in West Sound or Deer Harbor. You can make me a cup of tea. I do want to see your new place."

"Sounds great."

And then I was alone in the cottage again.

I glanced over at the play script, still sitting on my table, untouched...nope, really not ready for that right now. As eager as I'd been to hear Lisa's feedback, I found myself now reluctant to dive in and see more.

Tomorrow for sure.

I got up and went outside, fetching Master Bun in out of his hutch so he could run around the floor, or snuggle, whichever he preferred. He chose snuggling, which was fine by me, though it pinned me to the chair. Especially when James decided that there was still some lap left for him.

I sat there, scrolling through social media on my phone, wishing I'd grabbed a book to read before these animals trapped me.

Then an item on my newsfeed stopped me, a photo of a familiar elegantly slouched posture…

Dang it, why hadn't I unfriended JoJo Brixton? I really didn't need to keep being ambushed like this, reminded of how much I'd liked him, how much I'd enjoyed his friendship.

Well, what I'd *thought* had been his friendship. Because clearly, he hadn't felt anything like the affection for me that I'd had for him.

I clicked on the post, intending to just push the "unfriend" button and get this heartbreak out of my life once and for all. The whole story opened, of course: glibly captioned photos of him and other rich and beautiful people drinking elegant cocktails somewhere exotic, for the most part.

Hello dahlings, it's been ever-so-ever-so around here, hasn't it? And yet there comes a time in every young man's (shut up, I heard that) life when he needs to buckle down and do a bit of—perish the thought—work. I'll be scarce for a bit, but know that I still love you. Yes, you.

If you need to find me, and I know you do, my dahlings, every last one of you, try putting a message in a bottle and dropping it into Puget Sound, because as everyone knows, the modern world has yet to arrive at the remote islands of the San Juans. Or you could try my cell, who knows? You might get lucky. Till then, sweeties!

Absurd. And the photo. He was stretched out on a divan in some over-decorated locale—it almost looked like a stage set, and knowing JoJo, there was a strong possibility that it was—holding an empty martini glass in one languorous hand draped over the side of the sofa. His glass tilted toward the floor, to give people the impression, I suppose, that he'd poured the drink onto the carpet, but I knew the man, and there'd only ever been one place he poured a drink. He was gazing at the camera through half-lidded eyes, trying both to look seductive and somehow at the same time mocking the very idea of seduction, or attractiveness, or anything serious whatsoever. He was wearing a dark suit of—no, "suit" isn't the right word, because that implies something else, something businesslike; I only mean to say that the pants and the jacket were fashioned of the same material, which—was it velvet? Surely it couldn't be velvet. In any event, the pants were foolishly tight, except he looked so very, very good in them; and the jacket was cut slender but comfortable, letting his strong shoulders just sort of…imply themselves, under there; the jacket also featured pleats and darts and stitching, nearly invisible against the darkness of the underlying material, but it was there.

And why, why, *why* was I sitting here studying this photo of such a remorseless snake? Stupid spoiled JoJo Brixton. "Get thee out of my life," I said, and pushed the "unfriend" button. Of course the site wanted to know if I wanted to report the post or JoJo.

"No," I said to my phone. "Just…go away." Where was the "just go away" button?

I shut the phone down and slumped back in my easy chair—gently, of course, not wanting to disturb the menagerie sleeping comfortably on my lap.

"You look like a painting," JoJo had told me, when he'd seen me cuddling Master Bun, last winter. Of course, he'd had to go on to ruin it: *"Madonna and Flea-bitten Rabies-beast."*

Ha. Ha. JoJo was genetically incapable of saying something nice without tacking on a barb.

I was better off without him in my life. I'd been better off for months and months now.

So why did his betrayal continue to sting so badly?

"Because you keep getting reminders of it," I told myself aloud. James opened an eye and gazed up at me before giving a little cat-sigh and snuggling deeper into sleep on my lap. "But that's done now. I should have unfriended him months ago."

Except, had he just said he was coming back to the island?

To the San Juans. That's what he'd actually said. Nothing specific about Orcas. For all I knew, the Brixtons had property on all the islands. He could be going anywhere.

Master Bun fidgeted a little in his sleep, one of his strong back legs kicking out at James, who snurfled in protest and began squirming as well.

"That's enough, you two," I said, and set them both on the floor, where they looked confused and slightly annoyed, but at least they could do it somewhere other than on me. I got up and went to the fridge, like you do when you don't know what else to do.

But I wasn't really hungry. And I wasn't even bored, exactly.

I was...

What's the word for when you've been waiting for something for so long, and then it finally happens, and it's—well, it's fine, it's great actually, it poured you excellent wine and served you delicious snacks and said your play was good and that you're friends—but, now, somehow you have moved into the next phase of things; you no longer have something you've been waiting for, looking forward to—instead, now you have to—well, go on and do the next thing? And yet you waited for so long, you kind of forgot how to take initiative and *do* things?

That. That's how I felt.

Well, things might look different in the morning. I could only suffer this strange ennui from achieving a goal for so long.

I closed the fridge and went into the little bathroom to brush my teeth.

❦

I was right, at least to a degree: things *were* clearer in the morning.

After fortifying myself with coffee, I spread the manuscript across the tiny pine kitchen table and read every one of Lisa's notes again. And what was clear to me then, was that I had no idea what I was doing while writing a play.

Dang. I had a *lot* of work to do.

She'd been being kind to me, it was now obvious. I'd suspected it at the time, but, wow.

I had to start the play in a different way, with the same people, but doing different things.

I had to trim a bunch of stuff that she felt bogged the action down—but then add a bunch of other things that might be "peppier" in their place. Whatever that might be.

She liked the humorous bits, thank goodness, but she thought a number of them could be "amped up".

She liked most of the characters…except the ones I liked the best. *"What about merging the characters of Stewie and Ricardo? They seem to serve the same function, and would be sharpened by greater focus,"* read one note. *"And male actors of this age range are hard to come by."* Seriously? They were nothing alike and had nothing to do with each other, how could they be one person who served the same function?

Greater focus on what?

I sighed. I was not, not, *not* going to ask her what she meant. I knew she'd said I could come to her with questions, but…it would just make me look even more amateurish than I was.

She already knows you're new at this, I told myself, but I didn't want to listen to that. I wanted to impress Lisa. I wanted her to say, "Wow, what an amazing new voice!" And then produce my play, untouched.

I wanted to sigh again at the thought, but that would just be wallowing. I considered just burning it. That made sense, yes? I needed paper to start my fire, it was right here, and then I'd never have to incorporate all these dang notes.

"Might as well get started," I told myself.

And opened up my laptop to start writing a new Scene I.

❧

After the usual amount of dithering, false starts, unplanned snacks, and other time-wasting measures, I finally found my way into the rewrite. So of course my phone rang, startling me out of my imaginary salon. The screen said it was Colin.

"Hey," I said, swiping the call open. "Is it sailing day?" Had I forgotten?

"Nah," he said, sounding apologetic. "I'm calling to cancel. Gotta do a little maintenance work, and then the weather turns. Won't be fun till it gets nice again. Sorry."

"That's all right," I said, though I was a little disappointed. I'd been to dinner on the boat several times—after the first, disastrous dinner, when his ex-girlfriend had shown up and I'd chameleoned right there below decks with them—but I'd never been on it when it had been going anywhere. And I really wanted to.

"We'll get you out there. Don't worry. Anyway—can I offer you lunch instead? Consolation prize?"

"Sure," I said, glancing at the time. Wow, had I really been writing all morning?

Why hadn't I made more progress then?

"Yes, please," I went on. "I'm in revision hell, come rescue me!"

Colin chuckled. "Ah yes, Miz Cannon and her return to the island. So, she didn't like the play, then?"

"She loved it, and only wants me to completely rewrite the beginning, the middle, and the end. And then a little part after the middle, and another one just before the end."

I could almost see his smile. "Sounds like fun to me. Should I not take you away from that, then?"

"No, please, do—I have to eat. Am I coming to the boat, or—?"

"I thought a picnic up on Turtleback might be nice. Before the weather turns."

"Ooh. Absolutely."

"Pick you up in fifteen?"

"I'll be ready."

⌒

The Turtleback Mountain trail system is spectacular. And not far from where we lived—both Colin and me, that is. Kind of halfway in between, so it meant he came out of his way to pick me up, but that was all right. I let him. I did enough taking care of places, people and pets. I needed taking care of myself.

After a brief but strenuous forty-five-minute hike up, we sat on the mountaintop at Ship Peak, looking down over the west end of Crow Valley, the harbor at West Sound, and the sound itself beyond. No ferries were currently going by, though a small fishing boat was motoring toward the little bay at Shaw Island. To our left, the view encompassed the town of Eastsound, and then little glimpses of Bellingham and Vancouver beyond.

"On certain clear days, you can see Mount Rainier right there." Colin pointed to the hazy distance, in the general direction of Anacortes.

"Huh." I squinted, but no mountain revealed itself. "We couldn't even always see it in Seattle," I said.

"Moody things, mountains."

"Indeed. They come and go as they please, don't they."

"They do."

We munched on our delicious sandwiches in silence for a while. Suspiciously delicious, now that I thought about it. "Did you make these?" I asked, holding mine up. Only the last few bites remained.

Colin gave me a sheepish smile. "Picked 'em up in town."

I narrowed my eyes. "*Where* in town?"

He looked down uncomfortably. "A gentleman never tells."

So that was where. I took another bite as I considered it. Perfectly delicious sandwich; and it wasn't the food's fault who prepared it, was it? No, of course not. It would be unfair to this fresh hearty bread and the thick slices of tender roast pork to reject it based on my disdain for a certain hipster dude who just happened to be horrible at true love. "You're right. Don't tell me." I popped another bite in my mouth, now recognizing the familiar spice profile of the chutney. "Forget I even asked."

Colin nodded, took another bite of his own sandwich, and continued contemplating the view. After another minute, he reached into his backpack again. "Almost forgot: mint-chip oatmeal cookies. From Teezers."

"I thought they closed?"

He gave a secret smile. "Mostly. Unless you know someone."

The cookies were huge; he broke one in half and handed me a portion. "If you want more, I got 'em."

"This is delicious. But I need to be able to hike after this."

"It's all downhill from here."

I chewed, savored, and swallowed. "True that," I said, reaching for more.

◌৸

The hike-and-picnic was a nice diversion, but I can't say it helped the creative process any. By the time Colin dropped me off at home and I'd showered the mountain and my effort off me, all I really wanted was a nap.

"Okay, thirty minutes," I promised myself, and even set my alarm.

And then reset it after the thirty minutes were up. I'd hardly gotten to sleep!

By the time I'd given up on discipline, the sun was slanting low in the sky, I'd wasted most of the day, and I was determined to make at least a little progress. I brewed a fresh pot of coffee and brought a cup to the table. I opened my laptop (again!) and read through the few (very few) words I'd written that morning, before the hike.

I cracked my knuckles and prepared to type.

So of course, that's when my phone dinged with a text.

I thought about ignoring it, honest I did, but what if it was Lisa? Yes, she'd told me to take a few days off, but she was my boss—*and* the person who'd commissioned this play, more or less—so I at least glanced at the screen, and rolled my eyes.

It was Marie.

Hey Cam sorry to bothr you but I hear a

That was all.

I waited, but there weren't even any little bouncing dots.

Finally, I typed *Hey Marie, are you there? What's up?*

It said "sent", but nothing happened.

With a heavy sigh—so heavy that my cat looked over at me in annoyance from his own nap—I pushed the button to call Marie.

It went straight to voicemail. I hung up without leaving a message, sighed again, and started pulling warm clothes on before I even realized I'd decided I should walk over there.

I mean, of course I had to! It was an obvious cry for help, cut off in the middle, complete with a typo. Typos were not her usual style, but cries for help were sadly common from the poor thing, and she'd been sick. And I wasn't sure why this was my responsibility, but somehow, it was, and I needed to check on her.

It was a strange mix of sympathy and exasperation, what I felt for that girl. She was so clearly unequipped for this world, and I didn't really understand why. Was she just a lifelong sad sack? Did she hate it here so much? I wasn't sure why she'd agreed to stay on the island, when she had told me she didn't like it here, that it felt remote and isolated and unfriendly. But Diana Brixton had hired her after I quit, and here she remained.

I laced up my boots and went out, pulling the door shut behind me and, after a brief hesitation, decided not to bother locking it. Most "real" islanders never locked their doors, and though I still wasn't entirely comfortable with the habit, I was giving it a try.

I hiked through the woods, past Lisa's house, and took the path to the Brixton estate. The main house was dark and unoccupied as usual, save for the array of automatic lights that went on and off, fooling nobody.

I was on my way to the guesthouse when—

Movement. I saw movement in the trees. To the left of the guesthouse.

I froze, just off the edge of the main house, slightly in the shadows; shadows made even longer by the close-to-setting sun.

I stood stock-still, training my eyes on the spot as little hammers began to hit my skin. I was afraid to rub my arms and draw attention to myself. I wasn't chameleoning, not yet; but I was right on the verge.

Then I saw the movement again.

It was a human figure, dressed all in black…moving stealthily, and with intent. And it was *not* Marie.

That was all it took. My skin sang with prickling stabbing pain even as my voice froze and my heart pounded in my chest. My legs turned to stone, and my boots might as well have been attached to the gravel beneath them.

I was invisible—and trapped there.

Oddly, I stayed more mentally present than usual. I'd been working on trying to gain control of my supernatural disability since I'd moved here…with middling results. Last winter, I'd found out that being angry gave me more control over my invisibility. But I wasn't angry now. Just terrified.

The black-clad figure in the woods may or may not have been aware of me. It had stopped when I'd come around the corner, then moved, then stopped again as I froze. Now it moved again… creeping slowly, quietly, toward the Brixton guesthouse.

It could have been a man, or a woman on the thicker side. I couldn't see enough to be sure. It was not the short and solid Sheila, I was sure of that at least. She was safely jailed someplace far away. Wasn't she?

Could she have escaped?

I stared, unable to protect Marie, to call out for her, to even move my hand toward my pocket and its phone.

The phone! I had the sudden, terrible thought that she would text me again, or call me…and my position would be revealed—with me frozen in place.

My heart pounded harder, and my skin screamed and sang. I hadn't panicked this hard in a long time. I tried to drag my eyeballs just a tiny bit to the right, to see if I could see any signs of life at the guesthouse, but I was well and truly immobilized.

The figure was at the back of the house now. In a moment, they would be behind the house, and I wouldn't be able to see them anymore. They stopped then, just at the corner, and looked across the parking area—probably fifty yards from me; I would have been easy enough to see, even in the failing light, if I hadn't blended in with my surroundings…or emitted a *don't look here* force field…or however this actually worked. Because being on the inside of it, of course, I had no idea how others perceived it. Just that they…didn't see me.

The figure was in too much shadow for me to have a good view. They appeared to turn in my direction, searching for something, then after a long moment looked away again, back at the guesthouse, but still didn't move. Finally, they took another step forward. Halfway behind the house, there was a small window into the living room, next to the fireplace. A fireplace sending no smoke, or even heat distortion, from the chimney.

Whoever it was leaned forward to peer in the window.

For a long moment, the figure remained motionless there, staring in. Then, they drew abruptly back and hurried off into the woods.

In the direction of the road. And from there, perhaps even Lisa Cannon's home, if they circled around. And *my* home.

I needed to check on Marie, and warn Lisa, but I still could not move, could not make a sound. I had been so thoroughly panicked, it was going to take some time to release me. In the distance, I heard the sound of a car engine starting, then fading as the car drove away.

Away from our homes, thank goodness.

When the sound of the engine faded into nothingness, the tingling came back to my legs, then my arms. I took a deep breath and whooshed it out again, then another, slower breath. My heart was slowly settling, oh so slowly; I stretched my arms out, wiggling my fingers, then stamped my feet.

Finally, I could actually move, actually had full control of my body once more.

Still feeling foggy and light in the head, I walked across the parking area to the guesthouse door and knocked on it. "Marie?" I called out. My voice was still hoarse, a weird croak; I cleared my throat and tried again, more loudly this time, ringing the doorbell as well. "Marie?"

No response.

I moved to the side and peered through a window on the opposite side of the building from where the figure in black had been, but looking into the same room. It was not a large house.

Marie lay on the couch, her eyes closed.

Oh, please be napping, Marie.

But I feared she wasn't.

"Marie!" I yelled as loud as I could. When she didn't respond, I pounded on the door almost hard enough to damage it, then moved back to the window.

She didn't react at all.

This was not good.

I went quickly back to the door and tried the knob. Locked, of course. So I went around to the back, to the kitchen door, and tried that. Success! I ran through the kitchen into the living room, rushing to the couch. "Marie!" I yelled.

She lay on her back, under a thin blanket, unresponsive. Her color was terrible. I noticed a stockpot beside the couch, and evidence that she'd thrown up in it. My own stomach gave a turn as I shoved the pot aside and bent over her, reaching for her arm.

It was cold.

"Marie!" I shrieked, half-crying as my skin started tingling again. "Marie, don't be dead!"

CHAPTER 6

I had apparently called 911, because as I began to track things again, I found that Kip was here, and a deputy I didn't know, and of course Deputy Sherman. Colored lights flashed against the dark walls, from emergency vehicles parked outside. The room was full of people, but nobody was moving with a whole lot of urgency.

Had I chameleoned again?

I couldn't remember, but Marie was gone, and when I asked where she was, Kip said the ambulance had come and gone, heading for the island's tiny airfield. Hopefully, Marie was already on a helicopter to Bellingham or Anacortes or even Seattle, where a real hospital would keep her alive.

Now I sat on the upholstered chair on the other side of the cold fireplace, shivering. Kip was standing over me, and I hadn't seen him move across the room. I was still losing moments of time, seeing everything around me in a weird kaleidoscopic haze. The aftermath of chameleoning wasn't usually this bad, but…I'd found too many people dead. In too short a time.

"Come on, Cam," Kip was saying, trying to get me to stand up. "Let's go to the kitchen. It will be less crowded in there." His mellifluous voice was soothing, was helping me to calm down, to stay present. At least I wasn't chameleoning anymore, which was some relief; it would be terrible to vanish in front of all these people, and all of a sudden here were some more driving up outside, if my ears were not wrong…

I used to think Kip should be a radio announcer or something, but now I realized that he was in exactly the right profession. I leaned heavily on his arm as he led me back down the hallway to the kitchen—the kitchen that used to be mine—and sat me at the table, murmuring comforting nothing-words all the way.

Once he'd made sure I wasn't going to topple out of the chair he'd helped me into, Kip turned to the stove and frowned. "Didn't there used to be a teakettle here? I want to make you a cup of tea."

I just stared at him. "I don't know," I finally managed. "It's Marie's house now."

"Well, yes; that's a point." So calm. So soothing. "Never mind, there's a microwave, I can use that. Unless you don't approve of microwaved tea water. I know some who don't."

I knew he was just talking so that I'd keep hearing his voice. And I was good with that. As long as he kept talking about tea, about hot water, about nothing, then we weren't talking about the fact that Marie had almost died. I hoped it was almost. What if I hadn't found her?

Voices carried down the hall, from the front room. The new arrivals had—well, arrived—and someone was explaining the situation to them… "Oh!" I said, recognizing a voice.

Kip looked over at me from the sink, where he was filling a mug with tap water. "Yes, Cam?"

"It's…the Feds," I said, before I could stop myself. "Why are the Feds here?" I recognized the distinctive Canadian accent of Mountie McMichaels; and there was no mistaking the power and authority of Agent Veierra's strong voice.

Kip nodded, turning off the water and carrying the mug to the microwave. He put it in and pushed the button to start it heat-ing. "Yes. They're here to help us. Your call mentioned a trespass-er on the property. With everything that's been going on around here, they wanted to have a look around."

The microwave beeped. I thought about telling Kip that the water couldn't be hot enough yet, but he opened the door, sniffed the plain water, frowned, and put it back in. Oh. He was taking care of me. I didn't have to tell him how to make tea.

A comfortable warmth spread through me, a feeling of safety, of letting someone else pay attention to the hard stuff. I just had to…sit here. Drink the eventual tea.

Then there was a steaming cup in front of me. "Just sip, slowly for now," Kip said, sitting at the table across from me and meet-ing my gaze with his strong blue eyes. "It's hot, but not boiling. I made chamomile."

I wrinkled my nose. I hated chamomile. I picked up the mug anyway and blew on it, blowing the icky steam toward Kip. I was about to raise the mug to my lips for a sip when a voice behind me snapped, "Don't!"

I nearly dropped the cup; Kip's gaze shot up. It was Agent Vei-erra, looming in the kitchen doorway. "What is it?" Kip asked, getting to his feet.

"Nobody should be eating or drinking anything in this house until we we've had time to examine things in greater detail, don't you think, Deputy?"

I let the cup fall back to the table with a thump. Tea sloshed over the side and onto the table. "You…are you saying you think Marie was poisoned?"

"Just standard procedure, I'm sure," Kip assured me, resting a hand on my shoulder and giving it a gentle squeeze. "My apolo-gies," he said to the FBI agent. "I wasn't thinking; I just wanted to do something to help her with the shock."

She gave him a crisp nod. "Not a problem, but we do need to keep the scene unmuddied."

Was this a "scene"? As in *crime scene*? "Is Marie…" I couldn't say the word. "How is Marie?"

Agent Veierra gazed down at me with an odd expression. Kip squeezed my shoulder again and then took his hand away. "Will you need to ask her questions now, or can I maybe take her to her house till she's more...ready?" he asked the agent.

She looked up at Kip. "Just some basics now; we can question her more if we need to later."

No one had answered my question. "Is Marie alive?" I asked again, the fog in my head finally beginning to lift some.

The agent's gaze softened further as she sat down at the table across from me. "Ms. Tate, I understand that you've been through more than your share of shocks in recent months, and I am sorry to have to do this to you at this time, but...how well do you know Marie Tolliver?"

I blinked over at her. Such a tall, tall woman; such impressive hair. Agent Veierra clearly had a very talented hairdresser.

And she had just said *do you know* Marie, hadn't she? Not *did you know.* Wouldn't they refer to a dead person in the past tense? So Marie must be alive. I drew a deeper breath than I'd had for some time, feeling my mind clear further.

"I met her last fall, but I didn't know her very well. I mean, we're next-door neighbors, and I, I guess, I sorta liked her? Well, yes, I like her, but, it's not like we hang out or anything..."

She watched my face. I knew she couldn't read my thoughts, but she was obviously very good at discerning states of mind just by observation. Or maybe all my thoughts were written on my face, as Lisa had said. Her voice was still soft and gentle as she said, "You're here, though, and you phoned 911 about the situation. Can I ask how you happened to come here at that particular moment?"

I glanced around the kitchen. Kip was now standing in the doorway, clearly wondering if he should stay or go. "Marie texted me," I said. "She...she was afraid because she—heard something? Maybe? It wasn't finished."

"What wasn't finished?"

"The text she sent." Veierra and Kip exchanged a sharp look I couldn't decipher. "It just trailed off. So I came over to check on her. I checked on Marie a lot, actually. She was—*is*—a person who seems to need checking on a lot. But, on my way over...I saw someone outside."

Kip stepped over to the table. "Can you tell us who it was?"

Agent Veierra gave him a very professional smile. "You are welcome to remain in the room, Deputy Rankin, but I will continue asking the questions, if you don't mind."

Kip stiffened. "Sorry, ma'am."

She nodded, then turned back to me. "Can you tell me the exact wording of this text she sent you?"

"Of course." I dug my phone out of a pocket, set it on the table, and swiped it open. The string with Marie was active. I scrolled up, past my unanswered reply, and handed the phone to Agent Veierra. "It should be on her phone, too." Hadn't they looked at her phone?

Agent Veierra read it, frowned, and extended a finger to scroll further, but then stopped. "May I?"

"Yes, of course."

She spent another few seconds on the phone before setting it back down on the table. "That was it? Just that one half-sentence?"

"Yes, and when I couldn't get hold of her, that's when I started over here. I mean, I tried to call her too, but she didn't answer, it went right to voicemail. She hadn't been feeling well lately— that's what those earlier texts were about, I was getting her food and things in town." I glanced around the kitchen; there was no food in evidence, not even the healthy things I'd bought her. Had she eaten them? Thrown them away? Or...were they locked away as evidence of some kind now? They'd mentioned poison, hadn't they?

Or had that just been me who said that?

Oh, Marie.

"Do you think she had some terrible disease?" I asked. "Or did she starve herself? Because I was afraid for her, with how she ate. Do you think she'll be okay?"

Kip was shaking his head as Agent Veierra said, "We certainly hope so. But it's too soon to tell. We don't even know enough to have a working theory at this point. We're still gathering information, and it would be very helpful if, instead of asking us questions we can't answer, you just answer *our* questions for now. Would that be all right, Ms. Tate?"

"Yes, of course. I'm sorry. I just…this is just so…"

Her eyes crinkled around the corners as she smiled. "I understand. Believe me, I do. But the best way you can help all of us right now, including your friend, is to tell us everything you know, in order, starting with the text and proceeding from there."

"Right. Of course. Sorry."

Her smile grew. "You've done nothing to apologize for. Just tell it all, slowly, please."

I went through the whole story, only fudging a bit when it came to the vanishing part. *I froze, and the person didn't seem to see me,* conveyed much the same thing, without any of the complications.

"So there was only one person?"

"Yes. But I couldn't tell if it was a man or a woman."

Someone, possibly Kip, patted my arm. Somewhere during my narrative, Veierra's little notebook had come out, and now she jotted down a few things. It was a fresh notebook this time. When I finished, I leaned back in the chair, exhausted all over again. "What do you think happened?" I asked.

Agent Veierra shrugged magnificently. "I think nothing at this point. Perhaps she has an underlying medical condition that's put her in this state, but the presence of a prowler has us on alert. As I mentioned, we are simply gathering information." She rose to her feet just as Inspector McMichaels appeared in the doorway. It was a small kitchen; the four of us nearly filled it.

"The forensics team is on their way. Shouldn't be long." I blinked up at him, though he didn't seem to notice me. Forensics team? What in the world?

"One moment," Veierra said to him, and glanced through her notebook. "That should do for now, Ms. Tate. Thank you very much for talking with me. I must ask you not to discuss our conversation with anyone else, please. Allowing such information to run loose—especially early on—could compromise our investigation very badly. And please don't leave the island without letting us know first, all right? We may need to get hold of you again as things progress."

I nodded, looking back at Kip, who smiled reassuringly.

"Forensics team?" I asked him when the Feds had left. "The island has a forensics team?"

"Hm?" He looked confused. "Oh!" He smiled. "No, of course not. They're from the mainland." He glanced at his watch. "We're going to need to find a way to get hold of her parents, and we haven't been able to track down Ms. Brixton yet. You wouldn't happen to have any idea where their contact information might be, would you?"

I shivered again. "Well…it's probably on her phone, don't you think?"

Kip just gave me an odd look.

"What?" I asked him.

He shook his head, tossing his sweet curls. "Nothing."

I sat, trying to make my brain function. "Diana is going to be so upset."

He gave a short bark of laughter before looking back at me, seeming almost horrified. "Cam! Seriously, you're worried about what Diana Brixton is going to think? I thought you'd be well over caring about her feelings by now."

I shook my head, wondering at myself as well. "Kip, what is going *on* here?"

"No one has any idea yet," he said, coming to sit down across from me once more. "You said she was sick, that she'd been getting sicker and sicker all the time."

"Yeah, but I thought it was just the flu or something. That's what she thought, too, when I stopped by to get her grocery list. She said, *you don't want this.* But Kip, that girl is in her early twenties. You don't just…waste away like some romantic heroine in your early twenties, do you? Not in this day and age."

He shrugged. "Could be anorexia. You've said she doesn't take care of herself, that she hardly eats a thing. They'll run a full toxicology workup on her in the hospital; it's possible she overdosed with something, either deliberately or accidentally."

I nodded, shivering a little. "But what about the prowler?"

"You're quite certain you actually saw someone? That it wasn't just—I don't know—movement of light and shadows?"

I stared back at him. "You don't believe me?"

"I believe you believe you saw someone," he said quickly. "But as you yourself admitted, the light was already starting to fail, and you were nervous and on edge. The human mind…can fill in details that aren't there, as it tells itself what it expects to see. Even at the best of times. And after all you've been through…" He gave me a mildly apologetic look, or maybe it was sympathy I saw there. "I'd be seeing prowlers behind every bush I passed, Cam."

He was trying to be kind and gentle about it, but I shook my head anyway. "No, there was definitely someone out there. Someone walking around the house and looking in the window. Like—they were checking on her. And I heard a car, after they left. Oh, I wish I'd seen the car!"

"Yes, you did hear a car," he said, reluctantly. I felt a little stung. After all the time we spent on that azalea case, I expected him to take me a little more seriously. "They'll check up on the road for any tracks or other evidence." He thought a moment. "You're sure it wasn't, say, Paige Berry? Does she still wander down here unannounced?"

I gave a half-smile at his mention of the old lady. "I don't know if she comes down here much, but she does come to see me kind of regularly. She's gotten pretty fond of Master Bun, and she says she likes my coffee better than what she makes at home. And she's going to teach me how to make goat cheese from her milk, just as soon as her 'girls' step up their production a bit."

He smiled too, shaking his head. "The energy that woman has…"

"But it wasn't her," I said. "She's never worn all black a day in her life, I'm sure."

Weirdly, it seemed almost as if I could hear her voice at that moment. I'd been hearing a steady stream of conversation and other noises from the front room and basically ignoring it, while Agent Veierra had been questioning me. But now—wait; was that actually Paige's voice out there?

"Did I *summon* her?" Kip asked, getting up again and reaching a hand down to me.

I took it and got to my feet as well, wishing I could have had a cup of tea after all—even if it was chamomile. I was still a bit unsteady, but yes, Paige Berry had just shown up on the scene.

☙

A lot had gone on in the front room while I'd been ensconced in the kitchen. There was an entire team bagging, dusting, combing and scraping. The firemen were gone, and the deputy I didn't know was outside, helping the Feds search for evidence, from what I could tell by the darts of light from their powerful police flashlights outside the windows. The living room floor was littered with little bits of paper or tape or something. Had those been in here before? I couldn't remember.

Oddly, it was also quieter now. Deputy Sherman sat in the easy chair, writing extensive notes in her own little notebook. She glanced up at me as Kip and I walked in, frowned, and brought her eyes back to her notebook. Her pen never stopped moving. She was wearing her full proper uniform, complete with clunky black cop shoes.

It must have driven her crazy, having to wear such ugly shoes.

"So, any *other* suspects?" she asked Kip, without looking at him. Or me.

I stopped in my tracks. "What do you mean '*other* suspects'? Are you saying I'm a suspect?"

"Cam," Kip started, but Sherman interrupted him.

"I meant 'witnesses', of course," she said, in a snotty tone. "My bad."

Kip gave me a helpless look, then said, "I should go out to help them search, unless you'd like an escort back to your residence first, Ms. Tate?"

I shook my head, not wanting to supply Sherman with any extra fodder. "I'm fine now. Thank you for…all your help." I'm sure I saw Sherman smirk as Kip turned and headed for the door. I meant to leave as well, but just then saw Paige Berry slip out from Marie's bedroom, closing the door quietly behind her. She gave me a sympathetic look as I headed toward her, meaning to ask what she was doing here, and when she had arrived; but she shook her head softly as I approached, directing a concerned look at Sherman, then looking back at me and shaking her head again as she headed quietly down into the kitchen.

Was she trying to tell me something? About Sherman? And why was anyone letting Paige poke around in here, anyway? Wasn't this a—well, maybe a crime scene? Certainly an *active investigation*, at least. Paige was moving around very quietly, but not sneaking. Sherman had gone back to her note taking; but there was no way she hadn't noticed Paige was here…was there? Kip and I had heard the old lady's voice clear in the kitchen. Something seemed very odd here.

I slipped down to the kitchen as well, and found Paige snooping through cabinets, standing on tiptoes to peer into one over the stove. "Hello, Camille," she said, not turning around. "This girl didn't have much truck with real food, did she?"

"No," I said wearily, sitting back in the chair I'd spent so much time in already. "I kept trying to get her to eat healthier…"

Paige closed the cabinet and turned her milky blue gaze on me. "All we can do is suggest, and lead by example. People must be left to live their own lives."

"I'm…sure you're right. Um, was I just imagining things, or were you trying to tell me something back in the hallway?"

"Oh, not really. I just didn't want us to start talking there and distract Deputy Sherman from her writing. She's clearly very busy."

I just sort of looked back at her, then shivered suddenly. Maybe it was just a random case of chills, or the ups and downs of my supernatural disability, or was it shock still? "I sure wish I could have had that cup of tea," I said, rubbing at my arms again, "but Agent Veierra seemed to think all this stuff should be checked for poison first." Oops. Was I not supposed to have said that?

Paige nodded pensively. "Sensible, I suppose."

"Is…that what you're doing here?" I asked, remembering that Paige was one of Orcas's more notable horticulturists. "Have they called you in to look for…poisonous herbs or something?"

"Seems a reasonable precaution, under the circumstances, doesn't it?" she said vaguely.

I was unsure whether she'd just answered my question or not, and decided just to shut my mouth as I'd been told to. "This kitchen gives me the creeps now," I said instead, shivering again.

"I don't blame you. The energy here is diseased. Very different from when you lived here." Paige set a hand on the kitchen table and smiled at me. "We had our very first conversation right here at this table, young lady. Do you remember?"

I gave her a smile back. "With coffee. And then wine." The pleasant memory seemed to cut right through the anxiety I'd been feeling, and filled me with a sudden warmth. Gosh, wine sounded good right now. I would have bet everything I owned that Marie didn't have any in the house, though. "Hey, do you want to come over to my place? I don't think I have any wine, but I can make us some tea."

Paige nodded. "Are they done with you?"

"They said they were."

"Let's just go, then." She gathered her fire-engine-red coat around her and headed for the kitchen door. "Come on, we'll go out the back way. No need to bother the important authorities."

こ

As we walked away from my previous residence, Paige observed in a low, amused voice, "I'm rather doubtful they'll find anything of use out here in the pitch dark."

I chuckled. "I guess they have to do something."

We took the path through the woods, as usual; I lit the way with my phone's flashlight. When we stepped out into Lisa's parking area, Lisa herself was just walking out her front door.

"Hey," I called over to her, hoping not to startle her by just materializing out of the darkness.

"Oh! Cam!" she cried, and rushed over to both of us. "And... Paige, hello." Lisa grasped both my hands in hers and peered into my face. From the illumination of her porch light, I could see she was upset. "Is it true? I just heard that Marie was taken away on a Life Flight helicopter."

"Yes," I said, as my heart sank again. Had I truly let the terrible news settle into the background just the tiniest bit, for a minute there, in anticipation of a nice visit with Paige Berry? "Yes, we're just coming from there, from her house."

Lisa squeezed my hands harder, then let them go and brushed her hair back absently, letting it fall again. "Oh, I don't know what to think, it's too awful! That poor girl, that poor, poor girl."

"You don't want to go over there right now," Paige put in. "Place is crawling with official personages. Quite a bit of police attention, for a sick girl. We were going back to Camille's place for a glass of wine."

Or tea, I thought.

Lisa shook her head, biting her lip, looking at both of us. Then she firmed up her narrow shoulders and put on a brave smile. "No, absolutely not. Come in here, I've enough wine for all three of us."

CHAPTER 7

For some reason, Lisa seated Paige and me in the dining room, though there was nothing resembling cooking happening in her kitchen. We sat around the far edge of her huge dining table, Lisa at the head, Paige and me flanking her. An unlabeled bottle of deliciousness rested on a sterling silver wine stand, already over half-emptied into our three crystal glasses.

Lisa took a big gulp of her wine. "Tell me everything," she said, setting her glass down and looking at me.

Well, I had been asked not to talk about my conversation with Agent Veierra. But I went through the rest of it again. I was getting good at it. Lisa asked few questions, just let me tell it.

The wine helped.

Paige sipped her own elixir, watching us carefully with her strong gaze, not adding anything to my account. When I was finished, I leaned back and took a sip of my wine. "I feel awful." I gave Lisa a helpless look. "I...wish I'd taken her more seriously. I had no idea she was really sick..." I trailed off, unsure of whether I was supposed to mention the prowler or not. That had come out before I'd ever talked with Veierra, but who knew what she might think off limits? I had no idea of anything, really.

Lisa still looked so upset. She wiped the corner of her eye and swallowed another healthy mouthful of wine. "It's uncanny, really."

"Uncanny?" It was a lot of things, but I didn't know if I'd have used quite that word.

She shook her head and refilled our glasses, though Paige's and mine weren't empty yet. "I have to think carefully about what this all means," she said, almost to herself.

Paige and I both leaned forward. "Means?" I asked.

Lisa's grey gaze met mine. Did she look...a little startled maybe? "She was my assistant, you know, for some time. One of them, anyway."

"Yes, of course." In fact that had been one of the many things I'd wanted to learn more about, now that Lisa was finally back on the island. Marie had been so maddeningly vague about her duties for Lisa, during all the time she'd worked for her. Or their relationship, or really pretty much everything.

"And you know how strongly I feel about mentoring. About helping young women find their voice, their power." Lisa blinked, her eyes glistening. "Marie...she has so much potential. She is very, very smart—"

"She *is*?" I put my hand over my mouth, not having meant to speak ill of the ill, but really?

"Oh, yes. I know what you mean, Cam, but she was a brilliant intern. She showed such talent. But she lacked a certain level of common sense. After I employed her, I tried to bring her along, and then I even offered her this position when that wasn't working out." Lisa's voice broke suddenly, and she wiped her eyes. "I can't believe it. I should have known."

"Known what?" I honestly didn't understand how Lisa could still feel responsible for Marie, after she'd quit and left Lisa in the lurch. Of course, that created the opening that led to my being hired, but still. "It's sounds like you did everything you could for her."

"I should have done more." Lisa was really upset.

Paige rose to her feet and stood beside Lisa, putting a gentle hand on her shoulders, patting her. "There, it's all right," she murmured.

I just sat there staring at both of them. If you had asked me this morning if I would ever in my life see Lisa Cannon breaking down and Paige Berry comforting her, I would have laughed in your face. I took another sip of wine, and began wondering if I should go poke around in the kitchen and see if I could put something together for dinner.

Just then, my phone rang, giving me the perfect excuse to exit this touching, if awkward, moment between Paige and Lisa; I pulled it out of my pocket as I rose and headed off toward the windows. I was expecting Kip. But it was Jen.

Of course.

"Hey," I said into the phone.

"Oh my gosh, you found another body!"

I turned further away from Paige and Lisa. "She's not *dead*," I hissed.

"Okay, she's not dead yet, but from what I've heard, she was most of the way there. Do you think she tried to kill herself?"

"Are you kidding me?!"

"And you're the one who found her. You really have a knack."

"Jen!"

"I'm kidding, I hope she's going to be all right, Cam. I'm sorry, it's too soon I guess."

"You bet it's too soon." I paced into the kitchen after all, just to not have this conversation in the room with Lisa. "She was weak and malnourished, and probably depressed, and almost certainly had the flu, and…" *Don't discuss—especially with Jen.* "…I don't know what else."

"But *do* you think she was trying to kill herself?"

I couldn't tell if she sounded horrified or fascinated. Well, both, probably. "That never even occurred to me. If she left a note, nobody's mentioned it to me." I could hear the sound of something happening in the background, though I couldn't quite make out what it was. "She texted me right before..." I started, the pit of my stomach dropping in dread. Suddenly all that wine wasn't feeling so good anymore.

Jen caught her breath in a low gasp. I heard laughter behind her. "She texted you? Really?"

"Well, yeah. That's why I went over there—the text was, well, like it was cut off or something."

"What did it say?" Jen asked.

"She heard something, she was sorry to bother me—but that was it. An unfinished sentence. I texted her back and I called her, and when I couldn't get her, I walked over."

"Oh, Cam." Jen's voice softened. "I'm sorry to make a joke of it, but you do keep finding these bodies."

"She's ALIVE. And I've only actually found *one* body. No one's ever found the guy Sheila shot. I did find a body on the beach, yes. But just the one. The *next* two bodies were found by *other* people." One by Lisa, and one by a very drunk JoJo (and his sister, and her girlfriend). "It's been *months* since I've found a body."

"I know, I'm sorry. I know your actual found-dead-body count is exactly one." Was Jen actually *laughing*? "Listen, this must be so awful for you. Do you want me to come over tonight when I get off work? You're not going to be able to sleep."

It was on the tip of my tongue to say no, but then I reconsidered. Did I really want to sleep alone in my tiny cabin at the edge of Massacre Bay, after some mysterious prowler had been at least spying on the caretaker next door, who might or might not be alive still?

I hadn't even locked my door when I'd left, I suddenly remembered.

"Would you?" I asked, instead.

She gave a low chuckle. "Of course. I'm not squeezing into a loft with you and your cat, though, no matter how great that bed is. I'll bring a sleeping bag and pad."

The sound of laughter grew louder behind her. She was obviously calling from the Barnacle.

"Thanks," I said. "I'm at Lisa's right now, but that sounds perfect."

"Lisa's?" she asked, her voice rising in curiosity. "Dang it, I have to run now—we're slammed. It was all I could do to get a moment to make this call. I'll see you around eleven, okay?"

"Sure," I said. "Thanks."

She hung up. I stood there in Lisa's kitchen for a moment, processing, then went to peek at the dining room. Paige had returned to her chair; she and Lisa were talking in low tones. Lisa looked like she had regained her composure.

"Hey, do you want me to figure out some dinner?" I called out to them.

Lisa turned and gave me a grateful smile. "Oh, Cam, that would be marvelous, but you must be wrecked too. I mean, you keep finding all these bodies."

"I HAVE ONLY FOUND ONE DEAD BODY."

The women in the other room were very quiet for a moment.

"Well." Lisa cleared her throat. "I have some posole in the freezer, plenty for the three of us; and there's a fresh head of cabbage in the fridge. And radishes." She rose her to feet and walked into the kitchen. I noted the tiniest unsteadiness in her step, but she covered it well. "It's probably a good idea if we eat."

Paige got up and followed her. "Count me out, ladies; I have to get back up the hill to my girls. I hadn't intended to be even this long, but when I heard the ruckus, I figured I'd better come see."

"Thank you, Paige," Lisa said, looking grateful.

Paige gave her a nod and a warm smile as she headed to the front hall. As she was pulling on her coat of many colors (well, just shades of red, but still), I followed her out and gave her a hug. "Thank you," I whispered. "You've put us both right at ease."

"You two take care of each other, hear?" she said to me softly.

I nodded into her shoulder, then released her. "We will. And Jen Darling is coming over to spend the night with me after she gets off work."

"Good, good." She glanced back at Lisa, who was rummaging around in her freezer. Then she lowered her voice further. "See if you can get this one to talk to you. Her cards are very close to her chest." She pulled the tatters and panels of her coat tightly around herself, since apparently whatever buttons it once had were long since removed by the goats. "Thank you for the wine, my dear!" she called out to Lisa, and then was out the door before I could even wonder exactly what she meant by the whispered comment.

So Paige and Lisa were…friends? Who could have imagined?

❧

It wasn't long before we were back in the dining room, this time with big bowls of rich, meaty, brothy posole sprinkled with shredded cabbage and sliced radishes, and more of the delicious wine. I'd made sure to give us full glasses of water as well, and a pitcher to replenish them with. Never in my life had I drank so much alcohol as I was finding myself doing since I moved here. The wine soothed my social anxiety and made chameleoning less likely—and it was delicious—but I sure didn't want to start relying on it.

Maybe I can watch my drinking on all the days when I don't *stumble into a crime scene,* I told myself, as Lisa topped up my glass.

That seemed fair.

I let out a discreet belch and took another sip. I was watching my wine, but Lisa was not. As many times as I'd drank with Lisa, I had never seen her as unsteady as she was this evening. Marie's illness obviously had hit her hard, which should be no surprise; however estranged they'd been since the water heater disaster and Marie's abrupt departure from Lisa's employment, they had worked together for several years before that, and Lisa had liked her enough to entrust her with first taking care of personal office duties and then her whole house here. Plus the mentoring thing.

Still, Lisa hadn't seemed this upset even when Sheila, her trusted assistant and caretaker, had turned out to be a murderous kidnapper.

The wine had clearly loosened Lisa's tongue. I mostly listened as she regaled me with fond memories of Marie's first arrival at the lab, explaining how she changed over the time of her internship. "She was brilliant, simply brilliant, but so *frightened*," Lisa said. "Frightened of *everything*." She'd found the research overwhelming, and was terrified of making a mistake, or wasting time on a dead end.

"That's how she ended up doing office work." Lisa shook her head. "It could have been nuts and bolts training for larger responsibilities down the line. But she just went from being a brilliant student with a bright future in research, to a possible lab manager, to office help. And when even that got to be too much for her, I made her my receptionist. I was viscerally disappointed. But she was too afraid to live up to her own potential. She had become so frightened of everything, and I still don't know why."

I nodded. Marie had been a scared little mouse, afraid of plumbers and calories and JoJo Brixton and…well, yes, everything. Had she frightened herself nearly to death?

I cringed inwardly. I had my own struggles with paralyzing fear, to a degree that no one in the world could understand. Maybe Marie's fearfulness bothered me so much because she reminded me of myself.

"The funny thing is, she didn't start out that way," Lisa said, looking sadly away, as if gazing at some view I couldn't see. "Derek—my ex-husband—tried to work with her as well, and…well, we might have gotten a little competitive about it. Of course I thought I could do better. But I had no better luck than he did."

My ears perked up at this. I remembered that Marie had talked about Derek with adoration, even reverence—though he had always been the villain of Lisa's story. "She...seemed to think highly of him?" I ventured. "The one time she mentioned him, that is."

Lisa looked at me across the table. Not quite drunk, but not sober either. "What did she say about him?" she asked, sounding as though she was making an effort to keep emotion out of her words. "I would be curious to hear."

"I don't remember exactly, of course," I said. "It was when we first met. But she seemed to think he was brilliant. I always wondered if, well, if he did the same thing to her that he did to you. Pretended to be someone he wasn't, so she would think he was wonderful. He sounds like a narcissist to me, you know?"

Lisa still studied me, then gave a quick smile. "You're sure you haven't met him?" She laughed, but it had a pained edge to it. "Yes, I suspect it was something quite a bit like that. He needs to be the center of—not just attention, but of everyone's regard. You understand the difference?"

I didn't, not exactly, but I nodded, hoping to keep *her* talking.

"He couldn't just join a team," she said, and now I could hear the anger in her voice. "He had to lead the team. He had to have a brilliant and successful wife—he loved that about me, at first—but she mustn't ever turn out to be better than him—at anything. He had to *best* me." She snorted a breath out of her nose and took another sip of her wine. Her posole bowl was only half-eaten, and she hadn't touched her water. I drank a big gulp of my own water, hoping to encourage her by example.

And now I had become *Lisa's* caretaker.

Of course, I learned that at a young age, when the room was so thick with danger, I could hardly see my mother for it. Hiding had let me live, when...my thought snapped off before it could go further. Where had my mind been going? I didn't even want to know. Lisa was talking again, and the moment was mercifully lost.

"And when he couldn't defeat me," Lisa was saying, her voice brittle, "he tried to undermine my relationships with my mentees. Beginning with Marie. He wanted them to be his acolytes, not mine." She shook her head and sipped her wine again, then set the glass down with a sigh. "Oh, Cam, listen to me. Or, rather, don't. No one wants to hear someone whine about their ex-husband."

"I brought him up," I said. "And I did plenty of whining about my ex-boyfriend, who *is still here on the island*, for no good reason whatsoever. Fair is fair."

She laughed, and suddenly looked more sober, more in-control. "Ah, men. Why do we do this to ourselves? Honestly, we'd all be better off with vibrators and sperm banks."

"Lisa!" I burst out in shocked laughter. "You sound like the women's studies class I took in college." Then I wanted to bite my tongue. Was she going to ask me about my degree now? I'd have to tell her it had just been a community college, and I hadn't told her that I didn't have a four-year degree...had I? Of course she could have guessed it—she knew I was a hairdresser—but now I wanted to be a playwright. Would she think I was insufficiently intellectual?

But she was still laughing, and here I was, making up trouble before it had happened again. She had already read my play, and given me notes, and hadn't told me that she was taking it off the production schedule, had she?

"It was nice of Paige Berry to stop down," she said. "She's a strange old bird, but she's always been a good neighbor."

"I didn't realize you knew her so well," I said, scraping the sides of my bowl with my spoon. I didn't even really know what posole was, but it was delicious.

"Who around here doesn't know Paige?" Lisa asked. "She clearly likes you quite a bit, and I feel like that's saying something." She set her spoon down and tapped her chest with a closed fist. "That woman sees more than most. I don't know what exactly it is about her, but…" She gazed off into the middle distance, lost in thought for a moment, before shaking her head and looking back at me with a small smile. "And this is how I get when I'm upset about something. I drink too much and get all spooky and woo-woo." Her smile widened. "Stop me if I get maudlin."

"You're in no danger of getting maudlin," I assured her. "And I'm not at all convinced that there isn't something woo-woo about Paige. Have you seen the vegetables she grows?"

CHAPTER 8

Lisa gently eased me out of her house not long thereafter, not even letting me help with the cleanup—which, admittedly, wasn't a whole lot more than two bowls, two spoons, and a sharp knife. And three wine glasses. "Are you sure you don't want me to walk you to the cottage?" she asked, as we stood at her door.

I looked out into the deep, dark, silent night and thought about it. Hard. But I shook my head. "When we got there, I'd just have to walk you back here," I pointed out, "and we'd spend the whole night walking each other back and forth and get no sleep. No, one of us has to break that chain before it even gets started, and it's going to be me."

She chuckled, and then pulled me into a quick hug. "Thank you for keeping me company this evening," she said, "and helping with my leftovers."

"It was my pleasure." Somehow, being with her and Paige had normalized things again. They had calmed me all the way down and removed most of the fear and danger from the situation.

Sadly, that effect lasted only a few more minutes as I used my phone light to illuminate my way down the little-used path to my unlocked cottage, wishing I wasn't alone after all. I really had become quite the caretaker type somehow since arriving here. It seemed like every time someone offered me help that I might once have leapt at, I took care of *them* now by refusing—only to regret it later most of the time.

Nope, I told myself, *there's nobody here in these woods.* There had been a prowler by Marie's house, yes; but I'd not only heard a car drive away, I'd also watched sheriff deputies, a formidable FBI agent, and a Mountie search the woods where I'd seen the figure in black. And Kip had been out there searching, too. If Kip had thought there was any danger, he would never have let me leave the Brixton guesthouse in the first place. So the noises I was hearing were just the normal noises of a forest at night, and here was my little cottage already, and now I was hearing the excited kick-thumps of a bunny who has been too long in his hutch in the cold and dark outside, and no dinner.

I brought him into the house, and endured the complaints of my cat as I put together dinner for both of them. "You know, between the two of you, you eat basically the whole food pyramid," I told them, when they were both chowing down. "Except it's all protein for the little carnivore, and all veggies for Mr. Fluffbutt there."

If they cared about my observations, they did a good job of concealing that fact.

I lit a fire in my little stove, and then sat back and watched them eat. It was not even ten o'clock; Jen wouldn't be here for at least an hour. I yawned, hoping I wouldn't fall asleep waiting for her.

So of course she startled me awake when she knocked on the door.

I hadn't locked it, so she was walking in as I blinked my eyes open and struggled to right myself in the chair just a bit, body tense, arms tingling. I gave them some brisk rubs, hoping the wine would still be in effect.

"It's just me, don't get up," she said, in a low, calm voice. "We can go straight to sleep if you want—it's been a long day for me too, though nothing like what you've been through, I'm sure."

"No, no," I said, relieved that my voice worked. "I just dozed off for a second. I'm glad to see you."

Jen pulled the door shut behind her and turned the latch to bolt it. Then she looked around the little room. "This place is great!"

"Thanks."

"You don't think it's too small, though?"

I stifled a sigh. "Nope. I love it." I pointed at the dark front windows. "Wait till you see it in the daylight."

"I look forward to that. I can't wait to explore it. There's so much to see. It will take days…"

"Ha, ha."

She smiled and glanced at the floor. "Should I put Master Bun back in his hutch?"

My rabbit, clearly aware that he was under discussion, wiggled his nose at both of us and then hopped over to the dying fire. "I don't know," I finally said. "Maybe not yet."

"I have a very strict rule about wild animals in my bed," Jen said.

I giggled. "He's not wild, and he's not a co-sleeper. But we'll put him out before we turn in."

She dropped her bedroll and duffel bag on the floor and walked over to me, opening her arms for a hug. "How are you *doing*, Cam?"

I got up and fell into her arms. "I don't know," I said into her shoulder as her red curls tickled my nose. "This is crazy, right? Tell me this is crazy, that people don't almost die from drinking too much kombucha."

"This is crazy," she agreed, patting me on the back. "And kombucha never put anyone in a coma. As far as I *know*."

"And that this is just another thing in a long *list* of crazy," I went on. "Right? That there is no good reason that so many people should be dying and almost-dying right here."

"Indeed, no good reason," she agreed again. "I don't know if there had been a suspicious death on Orcas for the last ten years, or more, before Megan Duquesne drowned. But I'm sure the authorities…" She snorted without finishing the sentence.

"What?" I asked, finally pulling out of the hug and flumping back into my chair. I gestured at one of the table's chairs, and Jen pulled it around and sat down in it, pulling her legs up to tuck her feet under her. James immediately jumped into her lap; she petted him absently. "What about the authorities?"

Jen shook her head, then leaned closer, her eyes holding mine. "I know super impressive experts from the wider world have been brought in—at great expense, I'm sure—to use their super impressive investigative powers to impressively solve all our mysteries—and how long have they been here? How many months? Yet we still have no earthly idea what's going on, though *something is going on here.*"

"What are you saying?" I almost whispered, because I knew Jen Darling, and I thought I knew where she was going with this…

"Why do you suppose all these experts have made such crappy progress, Cam?"

I shook my head. "I wish I knew."

"Because the answers they're looking for are hiding in places they can't find. That's why."

"And which places are those?"

She leaned back and shrugged. "I have no real idea yet, but I'm pretty sure we could figure it out faster than they seem able to." She raised a hand to stave off my interruption, even though I wasn't interrupting her. So I just nodded, and she went on. "I grew up here; you didn't, but you have an unusual sympatico with things on this island. You know when something is weird and when it isn't. I'm not even entirely sure how—" She gave me a searching glance.

I will tell her about my chameleoning…I will, I will… I told myself. I trusted her enough to. We'd been through enough together, boy howdy had we. Someday… *Just not right now.*

"But you *do* understand this place," she added, when I didn't answer. "So you belong here too, even if it took you twenty-whatever years to figure that out. Agent Veierra, the Mountie, even Deputy Sherman—they don't belong. They can investigate all they like, and they'll never get to the bottom of a lot of things around here, because they're outsiders. I'm sure people have just shut them out, or they've had less idea where to look in the first place even than you and I would."

I nodded again, even though a million questions flooded my mind. Sure, insider access was great and everything, but what if this was not an Orcas mystery—what if it came from off island somewhere? No amount of mystical island simpatico would get us anywhere against some larger conspiracy, if that was what we were dealing with. And what if that prowler did turn out to be just some red herring, and Marie really had just taken too many pills, or dieted herself into such poor health that a normal flu was enough to almost kill her?

*No red herring tiptoes around someone's house dressed in black and peeking through windows at a nearly dead woman inside…*a little inner voice insisted.

"What about Kip?" I asked. "He grew up here."

Jen's face softened. "I know you're sweet on him—"

"I am not!" I shouted, alarming the cat and the rabbit, who had both drifted off to sleep.

"—but he's been shaped too much by outside influence. You know? It's not like there's a police academy on the island—on any of the islands. His actions are all decided somewhere else, not done for any *local* reasons—not the way I mean local." Suddenly she leaned forward again, grabbing my gaze with her own.

"I know that look," I said. "You have a crazy stupid terrible idea, and it's going to get us in crazy terrible stupid trouble."

"Don't be silly!" she cried, laughing even as she said it. "All my ideas are one hundred percent brilliant, and you know it." She leaned even more forward. She was going to fall out of that chair if she leaned much further, and face plant onto my floor.

"All right then, out with it," I said, waving a hand impatiently.

But she just sat back, and gave me a mysterious smile. "Actually I need to look into one more thing first. Then I'll tell you my brilliant idea."

"So we just go to bed and work on this very important bit of business some other day?"

Her smile softened. "Yep."

I knew she wanted me to beg her to tell me now…but I was exhausted, in every way. "Thanks. I really am tired."

She scratched James's ears. "You don't even want a hint?" she finally asked.

I laughed. "Okay, okay. *Please Jen, please, please tell me the amazing secret you're holding back!*"

She giggled as well. "Well, this is what I have to confirm. My friends at the Green Goose had me prepare two new rooms today, setting them up for a long-term stay."

"Ohh…kay," I said slowly, not getting the relevance of that.

"The two cheapest rooms…and each set up for only one person."

"…And?"

"Their last names are Smith and Jones."

I just shrugged, giving her an *I'm lost* look.

She snorted impatiently. "Who travels with someone else, to a vacation spot, under a couple of obviously fake names, getting two rooms alone, and for a long time?"

I shrugged. "Loners? A couple friends who want their privacy? A coincidence, nothing to do with each other?"

"Or…" she paused for dramatic effect, "a couple of investigators working on a case…needing to get closer to the action?"

"Oh! Veierra and McMichaels. You think it's them?" I asked.

"That's what I need to see about tomorrow. But I bet it is. And

Cam! If they stay at the Goose, I'll be able to—"

"Do *not* spy on the FBI and the Mounties!" I almost shrieked. "Jen! I'm pretty sure that's a crime."

But she just grinned again, and hummed innocently.

"What do you think you'd find out if you did?" I asked. "You just told me that outsiders can't find the missing pieces here. That's why you want us to do it. So what are we even supposed to learn from spying on them?"

Jen rolled her eyes. "Well I just don't know! That's the problem, isn't it? But it'll be more than we know now. Even if all we find out is what questions they're here working on, we'll have a much clearer idea of what answers we need to look for—which should help us find them a lot quicker than we're likely to without that information, right?"

I couldn't help my smile. "Don't take this the wrong way, but you just can't stand not knowing something, can you?"

"Can *you?*" she demanded, but she was still smiling too. "Seriously, Cam, it's our *home*—our people, our community, and our place that all these crazy things keep happening to. If you and I can find the missing piece that keeps escaping all these experts, wouldn't that be great?"

Would it? Jen's enthusiasm was contagious, but I had a hard time seeing how great it would be to end up in jail for spying on federal agents from two separate countries. "So, have you got some kind of theory about what these places they're not finding are?" I asked.

"Well…I know you love Lisa, and I think she's pretty okay too, so you might not like hearing this, but…haven't you noticed how much of this bizarre stuff happens around her?"

"What are you saying?" I knew very well what she meant, of course, but she was right: I didn't really want to hear it—for all sorts of reasons. "At least as many strange things happen around the Brixtons," I argued. "One caretaker died. Another caretaker, and that's *me*, witnessed a murder and was kidnapped and shot.

JoJo Brixton found the body of Sheila's cousin or whoever that was. And Marie? This happened to her while she was caretaking at the Brixtons'." I shivered, and not for effect. "I'm really glad you offered to come over tonight. This is weirding me out, kind of a lot."

"My pleasure." She reached over and patted my hand. "But I think the only reason that strange stuff happens at the Brixtons' is because they have the bad luck to be living next to Lisa Cannon. Think about it: Megan Duquesne apparently died after she got tangled up with Gregory Baines, who in turn got shot by Sheila—who was working for Lisa. Ephraim Snooks died when he was robbing Lisa's house; and judging by what he was taking, Sheila was probably behind that."

"What, prescription pills?"

"And underwear, remember?"

"So he was a pill-popping pervert?"

"No. Think. Someone needed clean underwear, maybe even the pills for some reason, and that someone was probably Sheila." I opened my mouth to suggest that this seemed an awfully big leap, but Jen waved me silent without even pausing. "She probably told him where to go, what to get. He *knew* where stuff was. And Sheila's dead cousin was prowling around on his boat and somehow drowned; and Marie was only on the island in the first place because she worked for Lisa. I think all these trails lead back to Lisa, not the Brixtons. Come on, Cam; don't you want to know? Maybe even clear her of suspicion?"

"Is she under suspicion?" I asked. "I mean, do you think those guys are checking into the Green Goose to investigate *Lisa?*"

"Well," said Jen, not quite suppressing a triumphant little grin, "we can't know, can we, if I don't even try to find out."

I sighed. "Maybe you have a point," I finally said. "I like Lisa, and...well, I know she's caught up in this somehow. That awful divorce wasn't just about romance and heartbreak—it was about money, lots of it. Business. And pride. If she's into this somehow…I'd probably rather know that before I end up being her personal assistant. And if she's not, it would be good to help keep her out of trouble maybe. I think the first thing we need to know more about is her ex-husband."

Jen nodded. "Okay, there you go. Add that to our list. Lisa's way more likely to let something slip to you than to any of these law enforcement experts, isn't she? You need to ask her more questions, Cam. You really need to find out more of what she was up to when she was off island all that time—in Bermuda? Really? What's a single, semi-retired business maven from Orcas doing for months in Bermuda? Has she started training you to be her personal assistant yet?"

"No," I admitted, feeling no more comfortable than before about what we were getting ourselves into here despite having sort of agreed to try it. "Mostly she said I should have a little time off first, now that she's back. And she gave me a huge pile of revisions for the play." I nodded toward the stack of manuscript pages on the table. "But she doesn't seem like the kind of person who can go very long without an assistant, and as far as I know, she hasn't had one since…well, since last December."

Jen nodded again, chewing her bottom lip as she thought. "Well, don't push it—we don't want to make her suspicious. Just…be available, and cheerful, you know?"

"Well, of course. You don't have to tell me that."

"I know, I know." She brushed her hair back with her fingers, combing apart a few tangles, and getting something on her hands—sticky drinks she'd served at work, grime from her steering wheel when she drove here, cat fur, whatever—into her hair in the process. She had such great hair, it sort of made me cringe to see her abuse it. "Hey: we're both tired, and it's pretty late," she said. "I know you wake up early. Should we hit the hay?"

Her words were like a magical spell: my sense of exhaustion returned even as she asked the question. "Oh, absolutely, let's."

She chuckled and got up. "You wanna brush your teeth first?"

"No—I have to deal with the livestock," I said. "You go ahead." I got up and corralled Master Bun in preparation for his return to the hutch. He could have slept indoors…if Jen wanted wildlife in her bed, and if I wanted to hunt up little turds all over the house all next week.

No, he'd be fine outside in that fur coat.

❦

No matter how late I go to bed, I wake up at five a.m. or close to it. I could hear Jen's gentle snores, and peered through the railing to see her. She was tucked deep into her sleeping bag, huddled close to the cold stove.

I could go down and make a fire, but that would wake her up for sure; I wasn't sure I could even get to the stove without stepping on her.

So I turned on my bedside lamp and read a while, trying to let enough time go by so that more reasonable human beings might consider it morning when I got up. Finally, though, my desire for coffee, and my need for the bathroom, got me out of bed and down the ladder.

Jen stirred even though I was trying to be quiet, so I gave up. "Hey," I said softly. "I'm gonna make a fire, want to scoot over a bit?"

"Snurggg urmm flr," she muttered, but she did wiggle off to the side at least enough so that I could reach the stove.

I wished for cardboard while fussing with the stove, but it was too far a walk to retrieve any from the trunk of my car. So I made do with the twigs and such by the woodpile. Within ten minutes, I had a crackling fire going, and coffee was making its sweet presence known. Jen emerged from her sleeping bag, her red curls a bit squashed on one side. She blinked over at me. "Coffee?"

"You want it there, or are you rejoining the land of the living?"

"Uggh, what time is it?"

I glanced at my phone. "Almost seven!"

She rubbed her sleepy eyes. "Good gracious, how is it that you can be so perky in the middle of the night?"

I got up and went to the coffee maker, filling up two mugs. "Coooffeee," I sang to her as I poured cream into them. "Cooooffeeee." I brought the mugs to the table, sat down, and took a sip of mine. Ahhh.

"All right, all right, here I come."

❧

We'd drank nearly the entire pot and were starting to become coherent again—well, she was; I'd been coherent for hours—and I was about to get up and work on breakfast when Jen's phone chimed with a text.

"Huh," she said, after she looked at the screen. "Did you block JoJo Brixton?"

A pang of anger and sorrow shot through me. "I might have. Why? Is he texting you now, the lying spoiled sneak?"

I could see her trying not to smile. "Yes, he is in fact texting me now, wondering why he can't get hold of you." Then she sobered, as did I, as we both realized exactly why JoJo Brixton would be trying to reach me. Marie... "Yeah," Jen said. "I suppose they've all heard by now."

"I'd be surprised if they didn't hear yesterday," I said. "I'm further surprised that Diana Brixton didn't charter a private jet to fly out here the moment she heard that her caretaker had the temerity to become seriously ill and disrupt the care of her mansion."

"Hm." She was still looking at her screen. "What do you want me to tell him?"

I got up and went to the fridge. Eggs would be good. I'd been eating an awful lot of eggs, but they're good protein, and who knew what would happen today? I might need a good solid layer of protein down underneath whatever else happened: more comatose neighbors, or dead bodies, or betraying friends, or whatever.

"Cam?" Jen prompted.

I turned to her. "I honestly don't know. What does he want?"

She shrugged. "He hasn't said yet—he just asked me if I knew how to get hold of you, because he can't seem to. He wonders if you have a new phone number."

"He can't tell he's blocked?"

"No," she said, with a certainty born of experience, I realized. "His texts will just hang out there in the ether, as far as he can tell—never landing, never getting a 'delivered' message."

"It might look like I'm out of cell service range," I said.

I turned back to the fridge and pulled out four eggs, setting them into a bowl on the counter. Cheese, what kind of cheese would be good? I still had some amazingly creamy chevre from Paige. Too bad I didn't have any chives or green onions or anything...what else could I forage?

"Cam?"

"I...only blocked him recently. I blocked him on Facebook, and then I went ahead and did it on the phone too." I turned around to her again. "Not that he was ever calling or texting me! I just...wanted to be on the safe side. And now he wants to find me! After all these months!"

"I know, I know." She got up and walked over to give me a hug. "He's a pampered pretty man, and he should be torn limb from limb by rabid weasels for being such a conniving jerk to you. And you showed him, you totally showed him, by landing on your feet—*more* than on your feet." She waved at the adorable little cottage around us. "You landed miles higher than the cliff he pushed you off. And, you were right about the daylight, by the way." She waved cheerfully at the windows. "It's a very pretty view."

I couldn't help snickering. "You should be a writer. Your command of metaphor is astonishing."

"Shut up," she said, laughing, and reached for the coffee pot to pour herself the last half-cup. "So again I ask, what should I tell him?"

I thought about it. "I want to know why he did what he did—but I also don't care. You know? At first I wanted to know—no, at first I thought I did know. I thought he wanted his old job back, and was trying to get rid of me. But then he didn't move back—he just went back to his rich stupid playboy lifestyle, which of course I know *nothing* about because I was totally *not* stalking him on social media, so none of that makes any sense. I just want him to—I don't know!" I huffed out a frustrated breath. "Yeah, I guess I do want to know what he wants."

Jen watched me as I went through all these contortions. "So unblock him, and I'll tell him to try texting again. We'll take it from there."

I looked at her, thinking it through, but I already knew I was going to do it. So I huffed out an exasperated breath and pulled out my phone.

It took a little doing, figuring out how to unblock a number, one that I hadn't heard from in *such* a long time, but I finally did so. "Okay," I told Jen, who was very busily scratching James's ears and not watching me.

"Okeedoke." She typed a line or two into her phone and pushed send. "You have great service here," she remarked. "You should have been living here all along."

"I know! If I had, then…" I stopped before I could even go down that road. If Lisa Cannon truly were the heart of all the mystery…who's to say what would have happened if I'd started out as her caretaker or assistant or playwright or whatever-I-was?

Jen gave me a sympathetic smile. James pushed against her hand, his little pea-brain not understanding why she had been petting him and suddenly stopped. What could be more important than seeing to the needs of a rangy orange cat? Cats had great lives, I thought. All they had to do was hunt some vermin now and then, which they loved doing, as far as I could tell, and as a reward they lived with us, and were fed by us, and got all the affection they could tolerate on a daily basis.

(No, I totally didn't wish I was a cat, who had no caretaking duties or unconscious neighbors or giant mysteries to untangle. That would be ridiculous.)

My phone dinged with a text. I took a breath before looking at it, but Jen was watching me, so…

Camikins, I know you hate me with the undying passion of a thousand suns, but trust me, I still love you as much as ever and I had my reasons, but none of that is important now, because you have to talk to me about what happened with Marie. You do NOT want to have to deal with my mother about this!

I handed the phone to Jen; she read the text too. "Well?" she said, handing it back to me when she was finished.

"Well what?"

She snorted. "Well what do you think?"

"'I still love you as much as ever'—what the crap, JoJo?" I almost yelled, the sudden strength of my anger surprising me. "That much is obvious! Zero equals zero."

Jen patted my arm. "I'm sure that's not how he means it. It's just JoJo hyperbole anyway—you guys were never *like that*."

"I liked him a lot," I said, "at least, before I knew he was a horrible betraying river otter. And I thought he liked me too, before ditto ditto. And what is this 'I had my reasons' crap?"

Jen shrugged. "Maybe he had his reasons?"

"Reasons for siccing his dreadful mom on me and getting me fired from the only job—the *only* job—I had at that point?" The anger boiled, surged, threatened to overwhelm me again, surprising me with its intensity. Yes, I'd known I was mad at him, and hurt; I'd spent plenty of time over the last few months dwelling on it, rehearsing imaginary conversations with him, inventing reasons and excuses and points of misunderstanding and whatever—but this, this felt…so very fresh. Like the betrayal had happened yesterday, not last December.

The phone dinged again, just one word. *Cam?*

"You should probably answer him," Jen said.

"I…I just…" I set the phone down and paced around the tiny cabin, burning off the glut of adrenaline. "Wow. Sorry. I didn't realize how…furious I still am at him."

She gave me a wry smile. "Even Kevin doesn't bring up this level of emotion."

Oh yes he did—at least, on the evening Jen had told me what he'd said about me. But I was glad to learn I'd somehow managed to cover my feelings for once. Now I flung my arms out in frustration, but I couldn't help smiling. "I know! Jen, I don't know what this is about, honest I don't." I walked back to the table and sat down, looking at the phone again, then back up at her. "What should I say to him?"

"Tell him you'll talk to him. Tell him to call."

I shrank, I swear I shrank like a deflating balloon. "I don't want to talk to him on the phone."

She gave me an appraising look. "Tell him to come out here, then. He can charter a plane or helicopter or whatever, like his mom did."

"Like she's probably going to," I muttered. Because yes, she'd be coming here, of course she would! Her caretaker was in the hospital…from whatever causes.

I picked up my phone and typed *Where are you?* And sent it before I could second-guess myself.

On my way, as it happens, came the reply, almost instantly. *Was headed up to the island anyway, so I'm waiting for the ferry as we speak.*

"Oh crap he's in Anacortes," I told Jen.

CHAPTER 9

JoJo was *on his way*. Holy cats.

Jen grabbed my phone again and read the text. "He's taking public transit?"

I giggled. "A fifty-dollar ferry ride isn't exactly public transit!"

"It is though. It's run by the state, it's not a private plane or boat or anything like that—it's public transit. You know the Brixtons don't need to ride the ferry." She leaned back in her chair, lost in thought. "Why is JoJo Brixton coming on the ferry? Is he trying to hide his movements for some reason?"

"He can't be," I said. "He posted that he was heading to the islands, to all his friends, just the other day."

Her gaze sharpened, and she gave me a look. "I thought you'd blocked him and stopped reading all his social media."

"Yeah," I said, squirming a bit in my chair. "Like, just the other day. Right after I read that post."

Jen gave me a fond smile. "Oh Cam. You are such a sweetheart."

ᘓᕬ

We finally settled on telling JoJo that he should come here

when his ferry landed. Which would be at least an hour and a half from now; he was taking the mid-morning ferry, and texting from his position in the car line. I could just imagine his fancy Jaguar in line, among the island's pickup trucks and Subarus crammed with loads of big-box-store shopping.

Not that I was all that familiar with the ferry lines over in America, having only ever been in one once, when it was dark and pouring rain, and I was crying my eyes out. But I'd been living on this island long enough to hear people complain about the ferry lines ten times a day until I felt like I'd spent half my life waiting in them too—and I was betting there weren't a lot of Jaguars parking in them either.

When I told him I had moved to an A-frame on Lisa's property, he wrote back at once: *Oh, the painting studio! Marvelous, dahling, perfect, it's so you. But isn't it a little small?*

"Hmph," I said, showing the text to Jen.

"Are we sure they aren't lovers? Or weren't?"

"No we are not. We are not the least bit sure about that."

She looked at me. "And do we care?"

I looked back at her. "I don't know. Do we?"

"You never were sweet on him. And you're not sweet on her. Or…are you?" She gave me a mock-stern look.

I laughed. "I adore Lisa Cannon, and dearly hope she is not involved in terrible monstrous doings and that her awful ex-husband isn't going to succeed in ruining her and stealing her business, and I want to be her personal assistant and have her produce my play, and I want her to keep offering me delicious wine and expensive luxury foods—but no, I harbor no desire to go to bed with her."

Jen laughed too. "I didn't think so, but due diligence and all that. Just being a good investigator, you know."

I was startled when my phone dinged again, having all but forgotten that JoJo was still waiting for me to answer his irksome question. Done waiting for my reply, apparently, he'd written,

See you soon! I didn't reply to that either. Let him wonder what *I* was thinking.

"Okay," Jen said more seriously. "JoJo Brixton will be here soon, and he's got some 'splainin' to do. We are going to let him do that. But what do we want to ask him, specifically?"

"Seriously? It's actually very simple: why did he try to get rid of me? Was he just being an ass, or did he have some legitimate reason for throwing me to his wolf of a mother? And if he did— what was it?"

She shrugged. "I don't know, you're right." Then she grinned. "You showed her, at least."

To my surprise, remembering that evening actually made me smile. I'd thought all was lost, but I'd stood up to Diana Brixton anyway, quitting before she could fire me, even though that left me with no job and no place to go; even though James and Master Bun and I were going to be sleeping in my car, so far as I knew. And then getting rescued by Lisa Cannon—all coincidentally—mere hours later. (And reconciling with Jen too. Craziest day ever, the very worst and the very best.) "I did."

"So we'll let him explain himself," she said, "then just take it from there. Don't worry, I'm good at thinking on my feet."

"That you are." I leaned back in my chair, barely resisting the urge to hug her, or to hug my arms around myself and rock back and forth in happiness. Because I wasn't alone. Jen was back. What had I ever done to deserve such a friend as Jen Darling? I had never known anyone like her, not remotely. Confident, cheerful, resourceful, fun—oh and beautiful, of course, with unbounded energy and a quick wit—yet also kind and loving, observant and sensitive. I couldn't have designed a more perfect person if I'd been sketching out a character for my play—I seriously couldn't, because no one would believe such a character could be real.

"If nothing else, it should be entertaining," she said, after a minute. "He does love to talk."

"Oh, yes he does. And I'm sure it will be."

I went ahead and brewed another pot of coffee while we wait-ed, and scrambled up the last of my eggs—I'd need to get back to town soon, or it was back to English muffins. "Do you have to work today?" I asked.

She laughed again. "Of course I do. I'm innkeeping—well, maid-servicing—but not till noon. Just one room to clean; and of course keeping an eye out for our *new arrivals.*" She gave me a significant glance. "Kelsey's got the delivery route today," she went on. "Then I'm at the Barnacle this evening, but Hanna's opening, so I don't have to be there till seven. Or later, if we're slow." She gave me a knowing grin. "Practically a day off."

"Only two jobs. What are you going to do with all that free time?"

"Interrogate a charming and debauched million-heir, to start with."

I swear, it was only coffee we were drinking, though you'd nev-er have known it if you were eavesdropping outside the window.

Which I didn't worry about at all! Not even a tiny bit!

And if you believe that…

❧

The closest place to park a car was in front of the boring guesthouse where I was not living, and that was not nearly close enough to hear the purr of a fine English motor, yet I still knew somehow when JoJo arrived on Lisa's property.

I mean, it's not that I don't believe in supernatural things—I literally *vanish when I feel threatened,* for crying out loud—and we knew what boat he was on and how long it should take him to drive here, but…there had to have been something else at work there, because I was not the tiniest bit surprised when there was a soft knock on the cottage door. In fact, I was already on my feet ready to open it. Even so, I paused when the knock did come, and looked back at Jen.

"You got this," she whispered, nodding encouragingly.

I smiled, took a breath, and stepped to the door, careful not to trip over Mr. Inquisitive Cat on my way.

I opened the door and took a half step back, motioning as I said, "Come in, it's freezing out there."

JoJo may have raised an eyebrow—I didn't know, I was looking into the room, not really willing to study him yet. Anyway, he walked in, shrugging out of what must be one of a hundred fine, soft leather jackets. He hung it over the back of a dining room chair, then pulled the chair out and sat down in it. "Jen Darling," he said to my friend. "Lovely to see you."

"Likewise," she said, with a cheerful smile that gave away absolutely nothing.

He turned and looked up at me. I'd occupied myself with closing the door and trying to decide whether or not to lock it. I settled on "not", and finally walked back to my own chair at the table. He watched me, looking—apologetic? It was hard to tell. Guarded, anyway.

"Cam, I know you hate me," he said. Then he paused, as though expecting that I would interrupt him—to deny it, or to agree? I didn't say anything, though, just watched him. He took a small breath, shrugged his fine shoulders, and went on. "You have every right to. Honestly, I hate me, too, but I didn't feel like I had any choice."

"We always have choices," Jen said, folding her arms across her chest.

JoJo gave her a helpless look before turning back to me. "I've thought about that day a lot since then—you have no idea—and I've wanted to reach out, but...well, I didn't."

"Too busy partying and socializing?" I said. I knew I sounded sullen and bitchy, but, well, was I wrong? And even if I was, who was he to complain?

He blinked his long lashes at me, but with none of the relaxed flirtatiousness I'd always enjoyed. "A man's gotta keep up appearances."

It kind of broke my heart. He was trying to be his old self, but it was clear that even he knew it wasn't working. "Why don't you just tell me what was really going on then? Were you trying to get rid of me?"

"I was trying to get you to leave the island, yes," he said, his shoulders sagging a bit. "It didn't work, obviously."

"*What?*" I was amazed, and not only because he'd decided to stop dancing around things and just tell the truth finally. Until this moment, I had assumed he only wanted to get me fired. "Why on earth did you want me to leave *the island?*"

He held my gaze, looking *so* earnest. "Cam, you weren't happy here, and you knew it, but you didn't want to admit it. My mother is impossible; you were never going to be comfortable working for her. I'm glad you're out of that situation, but I felt like you needed to change things up even more—leave the island altogether." He glanced around the cottage, at the cozy fire in the stove, the sleeping cat, the sun coming through the jewel-like front windows. "Obviously, you landed in a better situation, and I'm really happy for you. But I—"

"I wasn't *happy* here? What a crock of horse poop!" My anger had been growing as he made this obnoxious little speech, and I couldn't listen to any more. "JoJo Brixton, I love this island more than anywhere I've ever been, and you knew that as well as anyone." Jen nodded, giving him a hard look. "I can't believe you came all the way back here just to go on lying to me!"

"I'm not lying to you!" he blurted. I didn't think I'd ever heard him blurt before. "I'm just..." He looked flustered now. JoJo Brixton, flustered? Was that even possible? "You weren't *safe* here, Cam. There's a lot of very scary stuff happening around here these days, and you always seem to end up right there in the middle of it. I wasn't going to wait around until someone found *you* dead on the beach." He shrugged, a little more like himself again. "I just wanted you somewhere safer, and knew you wouldn't go without…a little shove."

For a moment, I just stared at him, then shook my head. "What *ever* gave you the idea that it was your place, your *right* to meddle in my life like that? I liked you, and I thought you liked me too—"

"I did! I do!"

"—but the hard truth is that we barely knew each other, and I did *not* need you making my life decisions for me! You knew I'd blown up my whole life in Seattle and come running here from things that *really* weren't safe for me. So what *safer* place did you think I'd go to next? I don't have the means to just go hole up in some cozy ski resort on the Riviera, like other people I could name."

"Well, actually, there aren't that many ski resorts on the Riv—"

"I don't care! That's not the point. I had no place to go but back to Seattle and everything I ran from there to start with. Did you think of that, Mr. *Life Planner?*"

Jen, sitting between us, reached over and patted my arm comfortingly, but didn't say anything.

JoJo looked abashed; he actually literally hung his head. If this was an act, it was his best one yet. "Cam, I have no good reason. I'm really sorry. I…I just felt like it was the right thing to do at the time, and it was obviously wrong. I know you don't want to forgive me, but I hope some day maybe you will." Now he looked up at me, sincere and puppy-dog-like.

I snorted out a quick breath, trying hard to hold onto my anger. But the wound was months old, however fresh it felt at the moment; maybe I'd used up the last of its spark earlier this morning, talking to Jen about it. And, well, my life was indeed better now than ever. It had all worked out—despite Mr. Pretty Boy's interference.

Not that I was ready to forgive him. "Well, it confused the heck out of me, not to mention hurting me badly," I said. "Frankly, it didn't seem like you at all. I thought maybe it was because you wanted your old job back, but then you left and your mom hired Marie instead! And now..." My voice caught. Poor Marie, in the hospital. I shook my head.

JoJo looked sad too. Jen was just observing the whole conversation, her head turning back and forth like she was watching a tennis match. JoJo sighed and said, "That little sparrow."

"Is that guesthouse cursed or something?" I shivered. But I wasn't done being mad at JoJo yet. "Forget it—I don't know what's going on, but thank you for apologizing, anyway. I'm sorry we can't be the friends I'd hoped we could be, but, thanks for at least clearing the air."

He gazed back at me for a long moment before nodding. "Well, I—"

There was a knock at my door.

"What now?" I said, getting up and walking over to answer it.

Deputy Larissa Sherman stood there, in full uniform, her walkie-talkie crackling on her hip. I peered behind her, but she was apparently alone. No Kip. Could this morning get any better?

"Camille Tate? Please come with me."

I stood frozen in the doorway, just staring back at her in disbelief. Perhaps the recent anger in my system was what kept me from chameleoning right on the spot. I couldn't find my voice, though.

Suddenly Jen was standing next to me. "What's this about, Deputy Sherman?"

"My business is with Ms. Tate," Sherman snapped.

"No, it's a good question," I said, finally managing to get some words out. "Am I under arrest?"

I could see Sherman trying hard not to roll her eyes. What was this woman's *problem* with me, I wondered. What had I ever done to her? "No, you are not; this is an *invitation* to come downtown to speak with us regarding our investigation into Marie Tolliver's illness."

I crossed my arms. "It doesn't *feel* like an invitation."

"Marie is…being investigated?" Jen asked. "So, you think there was foul play?"

Sherman kept her eyes on me. "I'm waiting for an answer, Ms. Tate."

"Then you should ask me a *question*."

Deputy Sherman breathed in and out through her nose. Loudly. My gosh, she hated me.

"Look. I'm happy to come 'downtown' and talk to you guys," I said. "But I've already told Deputy Rankin everything I know." Not to mention Agent Veierra.

"Deputy Rankin is off today, and his notes are rather incomplete. We need to be sure our report contains all the relevant details." Now her eyes did flutter; not quite a full-on eye-roll, but close. "I know you two are *friends*, so perhaps he took less care in questioning you than he should have. We would like to rectify that oversight."

Well. I wanted to ask just what in the world she was insinuating, but doubted it was wise to antagonize her further. Also, I could feel Jen boiling over with curiosity beside me, and now JoJo had gotten up to join the party at the door.

Sherman raised an eyebrow at him, then looked back at me.

"Fine, let's go to town," I said, hoping to stave off further trouble. "Are you driving me, or can I bring my own car?"

"I'll follow you."

On an island, I guessed there was little risk of anyone fleeing the scene. The ferries only left a few times a day, and they were often late.

"Fine," I said. "I need to get on some warmer clothes, and wash the breakfast dishes."

I didn't want that woman in my house, but it felt rude to leave her standing outside. Then I wondered what I was thinking. Rude was coming to my house and demanding that I drop everything to go to town to answer all the same questions I'd answered right next door yesterday. Rude was having it in for me in the first place, following me around and scowling at me for no good reason. Rude was insinuating that there was something improper going on between Kip and me—Kip, the most proper man I'd ever met in my life. "Wait here," I told her. "I'll be out in a few minutes." And I shut the door in her face.

I turned around and gave Jen and JoJo a nervous smile.

Jen grinned back at me. "Good job! Now let's get you put together. But no need to rush."

JoJo looked approvingly at her. "I like how you think. In fact, let's look through all of Cam's clothes. I think it's important to dress very carefully for an interview with the esteemed Deputy Sherman, all the way *downtown*."

I couldn't help smiling back at him—oh, how I'd missed my wicked evil friend JoJo—but I quickly forced the smile down. "I'm still mad at you."

"Of course you are, dear Cam. As you should be. Now, do you have a little black dress?"

❦

I rejected all their more absurd suggestions, finally settling on some warm jeans and a black cashmere sweater that I'd gotten secondhand at the consignment shop in town. It had a tiny hole on the seam just below my armpit, but a black T-shirt under it disguised that fact. It made me feel elegant and authoritative. Jen wanted me to add a string of pearls, but I thought that would be pushing it, especially with a woman who wore $300 purple shoes on her days off.

Jen also offered to wash the breakfast dishes before she left for work. I hoped she remembered to clean the guest rooms while she was busy snooping in them.

"Sure," I said, glancing out the front window. Deputy Sherman stood over by the edge of the hillside looking down at the bay below. "I should get going. The sooner I go, the sooner she'll be done with me."

"Or I could just go outside right now and push her off the cliff," JoJo offered.

Jen and I both looked at him.

"Too soon?" he asked.

I just shook my head.

"*Way* too soon," Jen said.

How did someone turn into a JoJo Brixton anyway? Yes, I knew the basics—terribly privileged upbringing, a cold and snotty and exacting mother, a distant father, too much money and not enough to do—but seriously.

"Text me when you're done," Jen said to me. "I will want to hear every word. In fact, can you just record the interview on your phone?"

"I don't think so," I said. "There's probably rules about that."

"You can do it secretly," JoJo said. "Just leave it on in your purse, she'll never know."

"Did you miss the part where I'm trying to get into *less* trouble, not more?" I asked him.

"You're not in trouble," he said, patting my arm absently. "She's just going to ask you questions."

"And you believe that? JoJo, I found Marie, and saw a prowler or a peeper or a stalker. You know how they feel about things like that."

He shivered. "Who knew this island could be so creepy? Murderers on the loose everywhere you look."

"She's not dead."

JoJo leveled his killer eyes at me. "But what if you hadn't gone over there? What then? She would have died, and that's too close for comfort. Cam, you really should have let me drive you away from here."

"No one is trying to kill me. At least, not now that Sheila is in jail. I told you, I'm just fine, and I'm still mad at you, so tread carefully." Before he could rile me up further, I grabbed my purse, gave Jen a hug, and headed out to face the music.

Deputy Sherman turned when she heard the door. I could see her struggling with herself, clearly wondering whether she should give me a hard time for dawdling or save her fire for the "interview" itself. Restraint won out. "Where are you parked?" she asked, though I was sure she knew darn well.

"At the main house—by Lisa Cannon's garage," I told her.

She nodded and followed me through the woods to my car, where her cruiser was, of course, parked right next to it.

I gestured toward my sorry little Honda. "This is mine," I said, completely unnecessarily. What? I'm not a saint; I couldn't help pulling very gently on her chain, just the tiniest bit.

She just nodded again and stood by her car watching until I'd gotten into mine, started it up, and put it in reverse. Then she followed me into town.

She hadn't told me specifically that we were going to the sheriff substation out on Mount Baker Road, but where else could she have meant by "downtown"? Where had she trained, anyway? New York? Cop TV shows? There was nothing resembling "downtown" in the whole county, but, whatever. I drove to the substation and parked next to the ancient ambulance-thing. Sherman pulled in and parked right next to me.

"This way," she said, leading me to the door, pulling out a big set of keys, and letting us in. "Go on in there and have a seat. It'll just be a minute." She motioned me to the tiny interview room. The one where I'd spent so much time since I'd moved here...talking to Kip. Except for that one time I'd spent all night answering questions *about* Kip, when it'd been Inspector McMichaels and Agent Veierra doing the grilling, with periodic input from Sherman.

I sat down in my usual chair and waited. I wondered what Sherman was doing out in the main office. My question was answered a minute later when a man came in with a cup of that terrible office coffee, which he set on the other side of the table.

He was tall, in his mid-sixties or maybe a bit later. Slender, with thick white hair, heavy dark eyebrows over pale eyes, and a big bushy white mustache. He was dressed in khakis and a polo shirt under a scruffy leather jacket. As he sat down across from me, the jacket gapped open a bit, and that's when I saw the gun and the badge on his belt.

"Sheriff Clarke," he said, putting a hand out. "And you're Camille Tate."

CHAPTER 10

I stared across the table at the San Juan County Sheriff. He'd asked me my name—no, he hadn't, it wasn't a question. I reached out and shook his hand, trying to keep from trembling—or vanishing. "Yes," I managed.

"Thank you for coming down. I've got a few questions I'd like to ask you, if you don't mind."

"Of course." The sheriff himself. The *sheriff!* My mind raced. Why hadn't Sherman told me who I was going to be talking to? She'd said "we," which I'd assumed meant her and whatever other deputies were involved. Was she trying to put me off balance?

Well, duh, of course she was. But why?

Sheriff Clarke watched me, his expression giving away nothing. I gazed down, my eyes finding the cup of terrible coffee before him.

He hadn't offered me any coffee. Not that I wanted any: I could see lumps of powdered creamer floating around on its surface, spreading an oily, foul sheen. I looked away from this horror, and studied a yellowed poster on the wall that seemed to be encouraging recycling. I wanted so badly to say something, to break this awkward silence, and I also hated that he was doing this transparent trick on me—and that it was almost working.

The little gust of anger I felt about this helped keep me from chameleoning, anyway.

Finally, he leaned forward and gently cleared his throat. "Ms. Tate, thank you for agreeing to come in today. We appreciate your help in this matter."

All this *if you don't mind* and *appreciate your help*. Sherman had already answered this, but: "Am I—I'm not under arrest or anything, right?"

The corners of his eyes crinkled as he smiled. It made him look kindly, almost grandfatherly. "No ma'am, you are not under arrest. You are merely assisting our office in an investigation, for which we are most grateful."

"Okay. Thanks."

"And you are under no obligation to answer any questions at all," he went on. "You are free to go any time you like." Yeah, but it sure *felt* like I was supposed to answer his questions. He was the *county sheriff*, and I had been brought from my home to sit in the little interview room in the substation. *Downtown.*

"Okay," I said again.

He nodded. "Ms. Tate, you moved to Orcas Island last winter, is that correct?"

"Yes."

"And on your very first morning here, you dialed 911 to report a murder that you believed you had witnessed."

My cheeks flamed; I held tight to whatever anger I could grab inside me. "I was told at the time that it wasn't actually a murder after all—but then later that it really was. I still don't know what the whole story is."

He blinked at me. "Subsequently, you discovered the body of a young woman washed up on the beach. The young woman who had previously held your job."

"Yes." *It was terrible*, I wanted to say. *Why are you asking me all this?* But I bit my lip and waited for the next question.

"You were later kidnapped and held captive; and not long

thereafter, one of our own deputies was determined to have behaved in an unprofessional manner with your person."

Well, that was one way of putting it. "Yes."

"And then yesterday, you discovered Marie Tolliver in an unconscious state, and again called 911 to report this fact. Is that correct?"

What, you're not going to ask me about Ephraim Snooks or Sheila's creepy cousin? But of course, I hadn't found either of those bodies. I'd just been...nearby. "Yes," I said.

He leaned back in his chair slightly and folded his arms across his chest, just looking at me for a long moment. I looked back at him. Finally, he said, "I'm just curious. What's your connection to all this hullaballoo?"

Hullaballoo? Really? "I—I wish I knew," I said. "I'm as confused about all of this as you are—as anyone else is."

"I'm sure you must be," he said, sounding skeptical. "You have sure had one amazing run of bad luck, haven't you, Ms. Tate? Pretty much right from day one. Such an unlikely string of wrong places at the right time—or vice versa; and not a one of these events about anything to do with you at all, it seems. At least, that's what everyone reporting to me keeps insisting." He shook his head—whether in disbelief or bafflement wasn't clear. "Doesn't that seem a tad strange to you, Ms. Tate? Seems strange to me."

"Well...yes. Of course it does." Sure, sure; they just wanted my help with their investigation—of *me*, clearly! "I sure didn't come here looking for...all this, if that's what you're wondering."

"Why *did* you come to Orcas Island last winter?" he asked. "From Seattle, yes?"

Shouldn't he know all this already? Plenty of other people did... "Yes. Seattle. Diana Brixton offered me a job caretaking their estate here. I...had broken up with my boyfriend, and my career was kind of stale; I felt like I needed a fresh start, in a new place."

"And how did you know Ms. Brixton?"

"I was a hairdresser—I did her hair. I'd known her for years, sort of."

His gaze sharpened. "Sort of?"

I shrugged. "Well, I mean, I'd see her every six weeks, and we'd chat about things. But, you know, I was her *hairdresser*. Not a friend, or anything like that."

"I see." He continued to look at me, as if trying to figure out if I was telling the truth.

"Is Marie going to be okay?" I blurted out.

Had she died? Was that why they were turning up all this heat suddenly? I was all braced to hear the old "can't comment on an active investigation" line, or even a gruff "I'm asking the questions here, young lady," so I was surprised when he said, "We're not sure yet. Ms. Tolliver is still unconscious, and it could be weeks before we have a definitive answer as to why she's in this state."

"Weeks!" I said, startled.

"In an ideal world, she would wake up and talk to us," he said, ignoring my exclamation. "But we can't count on that, at this point. So we're following every other path of inquiry we can."

"But she'll make it, won't she? I mean, she's in the hospital."

"We can hope."

Was he watching me a little more carefully now? Gauging my response? "I hope she…recovers," I said.

After another longish moment, he nodded again. "You told the deputy that Ms. Tolliver sent you a text message. Would that have been from her phone?"

I shrugged. "I…assume so? How else does one send texts?"

"A computer? A tablet?"

"Oh, right." Of course, I knew that. "But how would I be able to tell?" Before he could answer, I went on: "She had her phone with her all the time, I don't know if I ever saw her without it. And I don't think I ever saw her using any other kind of device.

So, I assume it was the phone."

The sheriff held my gaze, as if expecting something more, though I could not imagine what.

"I don't know what you're hoping I can tell you," I said. "Can't you just tell these things by looking at her phone—or asking her phone company?" And then, I got it, remembering all the weird looks and non-answers I'd been given the day before whenever Marie's phone had come up. "Do you *have* her phone?"

He leaned back. "What makes you ask that?"

Oh, Cam, you idiot! I'd walked right into his trap. And, to make matters worse, I'm pretty sure I rolled my eyes before I could stop myself. "Well, it's not all that hard to figure out, is it? You guys keep asking me what Marie did or didn't do on her phone, and every time I've asked why you think I'd know more about that than you guys do, I just get these strange looks and a change of subject. Her phone is missing, isn't it?"

"I am not at liberty to comment on an ongoing investigation, Ms. Tate."

And there it was; just a little later than expected. So…her phone *was* missing.

He didn't like that I'd figured that out, I could tell by the narrowing of his eyes. "But it would seem, without definitive evidence to the contrary, that she had her phone only minutes before she lost consciousness."

"Yes," I said, implications unfolding in my head. "And her last text to me was about her hearing something. She didn't finish the sentence, so I don't know if she heard or saw someone, but the message did sound alarmed. Frightened."

"And this did not prompt you to phone for help right away? You walked to her house instead, to investigate for yourself?" He clearly thought this had been an odd choice, but he hadn't known Marie, had he. Well, that I *could* fill him in on.

I sighed. How to put this? Poor Marie. "She was…frequently alarmed about…well, all sorts of trivial things. She seemed frightened of the world itself. When she first moved here, I thought maybe she just didn't like the island; but she got, um, weirder as time went by. More dramatic, more emotional. About things like groceries. And spiders."

"So she exhibited paranoia." Sheriff Clarke leaned back again, still watching me but now through halfway squinted eyes. "Did you have a good relationship with Ms. Tolliver?"

I thought about how to answer, not wanting to lie, but also not eager to make myself seem even more suspicious. "Sure, I guess; I mean, not bad or anything. But it wasn't really what I'd call a relationship. She called or texted when she needed something—which was ridiculously often—and I did her favors."

"Did it ever go in the other direction?"

"What do you mean?"

The sheriff leaned forward again. "Did you ever ask her for help with things? You do work for her old boss, after all: Ms. Lisa Cannon. Did you ever need to consult her on matters related to your current employer?"

A little laugh escaped me, as I realized with a small pang of fear that his traps here might not just be set for me. Had Jen been right? Were they investigating Lisa now? "Uh, no, not really. She…caretaking really wasn't Marie's specialty. Even though I'd only been doing it for a short time when Marie got here, I was already more of an expert—compared to Marie, anyway. She was kind of helpless-seeming. Well, *very* helpless-seeming, to be honest. It would never have occurred to me to ask her advice or help with anything. She couldn't even seem to help herself."

He nodded, and his gaze became less sharp, as if he was thinking deeply. "All right," he said after a minute, "that's all the questions I have for now. Unless there's anything you'd like to add?"

I shrugged again. "Only that I hope this all gets untangled soon."

"So do we." He produced a business card. "Don't hesitate to call if you think of anything else. Thank you again for your help."

"Sure." I realized he hadn't touched his terrible coffee the whole time. It wasn't going to be any less terrible cold. But—not my problem.

I got to my feet, and the sheriff did as well, leaving his cold cup of terrible coffee on the table as he showed me to the door.

I could barely keep myself from scampering to my car. Larissa Sherman's cruiser was gone, though I hadn't heard her drive off. I let myself into my car and forced myself to drive sedately out of the parking lot and onto the road, already planning my report to Jen. I had agreed to keep my mouth closed about these interviews, but Jen would understand the need for discretion at least as well as I did, and if we were going to spy on agents of the law, what was the point of trying to be a good girl about the rest of it?

If someone had taken Marie's phone, that would seem to settle any questions about red herrings and flu or anorexia. I thought we'd want to add finding that phone to our list now, too—though I realized a minute later that it had probably been destroyed by whoever had taken it, or its GPS chip should already have led the experts right to whoever had it. Could local simpatico lead us to the broken pieces somewhere? The idea made me chuckle, though I supposed Jen might not think it was so funny.

Of course, I'd also have to tell her that they'd mentioned Lisa. She'd probably gloat about that, but I still hoped it had just been a random pot shot…a mere stab in the dark…

Why couldn't I think of any way to put it that didn't describe some kind of murder?

ℤ

Feeling a little shaky for lack of lunch by now, I drove straight to the Brown Bear Bakery in town. But, it was dark inside. I'd forgotten they were closed Tuesdays and Wednesdays, so even though nobody needed a chocolate muffin more than I did at that moment, I was out of luck.

Darvill's Bookstore had a little café, so I parked around the corner and went there. The door jingled merrily as I walked in and headed back to order a mocha and a big chocolate chip cookie. Then I wandered around looking at the books while my order was being prepared. They had a whole display of fascinating cookbooks on everything from salt-brick-grilling to traditional hearty stews. There was even an entire book on ways to cook bivalves. Too bad I was a terrible cook. Well, not terrible maybe, but not very adventurous.

"Cam?" called out the barista. I walked back and got my treats, then carried them out onto the sidewalk where I could call Jen. It would be obnoxious, not to mention way too eavesdroppable, to do it in the bookstore.

Just past the art gallery there was a cute little boutique called The Smol Froggy filled with all the world's most fabulous knick-knacks—including a lot of decorative frogs. I settled onto an unoccupied bench in front of the shop, and took a few bites of my cookie. Once I felt a little steadier, I pulled out my phone and punched Jen's number.

"Well?" I swear, she picked up before it even rang. "That was fast."

I laughed. "It didn't feel fast to me."

"What did she want?"

"Jen, it was a setup. She brought me in to talk to the *sheriff*."

Jen gasped. "You're *kidding*. The man himself?"

"The man himself."

She gave a low whistle. "We don't see him over here too often."

"Well, he's here today."

"That is totally bizarre. What did he want?"

I sipped my mocha. Pretty hot, but perfectly made, unlike the terrible cold coffee probably still sitting there in the sheriff substation. "A lot of the same questions they asked me yesterday, plus some general background. But get this: Marie's phone is missing."

"He *told* you that?"

"Well, not directly. Couldn't comment on an ongoing investigation and all that. But he made it clear enough."

"Well, that is strange. I mean, both parts of it. The phone, and him letting you know that."

"Yes, and yes."

"Is Marie conscious yet?"

"Not yet, apparently. It sounds like she's in a coma, Jen."

Jen paused. "Do they know why?"

I repeated what Kip had said about toxicology testing. "But it doesn't sound like there were any physical injuries. She's just... not there."

Jen chuckled. "I love the pause for effect. You should be a playwright or something."

"Very funny."

"Where are you now?" she asked.

"Sitting in front of The Smol Froggy, on a chilly iron bench, drinking a coffee from Darvill's and trying to calm myself down. Where are you?"

"On my way to the inn but I'm not far. I'll stop by and we can figure out our plan of action. See ya in a minute." She hung up before I could ask her what she meant by a plan of action. Were we really going to get all Trixie Belden/Honey Wheeler on this? Right *now*?

I wondered which of us was which.

Five minutes later, she appeared, her own paper cup of coffee clutched in one hand, and plunked down next to me on the bench. "Okay," she said, taking a sip and turning to me. "Brr, that bench is cold." She shifted around and got her jacket more fully under her behind. "That's better. Anyway, I think the first thing we need to do is identify your prowler."

"Oh, is that all? How do you propose we do that?" I looked away and shook my head. "And how do I keep letting myself fall into things like this? You're a very bad influence, Jen. You know that, right?"

"Cam. Don't you see what's happening here?"

"I absolutely have no clue. I would *love* it if anyone could just tell me."

Jen shook her head. "They're not coming right out and saying it, in fact they're being real careful not to because they don't want you to freak out or lawyer up or anything, but you're the prime—the *only*—suspect. Don't you see that yet? You were Marie's lifeline. She depended on you. You brought her *food*, Cam. They clearly don't buy that there was a mysterious prowler on the scene—who only you saw, but can't describe in anything but clichés, who left in an invisible car, leaving no trace whatsoever. If they'd found any evidence to back up your story, don't you think Kip at least would have let you know by now?"

"He's probably no more free to comment on a current investigation than any of the others."

"It doesn't matter. We need to find out who that prowler was and point them at him, or you're duck soup, hon!" She shook her head. "What if they're just stringing you along, Cam? Giving you enough rope so that you can hang yourself. Letting you tell stories about what happened, writing it all down, waiting until they can trip you up in a contradiction. Then—bang!—they'll slap on the handcuffs and cart you off to jail."

I just stared at her. "Wow. You really think that?"

"Honey. I believe the prowler you saw is responsible for the state that poor girl is in. But I also believe that Deputy Larissa Sherman has it in for you, and that Sheriff Clarke didn't just *happen* to be on Orcas today. I also believe that Deputy Kip Rankin, however much we like him, doesn't have the—how to put it?—imagination, I guess, or the independent initiative, to untangle a case like this before they've framed you for it." She held my gaze. "Why do you think he was even off duty the very day after a probable serious crime—when everyone must be rushing around gathering evidence?"

"Uh, because it's his regular day off?"

"You've never heard of overtime? Come on, girl. Larissa runs his life these days. I'll bet she insisted he take his day off, then called in the big boss because she knows Kip's sweet on you, and might get in her way if he knew what she'd done."

"Sweet on me? Why do you keep saying that? Is this just some personal tic of yours?"

She patted my arm. "Honey, half the island is sweet on you. *I'm* sweet on you, and I don't like girls that way. But that's not important. You need to focus on figuring out what happened to Marie—and how to get your name cleared once and for all."

I took another sip of my mocha. My head was spinning—was I really a suspect? And was half the island really sweet on me?

Jen laughed softly and leaned into me for a moment. "Oh, poor Cam. I didn't mean to blow your mind."

"Oh no? What *did* you mean to do?" I gave her my best shot at a stern look, and decided I had better tell her the rest, even though it bugged me some to reward her this way for 'blowing my mind' with such obvious glee. "There is one other possible take on all of this. The sheriff also brought up Lisa."

"Oh did he!" She looked as smug as a cat licking canary feathers off its paws. "Finally, someone starts asking questions about our mysterious lady of the island, Lisa Cannon."

"Well, it was just in passing. Nothing too specific. But yes, he mentioned her too at one point, very briefly."

"Well then, maybe you should start with Lisa Cannon instead."

"*I* should start? What happened to '*we*'?"

Jen spread her hands as if wondering what more she was supposed to explain. "Of course, *you*. I'm not Lisa Cannon's caretaker and soon-to-be personal assistant."

"Well I may not be for much longer either if I start grilling her about all the suspicious doings on the island. That would go over wonderfully, I'm sure."

Jen gave me an innocent smile. "I'm not asking you to do any such thing, silly. Just keep your eyes and ears open for suspicious doings on her property and the house next door for now. Easy-peasy."

"Thanks. That's very helpful. I guess you mean, any *new* strange goings-on, because let's see, so far, on Lisa's property, there's the play-rehearsal-turned-murder, and my kidnapping, and two bodies showing up, and now the next-door neighbor's caretaker falling into a coma—a caretaker who used to be Lisa's assistant."

We both sat there for a moment, taking it in.

Jen finally spoke. "Wow."

"I know."

"Cam?"

"I know. I'll be careful."

"Good." She put her arm around my shoulder and gave me a squeeze. "Listen, I have to get to the inn, hon; I'm already late. I'll check in with you just as soon as I get off of work."

I rolled my eyes. "Sure, fine, no problem. But when we get back to identifying that prowler, and it's time to rush up and wrestle him to the ground, I'm sending *you* in for that."

Jen got up, swallowing the last of her coffee, crumpling up the cup, and stuffing it into an oversized coat pocket. "Honey, you'll be fine. Wasn't she already promising you more explanations about all the weird business and finance stuff she's been tangled up in? Start with that. I'm sure it'll lead to information that will be helpful here. Haven't you heard that old saying, 'Follow the money'? Money is always at the root of everything."

Had I told Jen that Lisa had promised to fill me in? I couldn't remember, but as always, why even wonder how Jen knew what she knew? "Okay, I want to know that stuff anyway. And I need to know it, if I'm going to help her with it all."

"Exactly. Okay, hon. I'll call you later." She leaned over and gave me a quick hug before hurrying off.

I sat there a while longer, finishing my own mocha and cookie, thinking about everything she'd said. At the beginning of my meeting with the sheriff, it really had seemed like he saw me as a suspect, though I'd felt like that was more or less defused by the time we'd finished. And I couldn't be their *prime* suspect anyway, because why would they let me just wander around free like this if they really thought I'd "done it"?

And now I'd let Jen talk me into going back and spying on Lisa. Would there be anyone on this island I *wasn't* in trouble with by the time this was over? I pulled out my phone and stared at it for a minute.

Then I called Lisa.

"Hi, Cam. How are you doing today?" She sounded warm, but serious; just the right tone of voice for the circumstances. How had she learned to be so perfect? Was it something she practiced, or did it just come naturally to her?

"I'm all right," I told her. "I'm in town—I was asked to come in and answer more questions at the sheriff substation."

"Oh really? What more did they want to know?"

I decided to skip the details. The sheriff hadn't forbidden me to talk about it, like Veierra had, but the less Lisa knew, the better my chances of catching her off guard, right? "Pretty much the same as before. I think Deputy Sherman just wasn't convinced that Kip had interviewed me correctly." Not a lie. Just an omission.

Lisa gave a little sniff. "Ah. Deputy Sherman. Of course."

"Anyway, I just wanted to check in because I'm about to head home and—I know you do your own shopping, but I'm here, and, well, is there anything I can bring you from town?"

Now she laughed. "Oh Cam, it must be driving you crazy to not be able to do more for me."

I chuckled too, though my cheeks started flaming. I was glad she couldn't see me. "Well, kind of, you know? I've always worked for a living. And you're paying me so well, but I just…I don't feel like I'm working."

"Writing and revising an entire play isn't work?" She laughed again. "No, I know that's a separate issue, and it should be. You're right: we probably do need to get a little more formal about your duties and how we're going to work together. I've just been enjoying being back and letting the outside world fall away, for a day or two; and then there was all the excitement last night, and…well, I might also have been imagining you would want a little unstructured time as well. That's what I was telling myself anyway."

"Um, sure, time off is great, but I seem to spend most of it at the sheriff station."

"Ah, say no more: I am hearing you now, and understanding. And as someone who has managed any number of employees, I completely understand the desire for structure. It was selfish of me to project my own frame of reference on to you. So: yes, please, if you could pick me up a rotisserie chicken and a bag of salad mix from the store, and drop it by on your way home, I would be more than grateful."

"I would be happy to." I was trying not to laugh at all her corporate-speak; I could tell it was coming from the heart.

"And if you have the time to sit down and talk about further defining the structure of your position here when you get home, I would be delighted to do that. If not, we'll set a more convenient time."

"No, today is good. I don't have anything else going on—except rewriting the play, of course."

"And I truly do not want to keep you from that. I hope you understand, Cam, how much I enjoyed the play, despite all the notes, and how much I am looking forward to producing it this summer."

"I'm not sure I'll completely understand that until it actually happens, but, thank you."

"You're very welcome. I'll see you when you get here."

"Yep. Thanks!"

I shook my head, smiling in spite of myself, as I walked over to the grocery store. Once inside, I almost called Lisa again twice—

what flavor of rotisserie chicken? What kind of salad greens?—but I forced myself to take initiative and make the decision myself. It was so obvious that she was just giving me an assignment to help me feel useful. The lemon-pepper chickens looked the freshest; and I liked the butter lettuce blend, so that's what I chose.

Despite being packaged up in its plastic bag and that bag being inside a paper bag in my back seat, the chicken filled my whole car with tantalizing, delicious aromas. By the time I got back out to West Sound, I was hungry again, though I had no right to be.

I frowned as I drove down the driveway. JoJo's Jaguar was parked in my usual spot. He'd been at my house when I'd left, yes, but his car hadn't been here; what was going on? I pulled in next to him, grabbed the groceries, got out and walked up to ring the doorbell. It was a minute before Lisa answered. "Ah, thank you," she said, taking the grocery bag from me and heading to the kitchen. I followed her in. "Save the receipt; one of the things we should talk about is how we'll handle expense reports."

"Right," I said. Except I hadn't bothered taking the receipt. I wanted to say something like *never mind, it was only a few dollars*, but we were trying to be professional here, and she could certainly afford to reimburse me. I would just have to learn some new skills, like keeping receipts and filling out expense reports.

"Dearest, was it awful?" JoJo called from somewhere down below. In the living room, I imagined, though I couldn't quite see him. "You have to tell us everything!"

Lisa chuckled as she unpacked the grocery bag. Instead of putting things away, she dumped the salad into a serving bowl and started unwrapping the chicken. "Be patient, JoJo, she's just walked in the door. Nobody wants to tell stories before lunch." She pulled a platter from a cabinet and started carving slices of chicken, and arranging them artfully on the plate. Dang it, I *was* hungry again already.

Well, it had only been a cookie in town, and breakfast was a long time ago.

"Grab a few of those plates, will you?" Lisa asked me, pointing to the open shelving by the sink. "And some forks?"

A minute later, we were all in the living room, munching on succulent chicken and yummy salad. I wouldn't have thought any of this would make good lap-food, but that just shows what I know. There wasn't any wine, for once, which seemed a constructive change.

Though I did love Lisa's wine.

"All right, I've been polite and patient for the entirety of this meal," JoJo said, putting his empty plate on the coffee table and leaning back fetchingly at the other end of the sofa. "Camikins, tell us everything."

The nerve of him. Like everything was all better between us.

"There's not a lot to tell," I said. "Just the same questions as before. I think Sherman's yanking my chain."

"I think Sherman's got a thing for our Deputy Rankin," JoJo said.

"A thing?" I asked.

"La, innocent girl," he said, leaning over and patting me on the knee. "She *likes* him, isn't it obvious?"

"Are you kidding me? She does not. It's completely clear that they both hate just driving around together."

"Maybe it's all the sexual tension." JoJo did something suggestive with his eyebrows.

"Oh for Pete's sake." I crossed my arms in disgust.

JoJo shrugged. Lisa was watching us with amusement.

"Besides," I went on, "you haven't been here in months. What do *you* know?"

"I know more than you think," he said at once, then pantomimed zipping his lip.

"Did you even hear about their knock-down drag-out fight in front of the bakery last month? Kicking and hair-pulling and screeching at the top of their lungs?"

"What?" JoJo leaned forward, eyes wide. I had surprised him!

Too bad none of it was true. "Just kidding. But you weren't sure, were you. You've been away; you know nothing of what's gone on around here."

He gave me a dark look, or a faux dark look, who could tell? Was he ever serious about anything? "I have informants," he said at last, recovering his dignity. "Extremely well-placed informants. If such a *knock-down drag-out fight* had happened, I can assure you, I would have known about it within minutes, from five different directions."

"Whatever." I reached over and served another few bites of chicken onto my plate. Protein was always a good idea, right? "If she's got any kind of a thing for Kip, it's that she blames him for ruining her life, making her have to work here instead of San Juan. And, as much as I hate to admit she could be right about anything, she's kind of right about that one. None of this would have happened if he hadn't gone slightly wacko last fall."

"Nah, our small-town cop shop would have needed to muster its resources anyway, the minute more than one person died," JoJo said, growing at least a little more serious. Or giving a good impression of it, anyway. "We're talking about four deaths, one kidnapping and shooting, a kidnapper's death that turned out not to be a death, a cop's nervous breakdown, and now a young girl in a mysterious coma. All since *you* got here." He cocked an eyebrow at me.

"Don't you dare," I fumed. I really didn't want to keep hearing this from everyone.

"What? I'm just stating the facts. And the islands aren't set up for big-time crime stuff. The random bar fight, a few domestic disturbance calls, mainland shoplifters, stray cows: that's what they're set up to handle here, not kidnappings and bodies. They've just been making this all up as they go along, hoping to stay in the investigation at all."

"I think that may be true," Lisa put in, rejoining the conversation at last. "That last part, at least. It wouldn't take much more for the FBI to send in a half-dozen extra agents and take the local staff out of the picture altogether. They'd couch it as 'assistance,' of course, but it would be a terrible black eye for Sheriff Clarke and his whole department. The sheriff will have been doing everything he can to convince the higher-ups they've got a handle on all this."

And who had brought the sheriff into this conversation? I certainly hadn't. I took a bite of chicken.

"They're probably pretty nervous about Marie, then," JoJo said. Both Lisa and JoJo looked sad at the mention of her name. I felt sad too, but I was watching them both carefully, while trying not to be obvious about it.

These two. Their bond, their assurance. I *needed* to understand that more. There was something going on there. Of course, no matter what Jen might think, I was not a natural investigator, nor should I ever play poker. My face must have shown everything again.

"I'm afraid we're upsetting Cam even more." Lisa gave me a small smile as she added, "I clearly can't know everything that Marie was up to, but when we do have that organizational conversation later, Cam, I will share a few pieces of information about her with you that may prove helpful."

"Oh never mind *me*," JoJo purred. "Have your conversation. I'll just amuse myself with some of your exquisite wine."

"It can wait," Lisa stated with finality. "Cam and I have plenty of time to talk business later." Ah, so we weren't going to be having that conversation now after all, thanks to JoJo. Just another reason to be pissed at him, as far as I was concerned. "You can stay as long as you wish to, JoJo."

"Oh good," he said. "I was afraid I might have to go drink someplace in town all day until Mommy Dearest leaves. I do not have the constitution to deal with her in a rage." He smirked. "Or in any other mood, frankly."

I sat upright, my eyes wide. "Wait! Your mom is here?"

JoJo gave me a surprised look. "Well, of course she is. Did you think she wouldn't show up to find some replacement for Marie?" He gave a little *tsk*. "She has the most dreadful luck with caretakers, that poor woman. Imagine how hard it's going to be to fill that position *again* after all of this."

"JoJo, you're horrible," Lisa said, giving him a soft slap, and an indulgent smile full of radiant warmth.

I agreed that he was horrible...though he also wasn't wrong.

Who was going to work for Diana Brixton now? Megan Duquesne had drowned; I'd only been kidnapped and shot, thank goodness, but now Marie Tolliver was in a coma at some hospital in Seattle. Word had surely gotten everywhere by now. Diana Brixton could try importing yet another caretaker from the mainland, but the first time her next pick went to town for groceries, someone would tell them what had happened to the rest of us, and they'd be on the first ferry out of here.

"If she'd just hire dead people in the first place, maybe she could keep them longer," JoJo said. Then he looked at me from under his long lashes. "Too soon?"

"*Way* too soon." What a boor he was becoming.

Becoming? I asked myself incredulously. Ha.

CHAPTER 11

The conversation got no better from there. Somewhere post-lunch, JoJo started on a monologue about how incompetent Marie was as a caretaker, supplying a raft of details I hadn't even known. At first, I admit it, I took a certain mean-spirited pleasure in learning that she was even worse at her job than I'd known. I inwardly smirked while hearing about her inability to program a sprinkler system, how she'd ruined a full set of pans, one after another, by boiling water incorrectly (was that even possible?), and the fact that she'd lost three sets of guesthouse keys. But then I remembered those hopeless texts, and the greenish cast to her skin when I'd found her unresponsive, and it all felt a little ghoulish for me. I found myself laughing less and less, and feeling, I don't know, dirty.

Apparently, Lisa felt the same way. "I don't actually find anything about Marie's current situation hilarious, JoJo," Lisa said, standing up. "And I could use a glass of wine."

JoJo waved his hand. "I can…"

"I'll get it," Lisa said. She sounded almost frosty.

I took the opportunity to excuse myself. "I need to get going. My script won't revise itself."

"Really? You're leaving?" Lisa might have been protesting, but she looked almost relieved with my decision. Was she that anxious to see my rewrite? Or was there more? Did she have something she needed to discuss with JoJo?

Jen was getting to me with her suspicions.

I left the idle rich to their afternoon. I had work to do. Work that I *wanted* to do. I mean, as much as I dreaded the rewrites, I was also eager to do them, and very excited to end up with a finished product I could finally feel confident about.

A finished product that other people would stand up on stage and act out!

In front of an audience—who had no idea who I was, and didn't already like me, and might hate the play. What was I *thinking*? Holding my work up before everyone on this island, and—

I shook that whole line of thought away before it got up to speed again, and walked back to my cabin, relieved to escape JoJo's humor at Marie's expense. How many times had I complained about her? Mocked her? Rolled my eyes at her helplessness? Was I any better than JoJo? Of course I was better than JoJo, at least today. I was actually still pretty pissed at him. I marched on through the woods until my cottage came into view.

James was on the porch, stretched out in a patch of sun, snoozing away. Master Bun hopped to the front of his hutch, obviously thinking it might be time to go into the warm house, and maybe even get some snuggles or treats.

I opened the door of his hutch and reached in to give him a scratching. He laid his head down, letting me reach behind his long soft ears. I picked him up and cradled him under my chin. I could never believe how soft his fur was; ever so much softer than James's.

Maybe I should adopt a chinchilla.

Speaking of James, he woke up and wreathed around my ankles, insisting upon his own scratching. So even though I'd totally meant to get right back to the play, I found myself sitting in the rickety wooden chair on my tiny front deck in the sun on this clear, cool day, covered in livestock.

I had a little thinking to do.

I knew I needed to pay attention to Lisa Cannon and her role in this group of mysteries. I knew she was involved, because why would all this happen around her if she weren't? But she was my friend and employer. Whether I should or not, I trusted Lisa. As my dad would have said, "You don't always choose your team, but that's the team you play with. It's about loyalty, Camille."

Lisa was on my team.

James purred and stretched out his back legs, as if he was aiming to nudge Master Bun out of my lap. I shifted to accommodate his new position. "There's plenty of room for both of you," I told him. Master Bun wasn't giving ground, though. James moved his head, prompting me to scratch the other ear now. At least he'd stopped kicking at his stepbrother.

"What should I do, you guys?" I asked them. "I mean, I did just agree to help untangle this mystery."

James lifted his head, indicating that I should scratch under his chin now.

"And it's not like Jen has all this free time," I went on. "She's working like three or ten or sixteen jobs, and I'm just…sitting around here, scratching animals on the head and cashing my giant paychecks."

My cat purred louder.

"You're right," I told him. "We do deserve this nice financial windfall, after all we've been through. But so does Jen! She's a good person, a marvelous person. And she asks so little of me. Friendship is about making sacrifices for each other. Doing and returning favors—and not keeping score, but if we *were* keeping score, Jen is way ahead of me. Heck, she generously befriended me in the first place, when I was all alone here. She didn't have to do that. She knows the whole island."

Bunnies don't purr, but if they did, I felt pretty certain that Master Bun would be.

"So I should just bite the bullet and go over there and spy on them," I went on. "*...just keep your eyes and ears open...* " Jen's words echoed in my mind. "I'm sure I could figure out a way." I shivered, thinking about what I might *not* want to hear.

Then I sighed, shaking away the thought. "But friendship is also about being honest with each other," I told my pets. "And Lisa is *also* my friend. Yes, she's my boss, and I could really screw that up if I got caught spying—but she's my friend, she said so herself, and I don't want to do something that sneaky and dishonest to her. If she wants me to know something, she will tell me. In fact she's *going* to tell me. She would have already if that snake JoJo weren't there. So I just need to be patient. We'll find out everything we need to know, and I don't have to turn into a snake too in order to accomplish it."

Now the animals started fidgeting again.

"All right. Let's take this inside." I carried in Master Bun and James followed.

"So I guess the final thing to do is to be honest with Jen about this," I concluded. I wasn't happy about this part, but I knew I needed to do it. "No time like the present."

I knew Jen was working now and wouldn't be answering her phone, but I called anyway. I'd leave a message and—

But of course she answered.

"Hey!" she said, sounding a little breathless. "What's up—you got news?"

Ah crap. "No, I, um..." And then I just blurted it out: "Jen, I can't spy on Lisa. I'm just not gonna do it."

There was a pause. Then, "Why not?"

"It's not fair to her, and it's not honest, and it's not who I am. I'm not an investigator. And she likes me and trusts me."

"Well that's exactly *why* you should be the investigator! And hon, you're right there!"

I cringed, wondering if this was where our friendship was going to finally run aground, but I made myself press back. "Jen. I love you to pieces, to the moon and back, but I'm…well, I'm not feeling listened to right now. I don't *want* to do this. And…I'm not crazy about the way you talked me into agreeing to your plan, and then volunteered *me* to take the lead—as if this were all *my* project now."

Now there was an even longer pause. I could feel my heart pounding, could hear it in my ears. What had I done? Was I really choosing Lisa over Jen? Was this the stupidest thing ever—

Finally Jen said, "Okay. So, what *would* you like to do then?"

Her voice was so…calm. Was she furious, and holding herself together? Was she mocking me? I racked my brain, trying to think of something we could do, something that wouldn't just make everything worse. I wouldn't spy on Lisa, but… "Let's just—investigate someone else, maybe?"

"Like who?"

"I don't know. Anybody else! Someone I don't know—or care about. You said we should investigate the prowler first, remember? Before I even brought up Lisa." *And why did I do that?* I asked myself, cringing again. *How do I keep making so much trouble for myself?*

"Okay," Jen said. "I'd be fine with helping you investigate the prowler."

"Okay," I echoed, feeling an inkling of relief.

But then there was another pause. Oh jeez. This was not good. I opened my mouth to fill the silence, but then she said, "Any ideas where we should start—since you don't want to start with Lisa, I mean?"

She *was* angry, I just knew it. And she *was* mocking me, or humoring me at the very least. "Um, well, what about all your connections with the B&B community, and innkeepers—can't you ask them what other single, off-island guests checked in right around Marie's collapse?" I'd been grasping at straws, but suddenly it made sense. Of course it could have been a local, but if it wasn't, they'd have had to stay somewhere, wouldn't they?

"That's…not a half bad idea, actually," she said slowly. "I can ask around."

She still seemed so uncertain, though, so reserved. Well, if she was humoring me, at least that gave me a chance to repair this. "I'm so sorry," I said, and now the words came tumbling out. "I don't mean your ideas were bad—they were probably the best, I'm sure you're right!—but I just, I maybe need to work up to it? Or—"

"No, no," she interrupted me. "I'm not offended, Cam. In fact, you're right. I guess I may have been…kind of a bully. And I'm sorry." Now there was warmth in her voice. "I mean it. I am sorry."

Relief now flooded me, even as I wasn't sure whether I could trust it. Could trust the thawing I heard. "I forgive you! And… are we…okay?"

"Oh yes. Absolutely. It's just…" She snorted softly, and then said, much more cheerfully, "I guess I've never seen you be so… assertive before. It kind of caught me by surprise."

"I'm sorr—" I started, but she cut me off right away.

"Don't, hon! Stop apologizing. I kind of like this, actually. Assertiveness: it's a good look on you."

My mouth dropped open, but before I could think of what to say, Jen went on. "Anyway—I gotta go. I'll call as soon as I find out anything about other bookings around the island. I've already got some ideas where to start."

"You do?"

She laughed, entirely her old self now. "Oh yeah. I do think pretty fast on my feet, you know."

❧

After Jen hung up, I sat there, marveling at what had just happened.

I had stood up to Jen! I'd told her no!

And…Jen had just said assertiveness was a good look on me!

That seemed crazy!

All my life, I'd been such a pushover. I'd always known that. And yet—who did I admire, after all? People like Jen, and like Lisa. Kind yet *strong* women who didn't let anyone push them around. Had standing up to the nicest person in the whole wide world, who was not my nemesis at all, been strong or brave? I'd been so afraid that this was going to break our friendship. But it hadn't. Still...was *I* as comfortable with this "new look" as Jen seemed to be?

Not really.

Was I *happy* with it, though?

I honestly didn't know.

Crazy.

After another few minutes, I shook my head, still smiling. "Well, that play isn't going to rewrite itself," I said to my pets, to the open air, to the universe. I went back to face my laptop...and the pile of manuscript pages beside it.

Ugh, these notes! Was I really going to have to redo the whole dang play? I'd thought I was done! Didn't Lisa say she'd loved it, loved it so much? Did she mean her praise at all, or was she just blowing smoke up my...tailpipe?

I fired up the computer and opened the file, then took the time to do a save-as, preserving the previous version. Just in case.

And then I started in.

I began by reading Lisa's notes on the printout, one by one, and forcing myself to think about them. To really consider them. Yes, some of them seemed to contradict one another; but at a deeper level, they didn't.

I read on. I wasn't much past the third scene when I started to see what she was talking about. Yes, I was still sensitive about having to revisit this, but I did do an awful lot of dancing around the issue, didn't I? *Much like my real life,* my brain told me, and *Shut up,* I told my brain, but it wasn't wrong, was it?

Of course, some of that dancing was intentional—it was supposed to be funny; any piece of writing isn't just about the plot—but now that Lisa had pointed it out, I totally saw it. Yes, big chunks of the play could go…ugh! I had so much reworking to do. And yet it was oddly exciting at the same time. Once I realized how much I needed to cut, it become obvious how much more room there was for better stuff…

I was well into writing a new scene to climax the first act when I realized it had gotten dark outside. And oops! I hadn't even finished one full rereading of the play.

I got up and fed the livestock (including myself), then pushed my dirty plate aside and dug back in. It went so, so well; I finally found what I'd been trying to do here, all the way down. It was so clear now! This women, the one I'd been writing about, hoping to share with the world—she was an aesthetician. She was a "nobody" in the eyes of the world, and yet she had a life that no one ever saw. A really interesting life, which was what made the play funny, but also serious. As I wrote, and rewrote, and rewrote, I began to see ever more clearly how these two things could better feed each other.

I was charging along, my fingers on the keyboard clicking madly—it was almost like taking dictation. And then a loud crash startled me right out of the zone.

I was on my feet staring around the room before I'd even realized I'd gotten up. "What was that?" I said in a half-shriek.

From beside the front door, Master Bun looked up at me. I hadn't put him in his hutch for the night? Good thing, because that terrible noise had come from outside.

My heart was pounding and my arms were tingling—and then came a second sound, a sort of distressed-animal sound, followed quickly by another thump-crash.

I ran to the front door and threw it open, switching on the porch light as I did.

A masked face looked up at me, next to the knocked-over hutch. Water and shredded vegetables and rabbit bedding was spread across the porch, and the door to the hutch had been pried open.

The raccoon bared his teeth and growled at me as we stared at each other. I really did nearly vanish then—I could feel myself freeze, and my arms and legs stung with it.

Then the animal gave a huff, turned, and disappeared into the dark night.

After a long moment, I exhaled, and began to return to myself. I felt a tickle on the back of my leg, and startled again—but it was only Master Bun, coming to check out the disturbance, twitching his whiskers against me.

"Oh, little dude," I said, bending stiffly down to pick him up. My body barely obeyed me, but I could move. I cradled my bunny and shut the door, throwing the deadbolt, then walked slowly with him around the room, as my heart rate steadied and my limbs came back to me. "What if you had been out there? Oh my goodness. That was a big raccoon."

Raccoons ate bunnies, I was quite sure of it.

Why had the creature come? It had pulled the hutch entirely over and had used its clever hands to open it up. Was it after the vegetables…or the scent of Master Bun?

"Poor little sweetie," I crooned to the rabbit. "We are going to fix that. You are going to be safe."

I would call Colin first thing in the morning, I decided. He would have ideas—he'd know how to keep Master Bun safe.

Meanwhile…I pulled out my phone to check the time. Holy moly, it was nearly two in the morning! I really needed to get to bed. But I was absolutely wide awake, full of slowly dissipating adrenaline and the antsy feeling of my system absorbing a near-vanishing event. No way could I sleep yet.

I made myself a cup of herbal tea and sat back down at the computer.

And didn't look up again till I retyped "The End" at the bottom of the screen.

I blinked, looking at my half-drunk, stone-cold tea. The time on my computer read 4:07 a.m. It was still dark as midnight outside. "Oh man," I groaned, but I also felt...kind of great?

Because I'd done it. I'd done it! I'd made every revision Lisa asked for, and then some. The play was *so much better*. I knew it, knew it all the way down to my bones.

And I was finished too. I dragged myself up the ladder and collapsed onto my bed, nudging aside a very annoyed James—who had been up there the entire night, I realized as I dropped off. Even the raccoon hadn't disturbed his beauty rest.

❧

It was one of the few times in my life I slept past five in the morning—thank goodness. The sun was pouring in as I was patted awake by James. He was standing on my chest, tapping my cheek and breathing his cat breath in my face, just as annoyed as he'd been a few hours earlier, except this time his concern was breakfast, *his* breakfast, his *late* breakfast, his *many hours* late breakfast.

"Who made you the boss of everything?" I grumbled as I dragged myself out of bed and down the ladder.

Good gracious, it was nine o'clock! I fed the poor starving creature, and the other hungry creature, and set coffee going for myself. I felt hung over—and without even having had any wine last night.

But then I glanced at the table. Dirty dishes, pile of manuscript, still-open laptop *with a finished play on it!*

"Woohoo!" I called out. James didn't even startle, he was so busy scarfing up his food. Master Bun looked up at me, which reminded me I needed to call Colin.

"I can be over later this afternoon," he said, when I reached him. "But yeah—probably best not to leave food in there overnight. We can make your fella safe, but if the raccoon smells easy food, he's gonna keep trying."

"Thank you."

Speaking of food…once I hung up, I scrambled myself some eggs, to keep the coffee company in my stomach. And both while eating breakfast and as I tidied up my kitchen afterwards, I just kept looking back at my laptop. Was I done? I was done! I really was, really truly.

I felt amazed with myself all over again, and I couldn't wait to see the look on Lisa's face when I told her about it.

Because I couldn't just email it—I needed to tell her in person. I grinned, drying dishes and putting them away. *Done!*

Yet something was still bothering me, something that needed laying to rest before I could truly celebrate. I pulled out my phone again, dithered only a little, and then called Kip's cell number.

"Miz Tate," he said warmly, in his mellifluous voice.

I dove right in. "Kip, I need a big favor."

He paused only briefly. "What is it?"

"Am I the prime suspect in Marie's poisoning? Just tell me, okay? I need to know. I have a *right* to know that, don't I?" *Do I?* The second-guessing started right up, because of course it did. *Will this just make them come out and arrest me now? What the heck am I doing?*

Kip stammered something; there didn't seem to be any words in it at first. Then he said, "Cam, what on earth…? Where did you get this idea?"

"From the sheriff, Kip."

"The sheriff?"

"Yeah. Sheriff Clarke came over here to Orcas just to interview me."

He made another incoherent sound. "When was this?"

"Yesterday. Sherman came out here, because it was your day off, and hauled me 'downtown' and then the sheriff was there and he had all these pointed questions, and Jen says she's sure it's because I'm the prime suspect, and you're all just humoring me till I make a mistake, and…" Kip had gotten awfully silent. Had he hung up? "Are you still there?"

"Yup." Just that one word. He did not sound happy.

I winced. Oh, this had been a terrible idea. "Are you mad at me? Is this…not appropriate? It's not, is it? I'm sorry. I got basically no sleep at all last night. This is just sleep deprivation talking. Forget I ever—"

"Cam," he said. "Stop."

I took a breath. "Okay."

"This is the first I've heard about any of this," he said slowly. "I was *not* off yesterday. And if Sheriff Clarke was on Orcas, no one told me that."

"Oh." Hadn't Sherman told me he was off? She totally had. "Why not?"

After another, longer pause, he said, "I haven't any idea, and I am certainly not able to comment on an active investigation, Ms. Tate. I'm afraid I have to go." And then the line went dead.

I stared at my phone. Polite, courteous-to-a-fault Kip had just hung up on me. Without even a proper goodbye. He had never been so rude to me, ever…well, except maybe for that awful night on the boat.

I had clearly just stuck my foot in something bad—*again*. My heart started pounding, making me regret all that coffee. What had I been thinking? What anthill had I just kicked over! Why couldn't I ever—

There was a knock on the door. I hadn't even heard footsteps on the porch, I'd been so busy freaking out, *oh for crying out loud, it's the cops, already here to arrest me*—

I made myself get up and pull open the door, steeling myself for Sherman, for maybe even the sheriff himself. But Colin stood there, looking capable and sturdy, with his tool belt slung around his narrow waist.

"Mornin'," he said. "I know we said this afternoon, but I was nearby and figured we might as well take care of it. Got some supplies in the car I could use help packing over here, if you're free?"

He was so not what I'd been expecting that I momentarily blanked on why he was even here. "Supplies? For…?"

He gave me an odd look. "Raccoon-proofing your hutch?"

"Oh. Oh! *That*," I said, with a relieved smile.

He raised an uncertain eyebrow. "Sorry. It sounded…kind of urgent when you called."

"No, *I'm* sorry," I told him. "It was—is—urgent, actually. But…that was twenty minutes ago. And you would *not* believe… Never mind. Thanks so much for coming. Let me put some shoes on. And send a quick email."

I hurried to my laptop and typed out a message to Lisa, attaching the manuscript. I'd ring her doorbell while I was over there helping Colin get his supplies, in case she didn't check her email that often. This way, at least she'd have it before I got arrested.

I'd have hated for all that brilliant work to have gotten lost in the shuffle.

CHAPTER 12

When we got to Lisa's house, Colin went to his truck while I rang her doorbell.

She answered, looking as elegant and well put-together as ever. "Well, good morning, Cam."

"It's done! I just emailed it to you." I almost burbled in excitement mixed with panic.

"It's…done? You mean your play revisions?"

"Yes! Anyway, I can't stay—I just wanted to let you know."

Colin slammed the truck's tailgate. Lisa's gaze lifted at the sound.

"He's here to beef up Master Bun's hutch," I told her. "It was attacked by a raccoon last night! Made a terrible racket."

"Oh dear," Lisa said, looking sympathetic. "I hope the rabbit…survived?"

"Yes, he was in the house with me, actually—I was still up, working on the manuscript. Which is done!"

"Er, yes. So you mentioned." Colin was now rummaging around in the cab of his truck. "That's just wonderful, Cam. Amazing, in fact. I'm so eager to look it over."

She didn't *look* eager, though, and she didn't *sound* eager. In fact she seemed almost upset.

My face must have given me away yet again, because she

reached out and put a gentle hand on my arm.

"I'm sorry, Cam. This is terrific, truly, but…I've just had some very upsetting news, and…"

"Oh no *I'm* so sorry!" I cried. "What happened?"

Lisa seemed at a loss. "I'm…not quite ready to talk about it yet. But I'm afraid it may affect the play, actually."

"What? Oh no—how?" *Affect the play? What in the world??*

Now she forced a brave smile. "Listen, when you and Colin are done over there, why don't you come back, and I'll fill you in. I think it's time to have our talk about your transition to personal assistant anyway, if you're free for that?"

"Of course. Any time." Colin walked up from the truck with an armload of lumber, clearly trying not to interrupt. "How long do you think we'll be?" I asked him.

He shrugged. "I got a few loads of wood and then some tools you could give me a hand with, save me a trip or two. I can take it from there. Just a bunch of hammering and screwing after that. Nothing you want to mess with."

Lisa was still smiling, looking quite calm. "I'll check my email right away, Cam, and start reading. This is really an impressive surprise—I imagined you'd be rewriting for a week or so. No need to rush back, though. I'll be here whenever you're ready."

She patted my arm and withdrew into her house.

Colin loaded me up with two heavy toolboxes and followed me back to my cottage. "Yep, looks like raccoon work," he said, looking over the tumbled-over and clawed-at hutch.

Of course it was raccoon work. I'd stared right into the masked beastie's face.

"Can we make it safe?" Master Bun was still in the house. I'd resigned myself to hunting down little turds after all.

Assuming I wasn't in jail, that is.

"That's why I'm here, isn't it?" He gave me a gentle smile. "Now go on—whatever you've got on your mind is burning a hole in your head and sending smoke out your ears. Go talk it all out with Miz Cannon."

"Thank you!" I said, giving him a quick hug. He stiffened in surprise, but his arms wrapped around me and gave me a hug so strong, I almost melted.

No. No melting. Lust was not love. I'd learned that lesson as well as anyone, and I didn't want to hurt this nice man—as easy as it would have been to fall into those strong and capable arms, and just surrender to my body's long-neglected need.

I pulled away and tried not to run back down the path to Lisa's.

She answered my knock quickly this time. "I'm not through reading the manuscript yet."

"I didn't expect..." And then I saw her smile, and knew she was joking. "Sorry I'm such a pest."

"You're not a pest. Come on in." She led me down to the living room and we sat. I could tell this was a business meeting because there was no amazing wine, no insanely delicious snacks, not even coffee. And Lisa jumped right in without any polite chit-chat first: "I was informed this morning that two of my actors have been detained by the police in Seattle."

"Oh my gosh! Who?"

"Bella and Petey."

My heart sank. Bella was supposed to be the lead! And Petey's role was almost as important. Oh man, I was going to have to rewrite the play *all over again*... "What for?"

"They were caught trying to sneak past the security detail into Marie's hospital room."

I just stared at her. "Why?"

"I couldn't possibly say." She shook her head, looking grim. "They claimed to be friends of hers, just coming for a visit, but if they even knew her, I wasn't aware of it."

"Well, they did all hang out some—while you were gone."

Her gaze sharpened. "They did? Often?"

"Um...I'm not sure. But at least a few times that I know of."

"Here?"

"No, never *here*. I never had anyone here, Lisa, not once." She looked greatly relieved. "They hung out at the Brixtons' house, actually. They all…had…gatherings there."

"Imagine that." She looked more unhappy by the minute.

"Maybe they really did get to know each other," I said, "and just wanted to see how she was doing? I mean, *I'm* dying to know how she is—and I'm not all that close to her."

Lisa pursed her lips. "Well, the middle of the night was an odd time to visit. They very carefully avoided the nurses' station, and every ICU check-in procedure. The guard on her room happened to be absent for the first time all night." She frowned, then said, as if to herself, "None of this makes any sense."

Her level of distress—well, it felt a little, I don't know, excessive? I didn't really know just how close Lisa was to her actors, but remembering her near freakout the night Marie collapsed, I wondered what was really behind all this angst.

"How do you know about this?" I asked. Had Bella used her one phone call to reach out to *Lisa*?

She exhaled. "Sherman and Rankin came by this morning."

"And *told* you all this?" I was astonished. "They sure don't report things to me like that. They just keep telling me they can't comment on an active investigation."

She gave me a wry smile. "They weren't reporting, Cam. They were interrogating."

"They were here to question *you*? About what?"

"Well, of course they questioned me," she said gently. "They were 'my' actors, after all. And Marie used to work for me. They've questioned me any number of times since all this started." Her smile grew even more rueful. "Did you really think you were the only one?"

"Uh…" It had never occurred to me that Lisa would have been questioned too, which did feel foolish now since this whole "hullaballoo" had started with a murder on her property. "How come you've never said anything?"

Lisa straightened her fine shoulders and gently tossed her excellent hair, as if shaking off unpleasantness, and leaned forward. "That leads nicely to the first topic we should cover in regard to your new role as my personal assistant, actually: and that's *discretion*. Your work here would involve access to some very private aspects of my personal life, and I need to be certain you understand how important your discretion will be to me."

"Oh—no, of course, I would never—" I started.

"I know you'd never mean to." Her smile was so kind. "I also know how fond you are of Jen Darling, for instance, and rightly so; she's a delightful, competent, industrious young woman. But I can't have you reporting on me to the biggest gossips on this island, Cam—even unintentionally."

I nearly shuddered as I thought about Jen asking me…just yesterday…to spy on Lisa. "Jen's…a good person," I mumbled. "I've never thought of her as a gossip."

"I am certain you haven't. And yet." She reached for a manila file on the coffee table before her, handing me a piece of paper from inside it. "Before we go any further, I'd like to have you sign a simple nondisclosure agreement. Take time to read it over carefully. I'll be back in a few minutes."

She rose and went off toward the back of the house.

I studied the agreement, my heart pounding as I took in all I'd learned about how much else had been going on here, right under my nose.

I made myself focus on the NDA. I'd never signed one before, though I'd certainly heard of them. It looked simple enough…I was not to share any personal, financial, or other proprietary information of Lisa Cannon's with anyone without express prior written or verbal instruction to do so. If I violated these terms, I would be fired immediately, with no notice and no severance; egregious, willful, or substantive violations could even be grounds for legal action.

Simple, yes. And pointed. But entirely reasonable, I thought.

There was a lovely, heavy-looking pen on the coffee table. I picked it up and took off the cap—it was a fountain pen! I'd always wanted to try writing with one.

One new experience after another.

I signed the agreement and set the sheet of paper back on the folder as Lisa walked back into the room. "All good?" she asked.

"Yep."

She took the sheet and the fountain pen and signed below me. "Very good. I'll get you a copy of this for your files."

I almost snickered. *My files* indeed.

"So," she said, getting comfortable on the sofa once more, "do you need anything—coffee, a glass of water?"

"I'm good," I assured her.

"All right then. As my assistant, you'll soon discover that even I have no idea from week to week—or day to day sometimes—which parts of my circus may require your attention. But some of your work will likely touch on an extremely private part of my life: the ongoing struggle with my ex-husband for control of my pharmaceutical company."

My mouth fell open. "But…wait. That's still going on? Didn't you tell me—"

"Yes," Lisa cut in softly. "I'm sorry, Cam. The story I told you about my binder…" She paused, seeming lost for words. "I needed help desperately, and, after everything that had just happened with Sheila and the others, I had no idea who I could trust anymore. You seemed so innocent and honest, and so completely unconnected with anyone or anything here that I thought you might be safe to turn to. But I had no way of being entirely certain even of you then. So," she sighed, "I asked for your help in a way that wouldn't leave me too exposed if it turned out I'd been wrong about you too."

I had no idea what to say. Was she telling me…she'd lied?

"The story I told you then was a fiction, I'm afraid." Yes, she was! "As are various other parts of my cover story here. But as you start helping me here, bits and pieces of the real story will undoubtedly come up, and you're way too bright not to start noticing how some of what I've said in the past doesn't add up. So, before we go any further, I need to set that right. You need to know the truth now, and now I am *completely* certain I can trust you with it—if you can still trust *me?*"

I was taken so completely by surprise. My first impulse was to say, 'Sure! Of course I can!' I liked and admired Lisa so deeply. She'd been so kind and supportive in so many ways. I still wanted desperately to trust her. I mean, why even bring all this up again just to lie a second time? How would that make sense? And yet... if she'd lied once, how would I know she was telling the truth now? "I guess...I should hear the real story before I answer that," I said, trying not to sound as frightened as I felt of offending her by not just saying yes.

Lisa gave me a sad smile. "That was a very *good* and *reassuring* answer, Cam. If you'd just said, 'Oh yes; no problem,' I'd have worried a lot more about your trustworthiness, and your very *ability* to be discreet."

I nodded, not understanding why, exactly, but pretty sure this was not the time to ask.

"So," she went on, "here's as much of the real story as I know."

As much as she knew? About herself and her own ex-husband? And what did *that* mean?

"What I told you the other night was closer to the truth," Lisa began. "Closer than I really meant to come, actually. That's the trouble with mixing wine and emotional distress. Derek really was a dazzling, charismatic man, and I thought he'd be a fantastic addition both to my life and to my company's future, at first. It took longer to see how much more he cared about what I *had*— what I'd *made*—than about me.

"He was a *very* accomplished manipulator who wanted the company I'd built to follow *his* vision and leadership now, not mine. And the dreams he wanted us all to embrace were...well, recklessly infeasible. That became a very big problem—and not just for us as a couple. My employees had no idea how to navigate divergent instructions from their boss on one hand, and their boss's husband and business partner on the other.

"I finally tried to defuse the problem by giving him a sandbox of his own to run entirely his way, and take full credit for. I created a brand new R&D division focused on 'futuristic imagineering,' you might say, and put him fully in charge of it. I asked only to be kept abreast of what was happening, and provided with the usual reporting that any division supplies to its parent company. Everyone else there would report to him alone."

"Nicer than I would have been," I grumbled, unable to avoid thinking of Kevin.

"Yes, well. Even at that point, I still imagined I loved the man," she said dryly. "He was thrilled with the plan; and for a while, it seemed to fix everything. I thought I'd saved not just my company, but our marriage too. Such a clever woman, I was...

"Then, his reporting became spotty, if not altogether absent. More and more of what I received didn't quite add up, and I began to worry about what was going on.

"I should have kept a closer eye on things then, but every time I brought up my concerns, he became evasive or surly, and I was quite busy with my own side of the company. We were launching a new drug that had shown very promising results in clinical trials. We needed to get it right—and out to as many potential patients as we could, as efficiently as possible. My focus just kept being diverted until, one day, Derek came to me with all his old charm brushed off and polished up to request a laughable funding increase. When I told him I couldn't possibly justify any such amount without a great deal more documentation than I'd been getting—if even then—he became enraged, insisting he was on the verge of things that would redefine the future of *our* whole company—if not all of pharmacology! How dare I tie his hands like this just to defend my envious vanity? I told him I'd have loved to hear about all that far earlier, and that if even half of what he said were true, he should have no trouble at all developing new funding on his own.

"I wasn't wrong. About any of it. But I'm pretty sure throwing down that gauntlet was one of my biggest mistakes." She rolled her eyes and sighed. "I should have used the extra funding he wanted to leverage full access to his operation. But we all know the value of hindsight."

I hoped her personal assistant wasn't expected to understand this kind of business strategy, because I sure wasn't making heads or tails of half of it.

"After that," she continued, "I feared whatever he was up to might bring my whole life's work crashing down at any moment without warning. I was more than entitled to insist on full disclosure from him, of course. But, given his behavior, forcing his hand that way seemed likely to require legal combat that would almost certainly result in our divorce. And that," she gave a derisive little huff of laughter, "seemed too potentially disastrous for both my company's public image and myself to risk by then.

"So..." She fell silent for a moment. "I quietly summoned a brilliant young researcher to my office whom I'd been mentoring for some time—and asked her to do me a huge favor."

I was suddenly sure I knew who that had been. "Marie?"

Lisa nodded sadly. "You would not have recognized her then. She was a confident, capable, incredibly knowledgeable powerhouse with every quality I needed for the task at hand. I asked her to apply for transfer to Derek's division, saying nothing of my involvement, of course, just that she felt bored and unchallenged where she was, and had heard through the company grapevine of projects on Derek's turf that sounded more exciting, and of greater potential importance. I knew Derek would snap all that up in an instant. Once Derek hired her—which he did, of course—she would report secretly to me on what was happening there."

"Wow," I murmured. "It's hard to imagine the Marie I know as a brilliant anything, much less a spy."

Lisa looked down at her now folded hands. "Yes. It is…now. And her reports confirmed my fears. Marie thought most of his projects far-fetched and poorly justified by any sound science or testing she was aware of, which didn't worry me so much, since the division's purpose was just exploring theoretical possibilities and wild ideas anyway. What troubled me more was hearing that he'd apparently found that new infusion of capital somewhere, though Marie had no idea how or from whom. Why hadn't he come crowing to me about such a success? It seemed he should have—unless he didn't want me asking questions—like, where the money came from?

"Then, suddenly, Marie's visits to my office became less frequent; and her reports grew vague and unconcerned, as if there were just nothing there worth wasting my time with anymore. But one of my financial officers was cc'd—by mistake, apparently—on an email regarding financial arrangements with someone I had never heard of and couldn't track down. The exchange seemed almost intentionally oblique, but hinted at some round of new investment which, it seemed, might be intended to 'satisfy' *previous* investors in some way. That worried me a great deal.

"Since that email had been sent to us, however unintentionally, I called Derek in to ask him about it. But he just set his jaw and claimed I'd forfeited any say in his finances by refusing to fund him myself. When I reminded him that '*his finances*' were still just a part of *my* business, he simply turned around and left my office.

"I filed for divorce the next day. This had become too dangerous to ignore anymore. But I didn't dare shut down the division before finding out what, exactly, was being done there, and what unknown investors might be roused to legal action against *me* if I did.

"I had no further word at all from Marie for weeks after that, until I finally risked summoning her again, ostensibly to take some personal legal papers to Derek. When she appeared, I was shocked to the core. She looked gray and dreadfully thin, like someone with an advanced eating disorder. Her cognitive impairment became clear almost as quickly. She seemed barely able to string a sentence together. She was clearly terrified, whether of me or of something else, I couldn't tell; but when I asked her what had happened to her, she refused to answer. When I pressed the matter, she fled my office in a panic."

"So…what was it?" I asked, feeling terrible about the way I'd always judged Marie.

"I still don't know. To this day, she's been unwilling to discuss it. But I called Derek to my office the next morning, and demanded that she be returned to work for me immediately. He angrily asserted that I had neither the right nor the power to make such decisions for her. I asked him what possible use she could be to him in that condition. He asked what *I* wanted her for. Within minutes, we were trading accusations, then threats, both personal and legal. There was no fixing anything after that. Our war was launched, and impossible to conceal any longer." Lisa shook her head. "But within days, I had Marie back in my office, where I could watch over her.

"I sent her straight to specialists; but without her cooperation none of them could diagnose the illness or treat more than her symptoms. She was useless now as a researcher. She could barely manage even basic office work, but I wasn't about to let her out of my sight again. I had placed her in harm's way. I felt responsible for whatever had been done to her. And I hated Derek with a passion for having allowed her to fall into such a state—if he hadn't done something to cause her condition in the first place. Imagining what that might have been made me feel physically ill, day and night."

"So…you still have no idea?" I asked in disbelief. "After all this time?"

"You'd think I should, wouldn't you?" she said. "But Derek's been a walled fortress ever since. Our legal battles have produced a few pretty frightening clues, but I can still do little more than guess that he got himself into some very deep trouble with whomever that extra financing came from, and did something worse trying to solve that problem. No one's found out what, though."

I couldn't believe something like this could just sit there unresolved. "Why hasn't the court forced him to hand over records or something? Can't they just go to the IRS, or his bank, and find the answers? Hasn't anyone who worked for him come forward? Can't the law force them to? I mean, whatever he did to Marie; that's got to be some kind of crime, right?"

"Only if Marie were to accuse him of one, which she never has," said Lisa. "And Derek's handed over reams of documentation to the courts, likely all fabricated. We can't force him to hand over further evidence that no one can even prove exists. And no; if something incriminating went on there, no one who might know that has ever admitted it. What he could have on so many people to keep them all quiet is beyond me. But I'm still fighting to find out—and to put my assets and my company beyond his reach, though I still have a lot to lose if I'm not careful, and Derek's made it quite clear how happily he'd take it from me, if I give him sufficient cause."

"Are you worried he might come after you? Here on Orcas?"

"Well…" She looked away, unhappily. "I guess I can't rule even that out after everything that's happened recently, though I'm… not all that sure how much of it's had anything to do with him. The whole problem with Sheila…" She grimaced, and looked back at me. "No one I'm aware of seems to be sure yet whether all that might even just have been a string of terrible mistakes."

"You've told all this to the police—here, I mean?"

"Oh yes," she said wearily. "There are years of public court records concerning our dispute. The police probably knew all that from the start. It was one of the first things I thought about when I learned what Sheila had done: *What will they think when they see my court records?*'" She shook her head, then gave me a sideways smile. "Now you see why I was so amused by your surprise that I'd been questioned. I doubt anyone on this island has been more scrutinized by law enforcement than I've been since all this began."

"So, are they investigating Derek, about Marie's collapse?"

"I have no idea. That's the sort of thing they would *not* tell me—or anyone, I'm sure."

"Is all this why you came to live here?" I asked, thinking of my own flight here from Seattle, and wondering whether Lisa and I had more in common than I'd guessed.

She nodded. "When I took him to court, Derek began a carpet bombing campaign of harassment against me personally and publicly—and not just at work and in the media. He sent people to the apartment building I'd moved into. It was tabloid stuff as ugly as you can imagine, and it really hurt our business. I'd purchased this property years earlier, and when it reached the point where I no longer felt physically safe down there, I just moved everything up here without even telling him.

"I invited Marie to come too, unsure of her safety without me to watch over her. But, to my frustration, she insisted on staying, though I still have no idea why. Then, last year, she suddenly changed her mind, for reasons as mysterious to me as all the rest. But you see now why I made her my caretaker, then rented her out to Diana Brixton when that failed to work out. I am... not unaware of how much you've done to help Marie do better at Diana's than she might have otherwise. Your willingness to help her has given me one more reason to feel grateful."

"Oh...well, I sure wish I'd been kinder to her now."

"You were though, dear. As kind as there was any credible reason to be. That says a lot about you, and means a lot to me." Lisa dropped her face into her hands. "I had hoped she would be safe up here, and find more space to recover."

"Do you think Derek did this to her?"

"It seems possible." Lisa raised her eyes to me again. "That's one of the reasons I'm telling you all this. I don't want another promising young woman I have come to care about walking into danger on my account without any warning."

I felt my brows climb in surprise. "You think *I'm* in danger?"

"I don't know." I had never seen—or imagined—such a strained expression on her face before. "I had hoped that this was far enough away. Out of sight, out of mind. That Derek might just be content to go on with more immediate things in his life. But now…well, people working for me haven't seemed that far out of the line of fire, have they?" She arched her brows inquisitively. "So…are you still sure you want this job?" She gave me a pale smile. "I'll like you no less if you say no."

"No! I mean, *yes*; of course I do. I've been so tangled up in this already that I can't see what working for you is likely to change one way or another. And about your question before, yes, I absolutely still trust you. I'm just so sorry you've had to go through any of this—you or Marie."

Her eyes grew shiny and a little red, like she might be on the verge of tears. "Thank you, Cam. I'm so relieved to hear that."

"I just don't understand how you've put up with it all so well. You always seem…so carefree and strong. And happy! The other night—when Paige and I came by…I'd never have guessed what you must have been going through! Not in a million years."

Lisa gazed at me, then nodded. "No one's life looks the same from inside as it does from the outside. *No one's.* That's just how the world really is." She shook her hair back, and perked up visibly. "But that's a good example of what we were discussing earlier. I was being discreet, Cam. The things I said were basically true; they just weren't the *whole* truth. That's what I need from you; not to lie—not ever that. It would break my heart to make you, of all people, lie. But just to guard my secrets. Do you think you can?" Her smile softened some. "If the answer is no, I need to you to be honest with me now, and say so."

I thought about how often my useless poker face seemed to fail me. But then I remembered telling Agent Veierra how I'd *frozen and the prowler hadn't seen me.* All true, just not the whole truth. Yes. I'd been very discreet all my life about one thing, at least.

Of course, it wouldn't be discreet to explain *that* to Lisa. But…

"Back at the salon, customers got *very* chatty during their shampoos, or under the driers, and said the most amazingly personal things—you've seen this in the play. That's hardly exaggeration." Lisa chuckled.

"And us stylists had a very strict rule that nothing those ladies said in our shop was ever to be repeated or discussed outside of work. Ever." Now I laughed softly. "It's part of why I wanted to write the play: None of *their* secrets are in it, but oh, I just had to show people what it was like! So I'll just do the same thing here—with Jen and everybody else."

"Good." Lisa smiled, relieved. "I'm glad you've had practice. What a great find you are. What an unexpected gift to me."

"Oh. Well… Gee, what a nice thing to say." My whole body blushed. "Thank you."

"No, thank you, Cam. For being so understanding—and so brave." She leaned back and stretched her arms up, glancing at the ceiling for a moment, as if to spare me from having to think of some reply. "So!" she huffed, lowering her arms and smiling back at me. "I'm going to be away for a day or two starting tomorrow morning. I'll be taking your amazing play revisions along, but I have to tell you, Cam, the few scenes I've read so far are *brilliant!* Far surpassing my expectations!"

"Oh! Seriously?"

"Seriously."

I just grinned. I was so relieved.

"I think you may be a real talent, young lady," she went on, "and I am so excited to have discovered you before someone else did."

"Oh my goodness! Thank you. Thank you so much."

"Would you stop thanking *me* for *your accomplishments*, please?" she teased.

I ducked my head, and almost apologized again, but caught myself in time.

"But I'd thought that would take you longer, and now I'm afraid there's really nothing else I need before I return. So just enjoy this last bit of freedom, because when I get back, you are going to be one very busy woman."

"Great! I can't wait!"

"Well, you'll have to. For a couple days at least."

"You're not going to end up calling me from Bermuda again, are you?"

Lisa laughed, the first genuinely comfortable laugh she'd uttered this morning. It warmed my heart. "No, Cam. This is just a quick meeting and an errand or two.

"Now," she said, rising to her feet, "shouldn't you be checking on that rabbit-hutch rebuilding project? Your poor carpenter must be wondering where you've gotten off to."

"Oh! Colin. Right!"

Lisa saw me to the door, but Colin's truck was no longer parked out front. Had he finished up already, or just been so insulted by my long absence that he'd packed up and left?

I headed back to my cabin processing all the astonishing and deeply disturbing things I'd just learned—any one of which would make Jen howl with amazement and horrified delight!

If only I were allowed to share any of them with her.

I'd have to figure out how to convince Jen that Lisa wasn't who we needed to investigate without betraying any of Lisa's secrets. But I wanted us to find the truth even more now, because when we solved these mysteries, we would clear Lisa too. I was so relieved to finally know that Lisa wasn't doing anything wrong. I could keep her on my team.

Oh, but no NDA would keep me from telling Jen that Lisa had called my play *brilliant!*

CHAPTER 13

At home, I found that Colin had finished up—and how. I stood on the porch, staring at the shipshape transformation of Master Bun's hutch. It was righted and repaired, of course; but it was now surrounded by something that looked like Fort Knox rendered in knotty pine and hardware cloth. Its hinged front door had an actual lock! The key hung on a nail beside the latch.

"I'd like to see one of those masked bandits try something *now*," I muttered, lifting the key to unlock the new perimeter cage and check the whole thing out before reintroducing Master Bun, who was still (I hoped) inside the cabin. But before I could open the cage door, a loud, overly enthusiastic, and somewhat slurred "Camilicious!" rang out behind me.

I whirled around to find JoJo Brixton, staggering toward me, brandishing a bottle of, well, something. He was waving it around in the air. Luckily, it was capped, or he and I would both be showered in whatever it was.

"JoJo! You *startled* me!" I nearly shrieked.

"I come bearing gifts!" he cried. "Rare and precious elixir obtained at tremendous peril from demons in the exotic east!"

"Oh for crying out loud." It was barely noon. And he was just about the last person I wanted to see right now—well, except maybe Deputy Sherman. "What is the *matter* with you?"

"The matter! Alas, for I have much of matter… And forsooth! I knew I must come to see you at once!" He brandished the bottle once more.

"I am not drinking with you right now," I told him. "I'm very tired and very busy."

"Camikinnnnns!" he sang. "I'm not taking no for an answer."

I ignored him, opening up the hutch and peering inside, inspecting Colin's work. It was kind of genius. The man did have a way with his hands…and that hug. It had felt *so good.*

JoJo kept singing and slurring, oblivious to—well, everything. When I finally turned around, he gave me a lurid wink.

"Maybe you should go sleep this off somewhere," I suggested. "And *don't* come back when you're sober." Why had I ever thought this clown was good friend material? I turned back around and went into my house, closing the door in his face, and turning the deadbolt.

He just sang louder, outside. What *was* this? Did, like, Dean Martin sing this? Was all of Massacre Bay listening to this Vegas lounge act? I tried to tune him out, but there was just no way. Finally I yanked the door open again. "Get in here," I seethed, "before Lisa comes over to investigate the noise, and disgraces us both."

"Lisa…would *never* disgrace me!" he cried, prancing into the cabin, nearly stepping on a very confused Master Bun. "I allow no one to disgrace me but myself!"

"Seriously, *cut it out.* Now!" I snapped, quite out of patience with this lunatic.

He froze in place, staring at me as if I'd just sprouted wings and a tail. Good. I'd gotten his attention, for a moment at least. "I'd let you sleep it off here," I told him, "but you'd just kill yourself getting up the ladder, and I am *so* not calling 911 about any *more* dead bodies. So just go sober up somewhere else, and then don't come back, okay? I've had a very long day already."

Suddenly, he just…shifted. He walked to the table without any staggering at all, set the bottle down gently and precisely, and sat down, looking as sober as a country parson. "Well, that certainly didn't go as I hoped." No slurring, every word precise and clear. He gave a long, discouraged sigh.

"Wait, what? So…you're not drunk?"

"Do I *seem* drunk?"

"Not *now*." This didn't help my irritation. I stood over him and put my hands on my hips. "What *on earth* was all *that* about? Did you think just being more obnoxious than *ever* would improve something?"

"Look at all this assertiveness." He looked up through his long lashes, but didn't flutter them coquettishly or anything. "Who are you, really, and what have you done with my dear friend Camille Tate? I warn you, if you've harmed her in any way…I can be a very dangerous man."

"Seriously, what the hell, JoJo?" I shook my head. "I really don't have the time or energy for you today."

"I hoped—foolishly, it seems—that you'd find my little act charming and pathetic, and feel sorry for me. Saint Camikins: finder of lost things, shepherd of strays." Now he did flutter, just a little; the man couldn't help himself. "I was just getting to the part where I reveal that my pathetic state was caused by abject remorse for what I'd done to you."

I rolled my eyes. "I've taken you for lots of different things, JoJo, but a moron was never one of them—'til now."

He actually leaned back and smiled at this, though his smile seemed somewhat startled. "Really, Camikins! What's with all this sudden spine? I haven't been gone *that* long! Where have you acquired all this fabulous ferocity?"

"I have no idea what you're talking about," I said. "And I'm fed up."

JoJo leaned forward, staring up at me as if I were some fascinating museum exhibit. "Maybe I really don't know you as well as I thought."

"Well, there's the first *smart* thing you've said since you got back," I said, and sat down across from him.

Now he looked genuinely sad. "You're really never going to forgive me, are you?"

Aww. *Don't relent now,* I told myself, sternly. "Oh, I've already forgiven you, JoJo. But forgiving is not forgetting."

"I want to fix this, Cam. I'm serious. Just for a minute, of course, but really truly—cross my frothy black heart—I want us back." He looked so earnest.

I looked at him askance. "'Us' *who*? I don't remember any '*us*.' You can be very charming, JoJo, when you try, but you are *so* not my type."

"Oh, hell no!" He rocked back in his chair. "I didn't mean it that way. I'm not even *my* type. I meant our friendship." He looked convincingly distraught, but then, he'd looked convincingly drunk just a couple of minutes ago. "You were the truest friend I think I've ever had. And I screwed that up." He looked down and shook his head.

Was this real? Did he even know how to *do* real? "Oh, come on," I said. "I've seen your Facebook page. You have a million friends."

"All of them in the game for something." He blinked at me. "All of them players. Except for you." Now he looked away. "And so you're the one I trashed. Go, go JoJo."

He was doing it, dang it: convincing me he was sorry. Making *me* feel sorry for *him*. Which just pissed me off again. The moment I took the bait, he was just going to laugh and say Gotcha!

I would not give him that chance.

"Well, if you really want our friendship back that bad, I guess you'll just have to start again, and *earn it* this time." I tried for a breezy tone—*La, I don't care one way or the other.*

He gazed at me for a long moment, then nodded. "Fair," he murmured, more to himself than to me. Then he brightened.

"Okay. Game on. May I begin by asking you out to lunch? My treat, of course."

"When?" I countered. "I wasn't kidding about being busy."

"You seem to be fairly unoccupied at the moment."

Only because he'd pranced over here and distracted me...

"Where?" I asked, despite myself.

A sly smile crept over his face. "I know just the place. It's perfect, but we have to hurry. Come on!"

With that, he stood up and dashed out of the cabin, leaving his bottle untouched on my table. On the front porch, he turned and frantically beckoned me to hurry.

Was "clown JoJo" back?

What had I gotten myself into?

Well, I was hungry. I'd let him treat me to lunch at some *perfect* place. I grabbed a sweater and my purse and followed him out.

On the way through the woods to Lisa's house, he stopped and turned to me. "Would you mind driving?"

"What? You don't want to take the Jag?" I couldn't quite believe that he'd be willing to be seen anywhere getting out of my Honda.

He shrugged. "I don't care. If you'd rather drive the Jag, that's fine with me." He reached into his pocket and pulled out the keys, tossing them to me in one smooth motion.

I just managed to catch them. "Are you *serious?*"

"You drive a stick?" He grinned.

"Of course I do. I grew up in the country, JoJo."

His smile grew. "Ah, well then I'm sorry to disappoint you, but the Jag's an automatic. But that's good to know for future reference." He wiggled his eyebrows and marched on.

I fingered the keys as I followed him. Sure, okay, if he was going to let me drive his obnoxiously expensive car, I'd do it. "So, where am I driving us?" I asked as we stepped into the parking area by Lisa's garage. I pressed the key fob to unlock the Jag. It hardly made a whisper, and blinked its lights at us invitingly.

"That's part of the surprise," JoJo said, pulling out his phone. "I'll tell you as we go."

I snuggled down into the leather seat—even more comfortable and butt-cradling than the passenger seat. It took me a moment to figure out how to start the car, and then adjust the seat forward so my feet could have even a chance of reaching the pedals. JoJo was ignoring me, already texting madly away with someone. So I put the machine in drive and headed up the driveway, adjusting the mirrors when I got to the road. "Right, I assume?" I asked.

"Yes," he said distractedly, typing away.

At the stop sign at Deer Harbor and Crow Valley, I glanced over at him, but he didn't tell me to turn. So I went straight. When we got to Orcas Road, he did look up. "Oh, left here."

I signaled and turned.

The car drove like a dream, like a whisper, like a caged beast. I could feel its power, humming beneath me eager to be set free. I wanted to ease my foot to the floor, to speed, to see what it could do…I did not dare to do so. Not for so many reasons: not my car. Deputies out to get me. Oh and it would be illegal.

But oh, I wanted to see what this car could do.

Yep, I've definitely become a car snob on top of everything else, I thought ruefully. I consoled myself by enjoying how the Jag took the corners. I barely had to think about turning the steering wheel and the car responded.

We were at town before I knew it. JoJo had been texting the entire time. I slowed down and signaled right; he looked up and said, "No, go straight."

I was nearly into the turn; I yanked the wheel and overcorrected. "Who are you talking to?" I asked him. "Can't that wait until we get wherever we're going?"

"I'm making a reservation."

"That takes fifteen minutes? At how many places?"

He pointed at the island's tiny airport coming up on our left, without even looking up. "Turn there."

"That's the airport." Did he mean North Beach Road, just beyond it?

"Oh," he said, glancing up for a second before resuming his texting with a tiny smile. "It is, isn't it?"

He meant it, then? I dutifully pulled in. The wheels rumbled over the deer guard. We passed Jen's employer—well, one of them, anyway, the delivery service. I drove past the tiny terminal building. "What are we *doing* here?" I was going to run out of road soon.

"Part of the surprise." Now he tucked his phone away. "Park up there, by that little red beater."

I did so. We got out, and I locked the car. JoJo took my hand and pulled me playfully toward the tarmac, where a helicopter sat, blades whirring.

A helicopter?

I dragged my feet, slowing him up. "JoJo—what are we doing? I can't do this! When will we be back?"

"Why?" he yelled over the rotary roar, dragging me forward. We ducked under the blades, just like they do in the movies. "You got a job to get back to or something?"

"I didn't even tell Lisa I was going anywhere!"

"What's she going to need you for? To discuss the play?" He said it like it was a joke. Was that what he thought? That my play was a joke? It felt mean. "Come on, hop up."

I planted my feet and yanked my hand out of his. This was starting to feel rather like being kidnapped. "You said lunch, JoJo! What is this?"

"Lunch! Just like I said. You can tell Lisa I kidnapped you, if that helps." Had he read my mind? But he was still grinning. "She won't care," he went on. "She loves me."

"She does?" *I knew it!*

He rolled his eyes. "Not like that, Camikins. I'll call her as soon as we're aboard here, and tell her you'll be back by dinner time, okay?"

"The *minute* we're inside this thing," I insisted.

He nodded as the pilot jumped down, helping us in. "Sit there!" he shouted, pointing me toward an uncomfortable-looking seat. I sat, and he lifted up a big pair of earmuffs from a hook in front of me and handed them to me.

I put them on; they muffled the noise considerably. But that also meant we couldn't hear one another. I turned to JoJo and pointed at my ear, trying to mime *Do these things have some kind of microphone built in?* I mean, a curly cord connected it to the back of the seat in front of me; didn't that mean communications? He just smiled and mimed for me to strap myself in.

The pilot slammed the door closed and returned to his seat up front. I scrambled to decipher the complicated seat-belt situation as the helicopter started to lift off the ground.

And then we were aloft.

Oh holy crap, I was in a helicopter! In the *air!*

If there were ever a time when I didn't want to chameleon, I would guess this was it. Sitting next to JoJo Brixton in a freaking helicopter. The sheer thrill of this ride warred with my absolute terror. I felt my skin trembling, wavering, as I sought to balance my exhilaration with my, well, my *terror* at riding in a glass bubble over the island and then, quickly, Puget Sound below. I rubbed my forearms briskly, wished for some wine, closed my eyes and thought of Mom, her reading glasses on the tip of her nose, peering at a recipe in a magazine.

Then I opened my eyes. How was JoJo going to call Lisa? I looked over at him: he was texting. He glanced at me and nodded significantly at his phone, then gave me a thumbs-up.

Okay then.

I looked out the window at my side. Horseshoe-shaped Orcas Island was receding beneath us as we flew over the countless islands of San Juan County, heading…south. I stared, watching the astonishing landscape unfolding beneath me. If I'd thought the view of Orcas from Turtleback Mountain was impressive—

wow. The sun sparkled on the blue water; the meadows and roads looked like a pretend world, with little toy cars driving to and fro. We motored on; majestic Mt. Baker loomed before us, draped in clean white snow, and now we were over the mainland. I saw fields and fields of bright blocks of color—tulips, yes, I'd heard about the tulip festival.

I'd had no idea it was so *big*.

I was still terrified, but the beauty of what lay below us was breathtaking. Was there such a thing as *good* fear?

By the time we approached Seattle, I had pretty well figured out that must be our destination. The chopper landed atop a frigging high-rise building. JoJo escorted me down a sleek elevator and out onto the street, where *of course* there was a freakin' limo waiting for us.

This absurd vehicle whisked us off to a nondescript little house in Wallingford. Some friend of JoJo's? No, it was a *very* nondescript, and *very* amazing restaurant—so under-the-radar, it didn't even have a sign outside. I knew for a fact that Kevin had never even *heard* of this place. That thought gave me a great deal of satisfaction.

We were whisked to a table in a private room, where we were served a series of astonishing dishes, so small as to be almost absurd...except they were some of the most delicious, and satisfying, things I'd ever eaten. And there were so many of them. There hadn't even been a menu to consult; JoJo had had a brief, murmured conversation with the server who seated us, and then the little plates and bowls just...arrived.

A thin and tender slice of duck breast, decorated with a ribbon of salty smoky sweet-sharp sauce.

A single crisp lettuce leaf, somehow bitter and sweet at the same time, cradling a spoonful of chopped nuts, dried fruits, and a vinegar-sherry-mushroom dressing.

A teacup with three perfect mouthfuls of chilled creamy earthy soup—potato-leek? Rutabaga-truffle? I had no idea.

A tiny plate of risotto with the freshest green peas I'd ever tasted.

And a few times in between courses, the server brought little *amuse bouches* "courtesy of Chef"—a single spoonful of some astonishing bite.

Dessert was…well. I didn't sign an NDA or anything, but if I told you about dessert, I'd have to kill you.

But I will say that it was followed by a tiny little glass of housemade limoncello, golden as the sun and just as strong.

Our lunch conversation mostly consisted of murmurs: "Oh my goodness," and "What do you think this is?" and "Don't leave even a morsel of that sauce on the plate." Mostly, we just spooned it in.

Chef herself came out to say hi to JoJo, and to make sure I'd enjoyed the meal. I merely moaned and nodded, unable to speak.

When all was said and done (and apparently paid for, though I'd seen nothing so gauche as a check), I leaned back and stared at JoJo. "This is a good start."

He patted his stomach. "Start for what?"

"For getting me to forgive you. But I can't be bought off with a helicopter ride and the most singularly delicious meal I've ever had in my entire life, JoJo. Seriously. I can't be bought."

He raised his brows and gave a wicked grin. "We'll just see about that, Camikins. A little shopping, perhaps?"

I just raised an eyebrow back at him.

"To the limo!" he cried out, and we were off.

⁊

We spent the next few hours quietly rampaging through high-end boutiques. To JoJo's consternation, I refused to let him buy me anything. I had my own money, and I had a closet about the size of a junior high locker at home. I'd been a thrifter my whole life; my mom and I called The Goodwill our personal Nordstrom, and loved the challenge of finding the best deals on the best brands.

But this was shopping on a different level. When I walked into each boutique, I felt like they were empty. "Where is the stuff?" I muttered to JoJo. "What is there to buy?"

"I'm sure you're used to pawing through racks for bargains, but this is what a curated store looks like," he murmured.

"You're such a snob," I hissed back. But he was right. There wasn't much, but it was all exquisite.

It was an unbelievable luxury to choose what I wanted, and to insist on paying for it myself. Because I could. I was immediately bewitched by a huge, thick, heavy silk scarf the color of Lisa's best wine.

"What's that for?" asked JoJo, watching me as I stood before a mirror draping and tying and doubling and looping this expanse of impossibly rich fabric.

"It's for accessorizing."

"Hm. I thought it was for draping a vampire's coffin or something."

I bought it anyway. At the third or fourth store, I also bought an emerald green cashmere sweater that actually didn't have any holes anywhere. That was the extent of my shopping, because I had money, but not *that* much money.

JoJo gave his credit card a healthy workout, though.

"I wanted to buy you something," he said, pouting. "Just one thing."

I didn't point out that I still had a belly full of astonishing food he'd just bought me. "I'd rather have an experience than a thing, JoJo."

"An experience!" His face lit up. "I know just the place!"

And then we were off on a quick, hilarious wander through the Experience Music Museum, a place I'd always wanted to visit but I'd managed never to go to.

I did let JoJo buy my ticket.

And then suddenly it was time to return to our high-rise heliport. Back up the silent elevator, back into the noisy chopper, and then liftoff. Seattle receded against the backdrop of a glorious sunset. Once we landed on Orcas, I was happy to let him drive his own car this time—I didn't think I could handle much more excitement today. I just leaned back in the soft leather seat and let it all wash over me.

He parked at Lisa's place and turned to me. "So. Forgive me?" He actually looked *worried*.

I smiled. "I do. But don't ever try to buy me off again."

"Is that what I was doing?" He looked away, bemused. "You enjoyed it, I hope—at least a little?"

"I did. Too much in fact. But I don't want to be one of your high society leeches. If we're going to make another try at being friends, I want something real, and reciprocal."

He nodded and smiled. "I like this new Cam. She's a little bossy, but I like her backbone."

"Who are you talking about me to?" I sighed. "I'm right here, JoJo. And I'm just me, a licensed hairdresser with half an associate's degree turned caretaker. I have writing aspirations but the truth is, I work for a living and I'll always have to work for a living. This..." I waved my hands around to encompass all of it—the helicopter rides, the private restaurant, the boutiques full of special things—the entire fantastical afternoon. "It's all fun, but it's not real. I need you to be real with me if you want to be my friend. No more acts, no trying to sweep me off my feet like in a movie."

He gazed at me strangely for a moment, then said, "Is there any tiny possibility that you might be wrong, though? About both of us?"

I could find no hint of humor in his voice, or in his face. "What's that supposed to mean?"

He shrugged. "That maybe you're not just a hairdresser with pretensions? And maybe I wasn't just trying to buy you off today?"

I almost laughed, except he seemed so serious. "What do *you* think I am then, and what *were* you trying to do?"

"Very good questions." He nodded, betraying a little of his usual impishness again. "Maybe we should think about them—both of us, and talk some more about this. Someday." He drew in a big breath, and made a strange face. "But this is not that day—or night. Tonight is still for having fun. You *have* had fun, right?"

I saw the hope in his eyes. "I had a freaking blast."

He smiled a huge smile. "Good." JoJo Brixton was a rich and spoiled man, but he had a good heart.

We got out of the car. Lisa's house was dark—not even a porch light shining. I did look forward to reporting this whole amazing day to her, soon I hoped. She'd said she was going away for a few days starting tomorrow... Had she left early? Maybe she was just out to dinner.

JoJo opened his trunk. "Goodness, what a lot of loot I have. And look at yours: so profligate you were! How will you *ever* manage to get all this back to your house? If only we had a valet. Or one of those, what do you call it, wheelie thingies."

"You mean a hand truck?"

"Whatever." Manual labor was clearly outside his vocabulary range. He held up my two small shopping bags. "Are you sure you don't want me to carry these for you? I could probably manage it."

I took them in one hand. "No, but I could use your help with some kindling."

"Some what?"

"I have a bunch of cardboard in my trunk that I keep forgetting to bring back from the car for my wood stove. You could carry that to the house for me." I opened the Honda's trunk and gestured at the pile of recycling I'd hoarded in there for fire starting.

"I think I can handle even this." He leaned over the trunk and recoiled. "What is that smell?" He pulled out a box and glanced at the label. "You're ordering kombucha now? By the case?"

"Of course not, I got this from…oh. Oh JoJo!" My heart pounded with alarm. I dropped my bags to the driveway.

"What's wrong, Cam?" JoJo sounded honestly concerned.

"These were…from Marie," I stammered, "for my fire. She was ordering a lot of stuff online, and I just asked her if I could—"

"These were *Marie's*?" His voice was extremely calm, which somehow made his alarm even clearer to me. "Are you telling me this is Marie's recycling?"

"Yes, oh, I, oh crap! Do you think these…could they be contaminated? Did I just poison you? Wait—*I* broke them down and put them in my car! Have we both been poisoned?"

He set the box back in the trunk. "These have been in here since before she…left us, I presume?"

"Yes. Just before…you know."

"Well, that was days ago, and you don't seem to be in a coma too, so they're probably fine, but, for the love of Lucrezia Borgia, Cam…" He glanced again at Lisa's dark house, then bent to start pulling the boxes back out. "Let's just put all of this in *my* trunk, and I'll get rid of them."

"Get rid of them? But…what if… Couldn't they be *evidence* maybe?"

"Why yes, Cam. I'm sure they are! Are you just figuring that out now? And what do you think the menagerie of law enforcement currently infesting our fair island will make of the fact that you've been concealing these in your trunk all this time?" He gave me a piercing glare, the first look of unfaked disapproval I had ever gotten from him, I realized—now that I'd seen what that looked like. "I must assume you've never mentioned these during any of your interrogations, or they wouldn't still be here."

"No. …I haven't." I put a hand up to my mouth as his meaning began sinking in. "They were just garbage. For kindling in my wood stove! I haven't even remembered to bring them into my house; it just never crossed my mind!"

"I know that," said JoJo as he lifted a stack of them out of my trunk and started carrying them toward his own, which was still open. "The question is, will the law believe it? Given how much time they seem to have spent grilling you lately, I fear they may find it hard to swallow the idea that you just never thought about a trunk full of *food packaging* taken from Marie's house just as she was being *poisoned*."

"Oh my gosh," I murmured, starting to feel a very unwanted tingling up my arms. *Not a good time for that!* I shouted mentally at my inner chameleon. "Oh, crap, crap, *crap*! You're right!"

"That happens sometimes, even to me," he said, coming back for the rest of them, "as hard as that must be for you to believe." He gave me maybe the most serious look I'd ever seen him give anyone. "So, these boxes *never existed*, Cam. Got that? I'm going to burn them now, and make sure not even the ashes end up where anyone could find them; and the rest will be our little secret—forever. You understand? Even from Lisa. *Especially* from Lisa."

"I…I guess." I hated having all these secrets to keep! More and more of them. Pretty soon I wouldn't even be able to remember which ones had to be kept from who anymore. "Why especially Lisa?" I asked, unable to imagine her throwing me to the cops after all she and I had shared that morning. "Lisa wouldn't tell on me."

"That's not the point," JoJo said, patiently, shoving his trunk gently closed now that all my boxes were inside it. "What do you suppose the law will think when *another* of her employees turns out to be hiding something important from them? How will that make *Lisa* look?"

"Oh!" How had I not seen that? "Oh no; I'm so sorry I've put you all in such a—"

"Don't," he said, almost gently. "Your apologies for everything under the sun have always been adorable, Camikins; but I like the spine you've been showing off all day even better." He gave me a wicked smile. "I understand mistakes, darling. I make one every now and then myself. But Lisa mustn't know about this because, once she did, she'd have to choose between protecting you, and ratting on you so that she couldn't be accused of hiding evidence from the police, herself. That's a risk she can't afford at this point, and a choice I know she *really wouldn't* want to have to make."

He was so right! And I hadn't seen that either. Where had this weirdly wise and clear-headed JoJo come from? Then I realized that he must know the things she'd told me that morning too. It was so obvious how close he and Lisa were. Of course she would have told him—at least some of it. I couldn't ask him, though, without admitting I knew too; and if I'd guessed wrong about him…well, that would not be very discreet at all. "I understand," was all I could say. "Thank you, JoJo."

He shrugged and wagged his head a bit. "Not the kind of favor I'd expected to be doing for you today, but things so rarely go as one expects. You're entirely welcome, though."

Then he turned away and climbed into his car. I picked up my two little shopping bags and watched the Jaguar make its exit from Lisa's driveway, the beautiful memories of this magical, memorable day turning to ashes in my mouth.

CHAPTER 14

I had barely let myself into my cabin and set my bags down when my phone rang. My skin still prickled, and my head was reeling. Also, I was just plain exhausted.

I pulled my phone out of my pocket: Jen. *I'm too tired for this*, I thought. But I swiped the call open anyway, because of course I did.

"Hi, Jen," I sighed.

"And where have *you* been all day?"

I exhaled, and dropped into my comfy chair. James stood by his food bowl, clearly not believing that I was going to neglect this pressing matter for one moment longer. "Oh…that is *such* a long answer that I just don't have anything like the energy left to launch into now."

"Seriously?" She sounded thrilled, and scandalized.

"Seriously," I said, then added, before she could wheedle me, "and I will so completely fill you in *tomorrow*. I mean…you just cannot imagine. So—what's up?"

She paused, clearly trying to decide whether to push it. "Okay, I'm going to hold you to that. Because I'm afraid there's a certain, um, *matter* that can't wait."

My heart sank. "Really?" I stifled another sigh. "Bring it on."

"Well, I think you need to decide what you are or aren't after with Colin."

I dropped my forehead onto the hand not holding my phone. *Colin!* I'd forgotten all about him in the rush of…well, everything else. "I never called to thank him for fixing up Master Bun's hutch."

"No, you didn't, and when he came by and told me that, it seemed so unlike you that I called you too after he left, to find out what was going on, and you never returned my call either."

I pulled the phone away from my ear and looked in alarm at the calls icon, only now seeing the little red '5' there. The phone had been in my purse or pocket all day, but I'd turned off the ringer at that absurd amazing restaurant, because sitting down in there had felt almost like being at church. I'd clicked it back on during the flight home, but had gone straight to camera, snapping as many sunset photos as I could grab. I put Jen on speaker and poked the icon. My list of missed calls came up: Colin, Colin, Jen, Jen, and *Kip!*

"Oh Jen, I'm so sorry," I gushed. "I just—today—I never even had a moment to look at my phone, and—"

"—and I look forward to hearing about why," Jen cut in. "But Colin came by where I was working this afternoon to say 'hi,' and went on for twenty minutes about how…um, uncomfortable it's beginning to feel for him showing up and showing up for you while you seem to keep 'takin'' what he's givin' while goin' elsewhere for a livin',' if you catch my drift."

I practically moaned. What an awful friend I was. What an awful *human being* I was. "This is terrible. I never meant any such thing!"

"Well *I* know that!" Jen said. "This is you we're talking about. But he's hurt, Cam."

"I'll call him the minute we hang up. Thank you so much for telling me!"

"My pleasure. He's kind of a catch, as we both know, but if you don't want to grab him, I think it's time to throw him back.

That's only fair."

I nodded, though she couldn't see me. We'd talked about this before. *She* didn't want to date him, because she'd known him all her life and it would be like dating her brother. "I know, and you're so right. My head has just been so full of other things lately, and—"

"Who would know that better than me, Cam?" she asked softly. "So! You'll deal with that, and we're done there, I think. Would you like to hear today's bit of juicy gossip?"

I looked at the time. It wasn't all that late, but I was just wiped. Meanwhile, James gave up his vigil by his food bowl and came to jump on my lap. "If it's short. I am really not kidding about how tired I am—I was up until four a.m. last night."

"You *were*? Why?"

"I finished the play rewrites."

"Finished—like *all* of them? *Last night*?"

"Yes. And Lisa called my changes brilliant." Okay, at least some of them, the few scenes she'd looked at, but I was so taking it. "*Brilliant*, Jen—that's the actual word she used!"

"Wow, wow, wow! But—why all in one night?"

Why indeed? I still wasn't entirely sure myself. "Because…well, because I was angry, I think, that she wanted me to do all that at all after telling me she loved it so much; but then I realized that she was right, and as I got into it, I just started getting all kinds of ideas about how much better so much of it could be. I ended up changing things she didn't even ask me to. I sort of couldn't stop, once I got on a roll."

"Wow," she said again. "Cam, what's gotten into you? It's like you're just…busting out lately! Congratulations! I am so bowled over! Except for the 'brilliant' part," she added with a chuckle. "I knew that already."

It was like an injection of energy, hearing her praise. Suddenly I was just fizzing inside. Okay, maybe I wasn't ready to fall over asleep just yet. I scratched James's ears, silently promising to feed him *very soon.* "So what's this gossip you mentioned?"

"Oh, well, not such happy news, I'd better warn you. Don't want you to get whiplash here or anything. But my friend Sherry is currently dating Deputy Harris, as you may know, and—"

"Harris? Which one is that?"

She laughed. "Lady, you are missing out! He's the youngest deputy on the island, and such a little hunk! Hair like raven feathers, and built like a romance book cover. Sherry would be so easy to hate right now if I weren't such a tolerant and forgiving person."

"Okay, go on. I'm not in need of hearing about any more hunks right now." Oh boy was I not.

"Right. You really should leave one or two for someone else here, or the whole island might get less sweet on you."

Now I laughed. "Stop it. Just tell me the bad news."

"Right again. So Harris told Sherry that he thinks Kip is in trouble at work—that they're pushing him out of the loop on things. What does that tell you, hmmm?"

My heart clutched. "Oh my goodness, that must be why he was so upset this morning!"

"You talked to *Kip?* This *morning?*" She sounded aghast.

"Yes. Oh-h, that was dumb."

"And you just didn't bother to tell me until now?"

"I've been gone all day, and—"

"I *know,* remember?" she said. "What about?"

"What have I been gone about?"

"No!" she practically shrieked. "What did you talk to *Kip* about? Why was he upset?"

My face burned. In my lap, James fidgeted. "Jen, I was such an idiot. I called his cell phone and asked him just to tell me whether I was their prime suspect."

"You did *what?* Why would you do that? You don't want them knowing that you know! They'll just…where *have* you been all day?"

"It was nothing to do with that. And I don't know what I was thinking. I was up 'til four, remember? Maybe I wasn't fully awake yet."

She sighed. "Oh, hon, if you're ever up that late again, you need to lock your phone in the freezer or something so it's harder to reach before you're fully recovered." Then she paused briefly before adding, "What did he say to that, I'm almost afraid to ask?"

"He said he had no idea what I was talking about, and that he wasn't off yesterday like Sherman said, and that if Sheriff Clarke was on Orcas yesterday, no one had told him about it."

"Wow," she said softly, clearly thinking it over. "It's true then, isn't it? Cam, I think they're cutting him out of this investigation! That's got to mean something!"

"You think?" Okay, maybe I was fizzy with her praise, but I still felt kind of stupid-headed.

"What else did he say?" she asked.

"Nothing, actually." And now I felt the pain again, remembering the call…and how it had ended. "He just told me he couldn't comment on an active investigation, and hung up without even saying goodbye. He sounded pretty ticked off."

"I bet he did," she said, softly. "Oh, I really need to look into this. Wow, wow, wow."

"And that was all before breakfast! You would not believe the day I've had, Jen."

"You're really gonna say that, and still not tell me about it until tomorrow? *Seriously?*"

Should I make her beg for it, like she always did with me? No, I was just too tired to stretch this out even that much, but I had sort of opened the can, so…

I gave her the 'quick version:' JoJo the drunken clown magically transformed into JoJo the sober penitent; driving the Jag, the helicopter abduction, the rooftop landing, the limo to the mysterious temple of gastronomy, then the shopping and museum, then home again. The whole while, Jen was gasping and screaming into the phone. I was glad I'd put it on speaker so this wasn't happening directly into my ear.

I left out the part about Marie's recycling, of course.

By the time I was finished, Jen seemed almost too winded to speak. She laughed again. "Oh…oh, Cam… Wait, did I punch the wrong number? Who is this, *really*? It can't be you!"

"Ha! That's exactly what JoJo said when I ripped into him this morning."

"Well…he's not completely wrong. Honestly, I have no idea what's happened to you, or where it's all going, but you are sure going there fast all of a sudden! Go you! Wow." She chuckled again, finally recovering. "Well okay, now I can hardly blame you for ignoring my calls, can I? But you really should call Colin."

"I will—right now. In fact I'd better go before it gets any later. But we'll talk again tomorrow morning, okay?"

"Oh you better bet we will. We have big plans to make now, hon. This case is *crackin' open!*"

Right, I thought, *about that…*

Not that I was ready to deal with that now.

"One last word of advice, though," Jen said.

"Oh?"

"You might want to take a minute first to think about what to tell him. Make something up, even. He's upset, Cam, and I don't think telling him you spent the afternoon in a helicopter with some other guy is going to make anything better for him. Even if that other guy was just JoJo."

Hmm. She had a point. "I don't like lying, though." I couldn't just call everything *discretion…*

Was I honest?

I scratched James again, wondering what kind of person I was, really.

ↁ

The first thing I did after hanging up with Jen was listen to all those messages: a call from Colin wondering how I liked the cage he built. A second message from him, hoping everything was all right. Two messages from Jen wondering what was up, the second considerably more anxious than the first. And, finally, a very brief, heartbreakingly awkward apology from Kip for having ended our call so abruptly.

"Aww," I said aloud, putting a hand over my heart. That was… nice. Confusing, but nice.

The second thing I did after hanging up was feed all these desperately hungry animals. Master Bun was still outside in his Fort Knox, but I knew he was no less anxious for his evening meal. I brought him inside for it, so he could enjoy a little indoor time (and to make sure there was no food left outside overnight) (even if Fort Knox was impenetrable to raccoons). I returned him to his newly battened hutch, and locked him in safe and snug, and then I felt like an absolute toad because I *still* hadn't called Colin.

I punched his number, and it rang four times and went to voicemail. "Colin," I said, "I am *so* sorry to have missed your calls, and to not have gotten back to you sooner. I love, love, love the hutch—it's amazing! I'm sorry I didn't tell you sooner, but today was crazy. I'll tell you all about it when we talk—I really am sorry to be so out of touch. Please, call whenever, and…we'll talk."

I hung up before I could repeat myself any more and sat, holding the phone. What was I doing? I leaned back in my comfy chair, petting James, too exhausted to even get up and make my way to bed, still thinking, and worrying, and finally…dozing.

A knock on my door woke me. And another. I was half asleep, but I stumbled the couple of steps to it and opened it to see Colin.

"Hi?" I probably looked as confused as I felt. "Colin?"

He looked miserable and a little uncertain. "Hi. You said…call any time, right? So here I am. Wondering if we could talk."

"Of course." I'd known this day was coming, right? The day of "the Talk." But it had to be *this* day? At *night*? Really? I stepped aside to let him in, immediately wondering where we should even sit to have this kind of talk in my tiny A-frame. In the one up-holstered chair by the woodstove? On the floor? Snuggled in the loveseat? But Colin sat himself down in one of the small chairs by the table. I sat in another, and girded myself for what promised to be a painful conversation with a sweet man I did care about.

He gave me a sheepish look across the tiny table. "I'm betting Jen already told you my feelings were a little bruised up."

There was no point in lying. "She mentioned something, yes. And I am so sorry that I just disappeared on you when you were working on the hutch. I appreciate you." I reached across the table to pat his hand. He pulled it back.

"Not the hand pat, Cam. Please. A man's ego can only take so much."

"I...I don't know what to say."

"Maybe you should just listen, then." He cleared his throat. "I think you know I've always liked you, Cam. I thought I made that clear enough from the start. And I thought, well, it seemed like maybe? But nothing ever happened. I took myself off for a bit, kinda like a dog crawling under a porch until he heals up. I thought I was gone long enough that I was over it. But..." He shook his head. "I guess I wasn't."

"I'm sorry, Colin. I don't know how things got so off track with us. Can't we just be friends?"

"Of course. We've always been friends and we always will be. But listen, Cam. I've never met anyone like you. You're just like water. On the surface, you sparkle and move and throw off light. But underneath? You're deep. There's more things inside you than I'll probably ever understand, but...I wish you'd give me a chance to try."

I felt tears prick my eyes. "No one's ever said anything that beautiful to me before."

"Just words, Cam." He took my hand between his, and held my gaze with his intelligent, deep eyes. "Will you give us a chance? I think we could have something special. But if not, I understand. And of course I'm your friend, now and always."

He was saying everything I should have wanted to hear—about as nicely as anyone could possibly have said it, though it clearly caused him pain. I tried to find some answer that would make sense of my own...well, senseless rejection, but I was suddenly less sure than ever about exactly why I'd been pushing him away all this time. I just stared at him, still without any words. I didn't want to hurt him. He so didn't deserve to be hurt—at all.

When I didn't answer him, he stood up and headed for the door.

I rose right up and followed him, more confused and upset than I was when he arrived. "Colin, I..."

He turned back, and before I knew it, I was in his arms.

જી

"You have to go," I murmured, through lips that felt a little bruised after those kisses.

"I don't have to," he replied, in a playful growl.

"This has been...so wonderful, Colin; you have no idea how much or how long I have wanted this. I didn't even know, really, until now."

"That makes me very happy," he said, grinning up at me.

"But...we need to stop now. Really," I said, trying to push a smile off my face that wouldn't seem to leave, in spite of how *unhappy* I knew this was just about to get.

"Then you'd better get off my lap, woman."

We stood up, flushed and of course a bit awkward. I'd been sitting in his lap in my one little easy chair for at least twenty minutes. We walked the step or two to the door, where he turned back, smiling at me.

"If you were planning to tell me to kiss off, you didn't do a very good job of it," he said.

"No. I didn't, did I?" The smile on my face finally fled. He looked so *happy*. What on earth had I done? How could I have let this… "Colin, you may be the most attractive man I've ever met, and what we just shared…" I shook my head. "You're too good to be true."

"Well, if you want to be *mean* about it," he teased, bending down to give me another kiss.

But I pulled back before we connected, shaking my head. "I don't want to be mean to you—at all. You aren't just the sexiest man I've met in years, you're the kindest, and the most…reliable. But…I'm afraid that mean is how I'm going to seem now." His smile faltered as I felt tears start pricking at my eyes again. Not happy ones this time. The worst thing I could still do to him now, would be play this out even more. "Colin, I am so deeply grateful for your friendship, and—"

"No…" he said, leaning back as if I'd swung a punch at him. "You can't be telling—"

"—and the loveliest half hour I've had for years, and I can't for the life of me figure out why I don't love you, but even now, I just can't see us—"

He whirled around in hurt or fury—probably both, all more than justified—yanked the door open, and stalked out, slamming it shut behind him almost hard enough to break the glass. I wanted to wrench it back open and beg him to come back. *Not like this. I can't let it be like this!* But what would I be calling him back for? One more wound? Every time I'd had the chance to let him down gently, I'd just made things worse. And now…

I went back to sit beside the embers of my fire, and let the tears come. I really didn't know why no one I met anymore seemed… to fill that space beyond just physical need and attraction. But even after such a gorgeous, tender moment, I had still not been able to imagine myself actually loving Colin, sharing a whole life, growing old with him. I had kept gazing deep into that space as we'd held and kissed each other, whispering and giggling, and trading pleasure like kids—expecting, finally, to see him there, in that longer, deeper picture. But the more I looked, the more I knew...I'd been a thoughtless fool to let this happen. Yes, Colin had just made my body sing—and laugh—beyond all expectation. It had been too long since a man had held me, and kissed me, touched me in a way that let me know he knew exactly how I wanted to feel—needed to feel. But Colin hadn't been the first to do that. Kevin had made me feel that same way too, once.

Despicable Kevin.

I remembered how he'd walked into the salon to see his friend Meredith, one of our nail technicians, and given me that adorable, toothy smile of his, flirting with me and teasing me even though I was too busy to talk and too skittish to date. He just *wouldn't go away.*

I'd been so shy, awkward and inexperienced...and afraid. Of so much vulnerability, so much visibility. But he'd been persistent too. Like Colin. And when he'd finally convinced me to let him kiss me, Kevin had known exactly how to hold me so that I felt safe but not imprisoned, and touch me in ways that brought me to life, instead of shutting me down. I'd thought that was love—at last. But I'd been wrong.

It was hard to imagine a lovelier moment than Colin had just shown me. But I couldn't let what I wished for blind me to what really was, again. Better to hurt Colin for a moment, right up front, than play along, pretending love until...we ended up where I and Kevin had. But, oh... How it hurt to think about what I'd just done to him. The look on his face just before he'd stormed out.

Maybe I should just swear off men completely, I thought—especially the nice ones—before I brought any more of them to grief. I'd treated Colin horribly, and Kip... Yes, I guessed I *was* sweet on Kip, whatever I might pretend. And nothing seemed to have gone very well for him either since the day we'd met. Was that my fault too somehow, or just coincidence? I hadn't hurt him like I'd just hurt Colin, yet. And I wasn't going to. I knew that now. Jen kept saying he was sweet on me, but... Kip sure didn't seem to care for me like Colin had. Did he?

And with that thought, a terrible question occurred to me. Jen had called Kip sweet on me while speculating about Sherman's reasons for dragging me in to see the sheriff on Kip's day off... Which it hadn't been, apparently. And now, if Jen's latest bit of gossip was correct, they'd been cutting Kip out of the loop on everything...because why?

She hadn't said.

But was it because...he *was* sweet on me? Was Kip in trouble for 'being sweet' on a suspect in their ongoing investigation? Was he being punished for feelings that, well, *might* not even really exist? Was there really anything between Kip and me—besides vague fantasies?

Oh sure, I melted pretty quick whenever he showed up. But Colin had made me melt too, and I'd known all along that wasn't love. Was Kip any different?

I still had no idea! Why?

Why was it so hard for me to figure out how I felt about *any-body*?

Anybody male, at least.

Was it because...I'd felt so sure about Kevin once? Before he'd reduced me to a mere prop in *his* play, and decided that I was "*craz*—"

And suddenly, I was right back there—in the conversation that had ended me and Kevin. And even though I tried to set it down, I couldn't pull away this time. *I'd told him my secret.* I'd *trusted* him with *that*! Something I had never risked with anyone before. And he had just freaked out. I'd tried so hard to explain it, to convince him, but the harder I tried the angrier he'd become, and then...

Then this awful memory was joined...overlaid and merged...

then wiped away by an even worse and older one. I was in another room. A suffocating, nightmare room, where…I didn't want to be here. Didn't want to think about it. *Don't. Don't go here!* But I couldn't stop it…

I saw him kill her, whispered a tiny, terrified voice inside my head.

He did it right in front of me.

I'd been too young to understand what "mental illness" was. But, oh, I knew the word *crazy* well enough. That was the word that man always started using when he got angry at my mother—when he hit her, and when he called the men who came to help him punish her. He always told me they were here to help her, but I wasn't stupid as he wished I was. That man only ever called those awful men to come 'help' my mother when he had been screaming at her, and hurting her. My mother would cry out in anger—in terror—as those "helpers" came in shouting at her. Grappling her to the floor. Kneeling on her back as she cried out in pain. They were *his* friends, not hers. They called her crazy too, and took *his* side, as if *she* was the threat to be dealt with in that benighted house. They did nothing to him, that man who was always hurting everyone. They only ever made things worse. And I had hated them almost as much as I feared and despised the man who called himself my father.

Until the night he'd finally gone too far, had solved the problem of my first mother permanently. In that room. Right in front of me.

I had vanished. For longer than ever this time—hours. But it hadn't helped me get away. It had only trapped me there, with them, unable to move, or even call out to my mother as I watched it happen. Frozen and voiceless, I'd had to watch him try to cover up what he had done, as if he had forgotten I was there at all. I was still frozen there, ignored by everyone, when his awful friends came back again, and told *him* they were sorry. Sorry for *him*! But that they couldn't cover up for him this time.

Not with her body on the floor. In front of me.

After they took my first mother's killer away, I had finally un-frozen. People remembered I was there then, and asked where I had been. What I'd seen. I told them nothing. I was never going to speak to any of them again. Not ever.

I only learned they were called cops after I'd been taken into "protective custody"—by other cops who weren't any more inter-ested in helping me than they'd been in helping my *crazy* mother. Neither were the foster people. I was nothing to any of them but a grubby, frightened, awkward child; silent and strange. Not un-til my wonderful, *real* mom and dad had finally come and saved me from all that did anyone do anything but punish me for being my mother's child. And…I'd known why. Even then. I wasn't dumb. It had taken me a little while to understand why nobody had seemed to care I was there the night my mother had been murdered. But I figured out, eventually, what it meant to vanish. *Really* vanish. Not make believe. Not just go quiet and small. And though I was just a little girl, I was old enough to know that what I'd done wasn't just mysterious or strange or confusing; it was impossible.

It was *crazy*.

Just like my mother had been.

Somewhere in that long, horrible river of reflections I had failed to dam up instantly and lock away again, the tears I had been shedding over what I'd done to Colin had begun to flow more fiercely. First a trickle, then a river of their own.

A while later, I found myself up in the loft, curled on my mat-tress, one arm clutching a cat, sobbing and sobbing and sobbing, still unable to set down the nightmares I'd let in. Unable to come back at all…

CHAPTER 15

James woke me up, as usual. Romantic angst followed by a deep dive into traumatic memories were all very sad, but a cat needs his breakfast.

So does a bunny.

I sat up and slid my achy body out of bed, then made my way down the ladder, feeling hung over and surreal. Getting everyone's breakfasts would give me something to focus on—besides the mountain of processing still waiting for my attention after all of yesterday's adventures. But the night had left me yet another revelation or two. About Kip.

I got it now; why I'd never been able to figure out exactly what I felt for him—or tell what he might feel for me. It was because I felt too many things for him at once. And some of those feelings didn't play very well at all with the others. Maybe that's why Kip had never made his own feelings clearer: because he could tell how unclear mine were. Maybe while I'd been aware of melting every time he showed up, I'd been unaware of telling him to go away at the same time.

Kip was a beautiful, thoughtful, competent, reliable, and very well-behaved man. About as kind and safe as they came, it seemed to me—in spite of whatever had happened that night on Snooks's boat. And yes, I was definitely "sweet on him." I was ready to admit that now.

But he was a cop.

However attractive and wonderful he might seem to me now, that wounded little girl still living down inside me was never going to trust a cop—or let me embrace one either. Last night had made that clear too.

I was a danger to Kip, emotionally and professionally. Even if he did have feelings for me too, he deserved better than a woman who was just immobilized by what he was—what he had every right to be. How many things did the world need more than it needed a kind and honest cop? He would never have treated my birth mother the way those other cops had. I was sure of that. Who knew how many women out there would be spared terrible misery because of what a thoughtful, caring kind of policeman Kip was. But he was still a cop, and I'd been letting him risk his chosen profession, and his heart, for nothing.

That needed to stop before I ruined anything more for him than I might already have done. And it needed doing now; this morning. This week's theme was breaking hearts, I guessed—my own included.

After I'd scrambled myself some eggs, I fed the livestock. Master Bun had spent an undisturbed night out in the amazing hutch built for him by the man whose heart I'd broken last night. I found no evidence of further disturbance; not out there, at least. Master Bun seemed calm and happy to see me.

After that, I went back inside, swallowed the last of my coffee, and pulled out my phone. No messages, no missed calls. I dreaded hearing from Colin, but also wouldn't be surprised if I never did again. What was Jen going to think of me when he told her about last night?

Well, that unhappy item would have to wait in line behind all the ones in front of it.

I started to pull up Kip's number, then stopped, and lowered my phone.

No phone call. This needed to be done in person.

I would have to drive down to the substation and inquire about how to contact him through *official* channels. I wanted nothing clandestine about this talk, nothing for Sherman to exploit. From now on, everything between Kip and me was going to stay aboveboard and professional. And if they decided to arrest me while I was down there, oh well—it wasn't like they didn't know how to find me anyway.

I walked out to Lisa's house. It seemed just as dark and quiet as last night. She was likely already gone on her trip. I got into my Honda (only bemoaning very gently the fact that it wasn't a Jaguar) and drove "downtown" to the substation. Before I turned, I glanced over to the airport, but saw no evidence of helicopters. I parked before the low building and walked up to the door, giving it a knock.

A hunky beefcake of a man in an extremely well-fitting uniform answered the door. He was well over six feet tall, chiseled and handsome, with raven-black hair and bright green eyes, and those *shoulders*... Good gracious. This had to be Deputy Harris, and though I was glad Jen had warned me, I was in no mood for romance, or even romance-novel-cover-looking men.

"Ahem." I cleared my throat and tried not to stare too obnoxiously at the vision standing before me.

"May I help you?"

"Uh. Yeah. I'm...looking to get hold of Deputy Rankin? He's not here, is he?"

Harris gave me a puzzled look. "May I ask about what? Ms... Tate, isn't it?"

"How do you know that?" I blurted. If I had ever seen this guy before in my life, the memory would be seared in my brain.

Did they have my *picture* up here or something?

Harris didn't quite manage to abort a smirk in time—which, I was forced to concede, only made his face look even more smolderingly hot. "Well, Ms. Tate, pretty much all we do around here anymore is investigate one or another of the bodies you keep finding."

I rolled my eyes, but didn't even bother protesting. That ship had so obviously sailed.

"You really think any deputy here doesn't know who you are by now?" He put on a good-natured smile, now trying for, what, innocent and casual? I wasn't buying it for a moment, and yet that smile, yikes! This guy *was* a lethal weapon.

Which was probably why I'd never seen him. They must keep him locked up here until they had some female criminal who needed disarming.

I batted away an inner vision of Sheila facing this creature, and cleared my throat again. "It's, uh, something of a personal nature," I managed, unable to think on the fly of any more legitimate reason to insist on Kip's presence, specifically.

Now he put on a sympathetic face. "Oh. I'm sorry, miss, but we're not really allowed to deal with personal business while we're on duty. You may want to contact him after his shift ends."

"I...would rather not," I said, trying to channel my best Lisa Cannon-style cold professionalism. It was probably too late to keep any of these guys from jumping to all sorts of conclusions about Kip and me, but I had to try. And then inspiration hit. "It involves his work, actually," I said. "I have a complaint about the way he handled something—at the Brixton estate the other night."

"Oh?" The young man's perfect brows climbed.

Not what you thought after all, is it, Junior?

But he recovered quick enough. "There's a formal procedure for lodging complaints, miss. I can give you the form, if you'd like to—"

"I'd prefer to talk with him directly about this first," I interrupted, finding my footing. "If that's allowed? I just want to be sure I'm not mistaken about some pertinent details before I launch a whole formal *inquest* for nothing." I held his gaze. "Perhaps I could leave him a message?"

Harris looked uncertain—and younger than ever. He took a few steps back and turned, calling out behind him. "Rankin! Ms. Tate's out here wantin' to see you. Some kind of complaint— about you. You wanna…?"

And then Kip was there, not quite pushing Harris aside, walking into the small entryway, giving me a look of skittish concern. Not five steps behind him, naturally, came Deputy Sherman, giving me the usual stink eye.

"Ms. Tate," Kip said. "You wish to discuss some…problem with me?"

"I'm afraid I do, Deputy Rankin. Can we speak more privately somewhere?"

Sherman pushed forward. "Unfortunately, Deputy Rankin and I have an inspection appointment in fifteen minutes, Ms. Tate," she said before Kip could say a word. "We are, of course, eager to address any complaint you may have. But I'm not sure there's time at this moment to accord the matter adequate attention and respect."

Respect? Really? From Sherman? Very funny! "I appreciate your concern, Deputy Sherman," I said, still channeling Lisa's strength and coolness, and still looking at Kip rather than at her. "But this conversation won't take very long, I think, and I am one hundred percent sure you'll want us to have it—without delay."

Deputy Harris was standing pole-axed, staring at all of us, eyebrows halfway to his hairline. Which still didn't make him unattractive, the jerk.

Kip's face, on the other hand, seemed set in stone. Was he even breathing?

"Really?" Sherman put in, her brows raised slightly now as well. "And why is that?"

Now I looked at her. "You're a talented investigator, I hear. Think about it for a minute and I bet you'll guess the answer." I turned back to Kip. "So, Deputy Rankin, is there somewhere we can talk, or must I come back later?"

Kip turned stiffly back to Sherman—was he asking her permission now? Even for something like this?

She shrugged. "I can't wait to find out what this is about either. She's got ten minutes, and then we're out of here."

I said to her, "I'm not here to speak with anyone but Deputy Rankin. If he wishes to tell you all about it afterward, that's fine with me. But you're out of the room, or I'm not talking at all."

Harris was gaping open-mouthed by now, watching the most interesting tennis match of his young life. I could just see him mentally rehearsing everything for tonight's tell-all with Jen's friend Sherry.

Sherman stared at me, too. I knew exactly what she must be thinking: *Where did all this spine come from so suddenly?* I had no idea. But my newest superpower seemed to be still with me. I was very, very tired of saying yes all the time. Somehow, I had found the guts, somewhere, to start saying no.

And if I made it out of this intact, I'd think about what it all meant.

Kip nodded at me and turned around, indicating I should follow. I did. He led me through the substation's very bland innards to a different room this time, an even blander conference room. He closed the door behind me and waved me politely into a chair at the long table there, before taking a seat opposite me.

"What is this about, Ms. Tate?" he asked, as formally and politely as ever. "And I should warn you that there are surveillance cameras in every room of this building. So if you're about to incriminate yourself in any way, know that video will exist of whatever transpires here."

"Oh. Thanks for letting me know." I looked around, and sure enough, there it was, tiny and dark up in one corner against the ceiling, trained on the table. "But, well…it's more your privacy I'm trying to protect than mine."

At this, even Kip's brows moved slightly. "Let's begin then.

What is the nature of your complaint?"

I sighed. "I have no complaint, Kip. I just said that to get past your cute little guard dog out there." *Chew on that, Junior.* "I've been hearing rumors that you're being pushed out of the loop around here, and I'm afraid I know why. I can't let you, or the other nosy-pantses around here, keep bashing at you for completely imaginary reasons."

Kip frowned. "Ms. Tate, I have no idea what you're talking about, or where this is going, but this may really not be the appropriate time or place for this conversation."

"I'm sure it's not." That had been part of my plan, I only fully realized now. I didn't just want to make it clear to Sherman and whoever-all else that there wasn't any romance between me and Kip. I most of all wanted *him* to understand that.

Because if he *was* sweet on me, I was pretty sure my obnoxious behavior here this morning was going to squash that once and for all.

"Deputy Rankin, if you or anyone else has been under any impression that I might be interested in you, in some sort of romance between us, I need you—and them—to understand very clearly that I am not, and never have been the tiniest bit attracted to you."

Kip's mouth fell open. It took him a moment to remember himself and close it again. "Ms. Tate," he nearly stammered, looking bewildered. "Where on earth has all this come from? I have never—"

"Please, let me finish," I said. "Then I'll be happy to answer any questions you have, okay?" I had planned and rehearsed this, and dang it, I was going to get it all out before losing my nerve.

Kip hunched his shoulders and nodded, looking like a man who had just been beaned dead center with a crowbar.

"You have always seemed a terrific police officer to me," I continued. "I mean, I know you're a deputy sheriff and that's not police, but, you know what I mean." I gave him a weak smile.

"Anyway. You're a good cop. Better than most I've met, actually. I've never been all that fond of—" Wait, I probably shouldn't be alienating every deputy on the island, and this was off topic besides. "What I mean to say is, I have never had any complaint about you at all, Deputy Rankin. With one relatively minor exception that everyone here knows all about, and that we have put completely behind us, your behavior has always been perfect.

"But you are not, and never will be, my type. And I just wanted to make that clear, in case you, or anyone else, has had a different impression—for any reason. You are too good at what you do, and the community needs you. So. Um. Do you have any questions?"

There. I'd gotten it out. My heart was pounding and my mouth was dry, and I couldn't look him in the eye, but I'd said it.

"Thank you," he said quietly. "I do have one question."

I forced myself to glance up at him, then looked quickly away. "Okay."

"Have I *ever* said or done anything, in or out of your presence, to suggest that I have romantic designs on you in any way?"

"No." I swallowed. "You have not, Deputy Rankin—"

"Then why—"

I didn't let him finish. "—or we'd have had this conversation a long time ago," I said forcefully. "Maybe I've just mistaken your...well, being nice...for something it never was. If so, I apologize. I was never all that sure if any of your niceness meant anything—and it didn't matter until I heard that maybe you were in some kind of trouble because of it. So I thought I should come down here and say this, *now*."

I made myself look up at him again, and not look away this time. He definitely looked hurt, and that broke my heart. I held tight to my *Lisa Cannon Professional Face*, tighter than ever. I couldn't lose it now. That would not just undo everything I'd just done—it would make it worse.

"I do have one more question, I guess," he said suddenly, surprising me. I nodded. "May I ask who's been telling you about this supposed conspiracy against me?"

I swallowed again. Gosh my mouth was dry. "No one specific, I've just heard things in the island rumor mill." No, that was not entirely honest, was it? "Though I have to say, Deputy Sherman has been pretty clear that she thinks we're…you know. And it was dumb of me to call you yesterday morning, on your personal cell phone. During that phone call—which you handled very professionally, I'd like to add for the record," I said, glancing up at the security camera, "you seemed upset by the fact that I'd been told—by Deputy Sherman—that you were off duty the day before yesterday, when apparently you weren't, and that you had never been told that the San Juan County Sheriff was here that day. So. That all seemed to confirm the rumors." *Suck all that up, Sherman.*

"All right," he said, stonily. "I guess I can see how you might have come to such a conclusion. But I would like to assure you that I have never intended to give you the impression I was interested in anything but your general welfare—same as anyone else in the county, or beyond." His tone was formal, but I had never seen a sadder look on his face. "Does that help at all, Ms. Tate?"

"Yes. Thank you. That's reassuring to hear." Actually it was killing me, and I was going to totally lose it if I didn't get out of here, and fast. "And again, I'm sorry if I've stirred up all this drama about nothing. I won't do it again."

"No apologies needed, Ms. Tate. Much better for you to say something than let this misunderstanding go on."

"My thoughts exactly." I scrambled awkwardly to my feet. "I'll let you get to that other appointment then."

"Thank you for coming in, Ms. Tate."

He stood as well, gesturing bleakly at the door.

He followed me through the station to the entranceway. I could feel everyone watching me, watching us both. If eyes were knives, Sherman would have been arrested for assault about now.

As I reached the door, I heard Kip say, coolly, "Tapes are right there, Larissa. Feel free to look all you want as soon as we get back from the inspection."

I turned around, astonished, and saw Sherman rock back on her clunky heels, looking incensed. He had just called her *Larissa*! Right in front of me! I'd have bet he'd never done anything so inappropriate in his whole career.

Well, except that once.

Harris sat there studying his computer monitor as if the whereabouts of Jimmy Hoffa's body had just been posted there. What was the rumor mill going to say *now*? Nothing pretty, I was sure.

But at least it was done now. Kip was free to get on with his life.

❦

As evening fell, I sat at home, a half-eaten bowl of chili-beans-onions-cheese before me.

It had been a strange day. Maybe the strangest day since Marie fell ill.

Mostly because, since my awful interview with Kip that morning, almost nothing had happened all day.

I had still heard nothing more from Colin. That friendship was clearly done. Kip hadn't contacted me either. But that had been kind of the point, after all.

There had been no new disasters or unexpected visitors of any kind, not even a word from JoJo. No raccoons or prowlers or helicopters or deputy sheriffs. So much sudden quiet, all at once. It had been...kind of unnerving.

Of course I had called Jen the moment I got home from the substation, crying into the phone as I'd poured out the whole account of what I'd done to Kip, and why. Jen was unusually gentle and sympathetic, even for her, telling me how brave and generous I'd been to give up someone I so obviously loved in order to save his job and reputation.

I had insisted that I didn't love Kip—had *never* loved him. I needed her to believe this, needed everyone to believe it, so that all this nonsense would stop, once and for all. Jen had obviously not been convinced, but she'd eventually at least pretended to play along.

That would have to be good enough for now.

I told her nothing about my meltdown the night before, or about the memories that had brought it on. I was going to tell her all the truth about me, someday, maybe even someday soon. But not right now.

I was still too busy absorbing it for myself. Something felt... changed inside me now. I could actually reflect on my birth mother's life, and her death, without immediately veering away from the thoughts. I now felt almost still and quiet deep inside, and I didn't really know what to make of it. It felt almost like something inside me had unclenched.

Would it stay unclenched? I had no idea.

And yet I also had a sense of waiting. For the other shoe to drop? That seemed plausible, even likely. There were all sorts of things swirling around out there, rockslides ready to fall on my head at any moment. But none of them had. Yet. Without even any play revisions left to make, and Lisa off on her meetings and errands, I'd spent this strangely empty day wandering around— literally and figuratively. I'd cuddled my animals (who were very pleased that I hadn't disappeared all day again). And I'd spent a lot of time thinking about all the things that had been shaken loose inside me this week. I was getting stronger. Taking charge of myself, and of my relationships to those around me.

So maybe I wasn't so much in the eye of the storm as in the ragged calm *after* a storm. Could that be true? Was the storm over now—for me at least? Had I sent enough of the world packing to be left behind by all of that at last?

That...actually sounded kind of nice.

I had just started thinking about what I would write for my

second play when my phone rang.

"Hi Jen," I said.

"Oh, Cam, you were right, and I didn't listen to you! I'm…oh, I'm so sorry!"

"Wait, what?" Was she crying? I had never met anyone who seemed less the crying type.

"We are *so screwed!*" Jen wailed. "I don't know what to do!"

"Okay, stop," I said, weirdly calm. "Slow down and breathe, okay? Then tell me what's happened."

She sucked in a jagged breath. "We're *caught*," she moaned. "They *know*, and it's all my fault."

"Caught…by who?"

"The Feds! They know I've been spying on them!"

I sighed, closing my eyes. "Oh no." Here it was: that other shoe. And so quickly.

"You warned me, and I just laughed at you, Cam. I'm sorry! I've been such an *idiot!*"

"You're not an idiot," I reassured her. "Where are you right now?"

"I'm home. I didn't dare call you from work—any work. They must be watching me like a hawk now."

"Well…wait, why are they *watching* you? If they've caught you, haven't they…? Jen, what did they catch you doing, exactly?"

She sniffled again. "Oh, Cam…oh, this is so… I happened to have this little voice-activated micro-recorder that I bought online, and—"

"You just *happened to have* a voice-activated micro-recorder?" Who just "happened to have" things like that?

"Well…yes; I bought it on a lark, you know? Seemed like a fun little thing to have around." *Wow*, I thought, *Lisa was right.* "So I hid it in Smith's room yesterday while I was in there cleaning—behind a grate he should never have had any reason to look behind. But when I went in there to make his bed up today, I popped the grate off to get it, and it wasn't there. Cam, they have it. They know now. They have to know. I'm the only person besides Smith himself who's been in that room."

"So…what have they done about it?"

She was calming down a bit, but she still sounded super distressed. "I have no idea what they're going to do. They're obviously letting me sweat. Probably to see what else I might hand them before they come to put me in cuffs. But…if I'm arrested, I just want you to know that I will so not implicate you. They have no way of knowing you were ever in on this. So just keep your mouth shut if they question you. This is going to be so much harder for me if I've dragged you in too. Okay? Just forget we ever talked about any of this."

"Well…um, thank you. That's very noble. But hey: I'm *not* involved in this. I had no idea you'd left that thing in their room, so you don't need to worry about me. Not on top of everything else."

"Well…but I did tell you I meant to spy on them, and that could make you an accessory. I'm really so sorry, Cam. I never even thought about that—or about anything. It all just seemed like…such a hoot. My brain was so turned off. I completely see that now."

I would never have imagined her being so addled. Bizarrely, it just made me feel even calmer, even more focused. "Okay listen, Jen. If they haven't said anything to you yet, maybe that's because they don't know you're the one who put it there."

"But…no… I just told you, no one else has been in that—"

"No one was *supposed* to be in that room. But why should that mean no one else *was*? No one was supposed to be bugging it either, so this could just as well have been done by someone who *wasn't* supposed to be there, right?"

"Oh." She paused, turning that over. "Well…but my fingerprints are probably still on it."

I rolled my eyes, thankful she couldn't see me. "You were in there cleaning, right?"

"Yeah…so what?"

"Did you wear latex gloves?"

"Oh! How do you *know* that?"

"I worked in a salon, Jen. I did a lot of cleaning too."

"Oh. Oh! Of course." She sounded even calmer. Maybe even…
relieved?

"If you're lucky," I went on, "any fingerprints already on that
thing got wiped off, or smudged at least, when you were han-
dling it with gloves on. Or maybe not, and they'll kick your door
in tonight. I don't know. But if I were you, I'd calm down and
not throw myself into their arms before they've even looked your
way."

"Hm," she allowed.

"Jen, someone has been *killing* people on this island. I know it
wasn't you. Maybe they'll assume it was whoever poisoned Marie
that put that bug there. That's what I'd have thought. If you just
act innocent—because you *are*—behave like there's no problem,
maybe there won't be."

There was a long pause. Then she chuckled. "When did you
get this smart?"

When did you get this flighty? I kept that thought to myself, of
course. "Thanks," I said. "But, speaking of bugging people, I just
had another thought. Next time you want to tell me about some
crime you've committed, maybe just come over instead of calling. If they *were* 'watching' you, I'm pretty sure they'd have your
phone tapped too."

"Oh no! You're right!" And the line went dead.

I pulled the phone from my ear to check the screen. Yep. Call
over. I sighed, shaking my head.

I was shoving the phone back into my pocket when someone
rapped on the cabin door behind me.

CHAPTER 16

I whirled around in alarm at the knock on my door. *No!* Had I been wrong? Had the Feds been right outside listening to that whole conversation in some unmarked panel truck? Were they banging on Jen's door at this very moment too? I hesitated, almost frozen, but there was nowhere to run and, honestly, no point in trying. So I steeled myself, made sure I'd stayed visible, and went to pull the door open.

There, standing on my porch in the dark, was a uniquely colorful individual.

"Paige!" I just about sagged in relief. "What are you doing *here?*"

"Hope I haven't come at a bad time," the old woman said cheerfully. She walked in past me without waiting for an answer, gazing up and around the room. "I've always thought this charming little house far homier than that pasteboard mansion Lisa built for *herself.*" She paused by the small table and turned to smile at me. James appeared from somewhere, going at once to twine himself around Paige's ankles. She leaned down to scratch him. "It has so much more character; I'm not at all surprised you chose it. Why, I'd have been surprised if you hadn't."

"Um…thank you." I closed the door. Why was she here, an hour after dark? "Is…everything all right?"

Paige looked surprised. "Well, of course it is. Shouldn't it be? Is there something going on I haven't heard about?"

"No—well, yes, some things, I suppose, but nothing to do with…um…" *Oh, very articulate, Cam, you should be a writer.* "So, um, what brings you out at this hour?"

Now she gave a cheerful shrug. "I was in the neighborhood, and realized I still haven't come by to celebrate your cozy new home!" She gestured toward the front windows, though of course we could see nothing in the dark. "I've left a little housewarming gift on the porch. It'll be fine out there for a while in this weather—no room for it in here."

I got up to go look, as did James. "Oh good grief!" I blurted before I could stop myself. Out on the porch was a fully packed thirty-three-gallon plastic garbage bag with massive dark leaves erupting from its semi-tied-off top. "What in the world…?" I turned around, closing the door again on the chilly air.

"Just some kale from the remains of my winter garden," Paige said. "All sorts of delicious things to make with kale."

I liked kale, sure, but… "Um, I hope I can eat that much before it spoils."

She waved her hand dismissively. "It cooks down. Not nearly as much food there as the raw leaves suggest. But if you feel outpaced, I bet your little rabbit friend won't mind helping out."

"Well, thank you so much, Paige. That's *very* generous."

"Of course, of course. I certainly can't eat it all myself. I'm just pleased to find such a good home for the rest." She seated herself happily at my table, looking like she planned to stay a while. She didn't want me to cook up some of that kale right now, did she?

"So…" And I could hardly ask yet again what she was doing—she'd already blithely ignored the question twice. "Can I make you a cup of tea?" No way did I dare offer wine. Paige might be here all night if I did that. I'd really been hoping to make an early night of it.

"That would be lovely!" James by now had leaped up onto her

lap, which Paige hardly seemed to notice, much less mind. "You wouldn't happen to have Pineapple Ginger Pear, would you? That's my favorite these days."

"Uh, no; sorry. All I have is green, mint, and English Breakfast, but it's probably too late for anything caffeinated, huh?" *That's right, it's late, hint hint.*

"Mint sounds lovely, thanks. They have Pineapple Ginger Pear at the co-op, though. You may want to try some. It's very good."

"Okay. Thanks." I filled the kettle and got it going on the kitchen stove, and pulled out the box of tea and some cups. What the heck, I had to try again. "So, you were in the neighborhood, because...?"

"Nothing like a lovely stroll by starlight to wash away the cares of the day."

She walked down here. Because of course she did.

Now she waved me over to the table. "Come sit while that kettle heats. Let's catch up a little."

We had just spent an evening together at Lisa's a couple nights ago. There was in fact plenty to catch up with since then...though how Paige Berry should know that...

But I dutifully went and sat down across from her. Paige leaned in, gazing at me rather gravely. "How are you *doing*, dear?"

"Oh...well, except for what happened to poor Marie, I'm good, I think."

Paige just continued gazing at me, as if I hadn't answered. When I was about to cringe and fill the silence, she said, "I was very sorry to hear about you and Kip."

"*What?*" How could she possibly—oh, of course. Harris and Sherry, already? This dang island. "I'm not sure what you mean," I said, though. I'd make her spell it out, at least.

"I so enjoyed getting to know you both during that whole azalea fiasco," Paige said. Her voice was warm with sympathy. "You were so charming together."

"But we *weren't* together. We haven't *ever* been together. Everyone here has just completely misunderstood things."

She nodded sagely. "I agree entirely. That's mostly what people do—here or anywhere." She leaned back at last, to James's approval; now she could scratch his ears more easily. "But I'm still sorry you two have broken things off."

I stifled a sigh. There was clearly no point in beating this horse. People would just have to accept the truth eventually. "How do you even know about that? It was just this morning."

"Oh, you know how people talk. Anything that more than one person knows is, by definition, not a secret here."

Right. So, Sherry…or…please, not Jen. Maybe one of them had gotten Harris to make a copy of the security video. Was everyone watching play-by-plays of my conversation with Kip right now on those big TV screens at the Tavern?

"Happily," Paige continued with a grin, "no one of any consequence is speaking unkindly about it—which is always fortunate in situations like this. Porter and I were not so lucky, as I'm sure you recall."

So, what, someone *inconsequential* was saying mean things? About me, or about Kip? Or both of us? Anyway, I was so *not* going to extend this ridiculous conversation by asking. I would no doubt hear all of it from Jen soon enough.

"You're being very strong about it," Paige added. "I salute you for it. Lisa will, too."

No, no, no. This was too ridiculous. "Paige, please, listen to me," I finally tried. "There has never been, and was never going to be, anything between Kip and me. People he works with thought there was, and it was getting him in trouble, for nothing. Which is why I had to go down there today and clear things up. Kip asked me straight out where on earth I'd gotten this whole idea from, and whether he'd ever done anything to give me such an idea. And I agreed that he hadn't—ever."

"I know, dear. It's very moving. You're both putting such a brave face on things. But that's not what I was referring to, actually. I meant the brave face you've put on *everything* that's happening." Her expression, already warm, became almost maternal. "You've been doing that for quite a long time, haven't you, dear." What? "Doing...I'm sorry; I'm completely lost. What do you mean?"

"I'm a gardener, dear," she said serenely. "It is my work to observe growth."

I blinked. "What growth?"

"What growth indeed!" Paige said, leaning in again. "From all I've heard, you've been acting very much like a woman who's recovered something she'd misplaced. Something important, if I'm any judge; which, despite the painful lessons I learned last winter—thanks to your kind intervention—I still flatter myself that I am."

All I could do was just keep staring at her. "Paige, I...don't know what else you've been hearing about me, but I don't understand. What's this about?"

"Well, I have no real idea," she said, as if that should have been obvious. "That's what I've come here hoping to find out. I do tend to *intrude* at times, though. As you know." She looked down and shook her head. "One of my foibles, I'm afraid. Everybody's got them." Now she met my gaze again. "*Everybody*, dear. And if I'm doing it again, I certainly apologize."

"You don't need to apologize. I just can't make heads or tails of anything you're saying. What do people think I've *recovered*?"

"Oh! Nothing, I'm sure. Everything I've been hearing is very complimentary, I assure you. I'm the only one who thought that maybe you'd recovered something. I should have made that clearer."

A loud shriek filled the room just then, startling the bejabbers out of me before I realized it was the tea kettle. I stood up to turn it off.

"And perhaps I've got it wrong," Paige said, also getting to her feet. "I often do." She smiled at me, and then down at James, who had been so still and quiet on her lap that I had almost forgotten he was there. Now he blinked up at both of us from the floor, clearly annoyed that lap-time had ended. "Thank you for a lovely conversation, dear," Paige went on. "I should probably be getting along now."

"No, please. Wait," I said. My skin was prickling, as if I were going to chameleon…except, that wasn't it this time. It was my hair standing up all over my body as I realized what I had, in fact, recovered—just last night—and that no one, anywhere, could have told Paige that. "The…the water's ready," I stammered. "Can I give you that cup of tea, at least, before you leave?"

Paige's brows climbed slightly. "Well, I can't see why not. If you'd like that. That's very kind of you."

She sat down again, and James immediately resumed his position. I went to the stove to pour two cups of water over mint tea bags, and brought them to the table.

"Oh, that steam is lovely in this chill, isn't it?" Paige murmured, leaning down to waft it dramatically toward her face while inhaling deeply.

"Can I ask you a question?" I said, looking down into my cup—anywhere except at Paige.

"Of course."

"How do you make all of your vegetables grow so big like that?"

She chuckled softly. "That's little to do with me. The soil and sun do all that work. I just…add water, and a sprinkle or two of fertilizer now and then."

I took a deep breath and looked up, straight into Paige's milky blue eyes. "I…don't think that's what I meant to ask," I said quietly.

"Oh?" She gazed placidly back at me. "What did you mean then?"

"I mean… What was going on at the Brixtons' guesthouse the other day? Why didn't anybody seem to care that you were there? Why did you warn me not to talk until we were in the kitchen?"

She gave me a quizzical half-smile. "I'm not completely sure what you are asking, dear." Her tone was so gentle.

"What *are* you?" I asked, barely whispering.

Paige's smile grew a little sadder as she shrugged. "I'm a gardener, as I told you. I grow and tend things. What are *you?*"

"I don't know," I admitted, barely breathing.

She nodded thoughtfully, the half-smile still there. "Well, when you do, I think we should talk again."

She knew very well what I was trying to ask. I understood that. And I knew just as well why she wouldn't answer. My teacup became compelling again; I couldn't drag my gaze anywhere else. "My mother," I started. "Not the mother I have now; I mean my birth mother." Paige nodded. "She was mentally ill."

"She may have been, yes," she said quietly.

My chest tightened around an urge to cry. I shoved it down. *She knows. This woman knows.* "My…my stepfather killed her," I whispered. "In front of me. When I was…very young."

I glanced up under my lashes for just long enough to see Paige close her eyes and purse her lips. Her upper body seemed to tremble for a moment. Then she grew very still, her eyes remaining shut, and nodded, just once.

I knew if I didn't get this all out quickly now, I never would. "After that, I think I began to think…that maybe I was just like my mother. That what had happened to her…"

"Would happen to you." She stretched an arm across the table and laid a gnarled hand beside the cup I was staring into. I looked up into her eyes. They were open now, and moist with unshed tears. "But it hasn't, has it? If you were mad, my dear, we would all know by now. You are clearly not your mother. Nor is her life yours in any way. You know that by now."

"You know what I am asking, don't you."

"I hear what you are telling me," she said.

"Then why won't you just answer my question?"

That ghost of a smile returned. "I told you, dear. I will answer your question as soon as you can answer mine. Until then, no answer I can give would help you. It might even hurt things more. And you have had so much more than enough hurt already. Thank you for telling me about it." She reached up and gently touched my cheek. "A very brave face indeed."

She climbed to her feet again, her tea steeped but still untouched. "Put this tea in a pickle jar, dear," she said, her voice strong and confident. "It'll keep very nicely until we're ready to drink it—which shouldn't be too long, I think. Now, I really must be on my way. Thank you for entrusting me with so much, and rest assured that not a living soul will ever hear a breath of what has passed between us here. This island is a gossip's paradise, but I am not entirely the fool I so often seem."

I stood too, and went to pull the door open for her. At the doorway, Paige turned, put her arms around my shoulders, and laid her head in the crook of my neck. It was the most natural thing in the world to hug her back, to breathe in her scent of forest and wool and goat milk and…something else. "Everything will be fine, dear," she murmured in my ear. "Trust. And take the leaps that come. Take them *all*. Life is too short for hesitation."

Then Paige disentangled herself and marched through the doorway.

"Do you want a ride home?" I called after her.

"No, dear. I have more to think about than such a short walk will give me, and the stars are safe company. Sleep well, brave girl, and thank you. I'll be back for that tea, never fear. So don't you think of dumping it out."

By the time she was finished talking, Paige was already too far into the trees for me to make out anymore. But I knew she'd be fine—more than fine. I felt no fear for that woman's safety.

In fact, I could find no fear of anything inside myself now. Only an inviting urge to climb into the loft and put all of this behind me until morning.

CHAPTER 17

It was barely six a.m. I hadn't emerged from under the cozy warm covers yet, just not quite able to face the enormous effort of climbing down the ladder and building a fire and making coffee and *all that*. I squinted up at the ceiling of the loft. Had I really just heard someone knocking? At this hour?

It came again. There was actually someone at the door downstairs.

I sat up, trying to peer down at the doorway, but whoever they were, they were not standing helpfully in front of a window. Dang this clever privacy. The solid wood door revealed nothing.

"Just a minute!" I called down—though it came out as more of a croak. "I'm coming."

There was no sign of James anywhere as I levered myself out of bed, then struggled into the leggings and sweater I'd left piled beside the bed last night. I grabbed my phone and hurried down the ladder, wondering who in the world could be knocking on my door this early—without calling first. Could it be Lisa? Back already?

Colin?

Certainly not Jen, she was not a morning person.

Maybe *Kip*?!

By this time I'd made it across the tiny room, I opened the

door…

Only to find Sheriff Clarke gazing back at me.

I froze, a jolt of electrifying dread coursing through me.

He gave a tiny nod. "Sorry to bother you this early, Ms. Tate, but your presence is wanted at the county courthouse in Friday Harbor, and unfortunately time is an issue. I'm here to ask if you'd be willing to come with me."

"To Friday Harbor? Right now?" My mind raced through possible explanations, though it was obvious, wasn't it? *Oh Jen, now we are going to jail!* So much for how calm and clever and mature I'd been last night.

"Yes'm."

I buried my face in my hands. "I know why you're here, Sheriff. I told her this was stupid, and she knows it was now, and she's so sorry, she told me last night how sorry she is, but she has a heart of gold—pure gold—and I swear she only meant to help you guys by—"

"Ms. Tate," he cut me off, his gaze rolling upward to the porch ceiling, "may I remind you that you have the right to remain *silent*." He looked back down at me with a professional, if somewhat strained, smile. "I would list the rest of your rights if this were an arrest, but it is not. For reasons I cannot presently elaborate on, this request had to be delivered here, now, and in person. I regret any discomfort that necessity has caused you, but are you willing and able to come back with me to Friday Harbor, or not? Yes or no will be sufficient."

My mouth fell open. "You're…not here to arrest me?"

He sighed, and gave me a weary look.

"Then, what *is* it about?"

"All I'm authorized to tell you now is that some colleagues of mine wish to consult with you."

Who authorizes the sheriff? I wondered, though this answer too suggested itself. "About what?"

"As I just said, ma'am, I am not authorized to say more at this time." He stood there, tall and authoritative, waiting for my answer. Then he glanced over at the absurd garbage bag full of kale that Paige had left last night, with its leafy bits poking out of the top. It looked like...

"It's kale!" I cried. "Kale, from, uh, a friend's garden." The sheriff just stared back at me. "Do you want some?"

"No, thank you." He cleared his throat. "So..."

"Right. Going to Friday Harbor. Can I put some shoes on first?"

"That's a yes then, Ms. Tate?"

I blinked. "Oh, right; sorry, yes. But I'm not going all the way to San Juan without shoes—and my purse. I'll be right back, okay?"

"Actually, Ms. Tate, I must ask a second favor that'll probably sound even stranger. My boat's tied up at the Brixton estate's dock. I'd like you to wait here for about five minutes while I get back to it, then come join me there, as unobtrusively as you can, please. It's important that you avoid engagement with anyone before we leave."

He was right. This was getting weirder by the instant. "So... you're leaving now, without me, and in five minutes you want me to sneak down to the Brixtons' dock without being seen by... who exactly? My employer, Lisa Cannon, is away on business, and I'm pretty sure the only person staying next door right now is JoJo Brixton—who usually sleeps at least 'til noon. Who am I hiding from?"

"Ms. Tate, I understand how strange all this must seem, but time really is short for us right now, and I can't keep—"

"Is there someone on this property who shouldn't be?" I cut in, my skin beginning to tingle—just when I absolutely, completely *must not vanish* right in front of the county sheriff. "Am I in danger? Is that why you're here?"

He actually, literally rolled his eyes. "No ma'am, you are not in any danger at all. And I really can't explain the whole dang shebang to you now. We've gotta go. So either you trust me and do as I've asked, or you just tell me no, and I'll leave you be. It's your choice, and you'll be just fine either way."

I nodded, gently rubbing my arms, trying to make it look natural and normal. *Sure, just chilly in here, yep.* "Okay, sorry... But you can see how weird this is, right?"

"Believe me, ma'am, I can," he said, turning to leave. "Weird as hell—every last damn bit of it. Come meet me in five minutes, and don't dawdle, please."

And then he turned and walked off, not waiting for any further reply.

I closed the door, put my shoes on, grabbed my purse, then looked around wondering what else I needed to take. I saw my phone charge cable; I yanked it from its outlet and stuffed it in my purse. I didn't care what he said, I was obviously in some kind of very deep trouble. Being allowed one phone call before they tossed me into a cell wouldn't do me a lot of good if my battery was dead. I opened a kitchen cabinet, looking for a nutrition bar. Who knew whether breakfast was included in this package? Then I could think of nothing else—until James came trotting down the ladder from the loft, whining plaintively and racing to his food bowl.

"Oh my gosh! Where have you been, spooky boy? I almost let you starve!" As I filled his bowl, I realized I'd forgotten to ask the sheriff how long I might be gone. (Not that he would have told me, I thought.) Was I going to need someone to feed the animals? "You watch over Master Bun, James, okay? I'm gonna toss some food in his hutch, and I don't want any raccoons sniffing around here, got it? That's your job, James; are you listening?"

I petted him as he dove face first into his food bowl, ignoring me completely, as usual. Then I went out and fed Master Bun too, glancing again at the bag of kale. *Later. I'll deal with it later.*

Back in the house, I looked at my phone. Gosh, maybe it would have been smart to check the time when Sheriff Clarke left. Well, it had to have been at least five minutes by now. Time flies—whether you're having fun or not, it seemed. I headed for the door. "Bye, James!" I called into the cabin behind me. "I'll be back before dinner." *I hope.* "Be a good boy—and remember, no raccoons!"

Then I pulled the door shut, locked it, and set off.

It was a crisp, pale morning; pretty day for a morning stroll. If only that's what I was doing. I walked past Lisa's darkened, silent house, then down the path between the estates, carpeted now in tule fog. Then I turned toward the water and the Brixtons' dock, looking for one of the patrol boats I'd seen around before—with the word SHERIFF painted along its sides.

Instead, Clarke was moving around the deck of a small, unmarked boat, readying things for departure.

What is this?

I stepped onto the dock. The sheriff jumped ably out, helping me aboard and into a seat on the tiny deck. "See anyone along the way?" he asked, casually.

"No," I said, still wondering who he was so concerned about, and why. "I forgot to ask about my pets. Are they going to need someone else to feed them dinner?"

"Heavens no," he said, not even glancing back at me as he finished readying the boat. "Ms. Tate, it's a lovely morning for a scenic cruise." Now he turned and gave me a brief, tight smile. "May I suggest that you just sit back, relax, and enjoy the scenery? I will not be at liberty to tell you anything more of substance until we get where we're going. All right?"

"Yes, sure, I've got it." I was being asked to shut up, so shut up I would.

But he wasn't wrong. It was a lovely morning, and here I was, finally out on a boat, about to get a closer look at some of San Juan County's other islands—which made me think again, with a twinge of guilt, about Colin.

He was never going to take me out on his boat, was he?

In a minute, we were off across the channel heading out around Shaw Island. This was the same route the ferry had taken the one time I'd been to Friday Harbor. I'd been glued to the window then, of course, but the view was even more spectacular from an open boat.

Cold, though! I shivered and pulled my sweater closer around me, wishing I'd brought a thicker jacket.

We rounded Shaw on our left (and a bunch of smaller islands whose names I didn't know on the right), and sped into the open channel leading to San Juan Island. Gosh, this was certainly faster than the ferry. Maybe I wouldn't freeze entirely to death before we got there.

I don't know where official sheriff boats moor up, but unmarked private boats apparently just find space at the regular public dock. The sheriff pulled a baseball cap low over his eyes, then turned and offered his hand to help me off the boat. "It's a short walk, just a few blocks."

"That's fine."

"And…as before, we're trying not to attract attention. I'll go on first, and you follow in a bit. You know where the courthouse is?"

"Um, no?"

He gave me a tired smile. "Two blocks up, two blocks over. You can stay close enough to see me."

They were very *uphill* blocks, even the "over" ones. I was nice and warm by the time I got to the courthouse.

The sheriff was waiting by a back door. He hustled me politely through it, into forgettable hallways and then a small conference room. We were clearly in some non-public portion of the building. After showing me to a chair, he said, "Can I get you a cup of coffee?"

"Uh." Yes, coffee sounded fabulous, and I was now sorrier than ever that I hadn't gotten up and brewed a pot at home; but all I could see when he offered was that nasty styrofoam situation he'd left sitting untouched at our last interview. "No thank you." I smiled uncertainly up at him.

"All right. I'll be back in a moment with the others."

And then I was alone in the room. I sat there, wondering yet again what kind of trouble I was in. Where this was all going.

A few minutes later, the door opened and Clarke returned, followed by Agent Veierra and the Mountie, Inspector McMichaels.

Oh my gosh the Feds. Apparently I was right: that's who could tell a county sheriff what to do. Had Clarke just been lying to me until they had me safely here where they could lock me up and throw away the key?

Or…were they expecting me to rat Jen out?

Then I remembered my panicked babble at my front door. Oh no! Had I already ratted Jen out?!

Lisa was right! I really wasn't very good at discretion, was I? I had so much to learn.

Too bad it was too late.

"Good morning, Ms. Tate," Agent Veierra said, breaking into my self-flagellation. "And thank you for coming over to talk with us under such unusual circumstances with so little advance notice."

I just nodded, afraid to say anything at all now.

McMichaels gave me a friendly nod (Canadians are so polite). Everyone sat down around the table.

"I know you have a lot of questions," Veierra continued, "which we will do our best to answer now. But allow me to get things started by explaining why you're here."

"Yes please," I said. I sounded small and frightened even to myself.

"As I'm sure you've already guessed, Ms. Tate, we have been struck repeatedly during our investigation of all the recent strange events on Orcas Island by how often you have seemed to end up in the most unfortunate places at just the right times."

I knew it, I knew it; I'm their prime suspect, just like Jen said. I hunched in my chair, waiting for the hammer to fall. Was there any way to convince them they were wrong without getting into my chameleoning?

At least if we did that, they'd throw me into a loony bin instead of jail.

"I am also aware," Veierra went on, "from things you've said to both Sheriff Clarke and to Deputy Rankin, that you've apparently been made to fear you are a suspect in these killings and other incidents."

Kip ratted on me? Well, of course he did. In fact he didn't even have to; I'd done it myself. Making sure it was all public and recorded and everything. Yep, I'd clearly been failing at discretion pretty much everywhere, with everyone.

"So, first off, Ms. Tate, allow me to make it very clear that you are not, and never have been, any such thing."

I stared at her. "I'm not?"

Veierra didn't quite suppress a smile. "No. Whoever led you to believe otherwise was entirely mistaken. We did look into your potential as a suspect early on, of course, as we have done with others seemingly no less tied to these events than you were. But nothing in your profile indicates more than an unfortunate, but coincidental, attachment to people who may or may not actually be entangled in these matters."

"Well…thank you! That's a relief."

McMichaels cleared his throat. Politely, of course. "Remarks you made to Sheriff Clarke this morning, however, suggest you may have knowledge regarding the placement of a surveillance device in my hotel room recently."

Crap crap crap! I should have known I wasn't off the hook—and all because of my own big, sloppy mouth. Well, if they thought I was going to throw Jen under the bus here, they had another—

"While Agent Veierra and I find no pressing reason to look further into that helpful insight at present," McMichaels continued, "it might be best to inform whomever may have put it there that should anything like this occur a second time, we might feel very differently about pursuing it."

And now I stared at him. "Oh! Really?" I gulped. "You mean, you're not going to...press charges?"

"Not if it all stops right now," he said mildly.

"Thank you! I...I promise it has already stopped. She only meant well, but she knows she was an idiot now, and I can guarantee you, she won't try anything like that again."

"Well, that's taken care of then." McMichaels turned back to Veierra and nodded.

I exhaled in relief, then looked around the table, waiting to see why I really was here.

"However, Ms. Tate," Veierra said, obliging me, "over the course of our investigation, Inspector McMichaels and I *have* been struck, repeatedly, by one other rather strange thing about you."

Oh, here it comes. If I wasn't a suspect in any of these crimes, and this wasn't about Jen, then what else could I possibly have done that would seem strange to them? *How many ways can even I screw up?*

Then I saw it. I closed my eyes in despair before I could think not to. *Someone's seen me vanish. That's what this is. Oh crap, do I lie? Or would that just make things worse? How much do they know? What on earth am I going to tell them? I can't even explain this to myself!*

"While we'd have expected even one, let alone so many traumatic experiences would leave you eager to place yourself as far away from further potential risk as possible," Veierra went on, "you have exhibited a...well, almost a *reflex* to move closer in. To involve yourself even more deeply in the affairs of those most closely linked to these events. And it's come to our attention that you and Deputy Rankin instigated some sort of informal investigation into a local conflict involving *azaleas* this past winter? Is that right?"

My head was already shaking. "No—I mean, well, yes, we...

got involved in that; but I didn't *instigate* it. That was all Paige Berry—she practically pushed me into the whole thing. And then, well, I'm afraid I dragged Kip—uh, Deputy Rankin—in because he was worried about me—about my safety, I mean, and okay, I kind of used that to, to, to persuade him. But none of that was his fault. Please don't blame him! Did he tell you about this, or was it someone else? Never mind; it doesn't matter. That was my bad, not his, but I really wasn't instigating anything there. I just wanted to—"

"This!" Sheriff Clarke cut in, speaking for the first time since returning to the room with Veierra and McMichaels. "This is what I'm talking about. Can you really imagine that this girl could possibly—"

Agent Veierra's hand shot up, palm-out, to silence him. "I heard you before, Sheriff, and I am not oblivious to your point," she said, somewhat severely, "but I would very much like to hear whatever she has to say, on her own behalf, please, before you've started spelling out the answers for her."

"I beg your pardon, ma'am." He looked genuinely chagrined. "And yours," he said to me, before falling silent again with down-cast eyes and a single little nod to no one in particular.

"Let me clarify again, Ms. Tate," said Veierra, "that we are not here to get you, or anyone else I am currently aware of, into any kind of trouble. It's seeming surprisingly difficult to convince you of that, though we have bent nearly backward several times already trying to." All this was said with a slight smile. "The primary reason you were dragged over here without warning at such an early hour this morning is that Inspector McMichaels and I are being called away on other, somewhat urgent business in," she glanced at her watch, "a little under an hour. I believe it will help us get through our business here if you can just relax, and stop defending yourself at every step from one wholly imaginary threat after another. Can you do that for us, Ms. Tate?"

I stared at her in surprise. Oh, she was being so gentle. So patient. All sorts of assumptions I'd been harboring since Clarke showed up at my door—no, long before that—suddenly became glaringly obvious. And when they did, they began to shift. Dumbfounded, I nodded. "I'm sorry."

Veierra shook her head, still wearing a kind smile. "There is no need to *apologize*, Ms. Tate—for anything. Not to us, at least. Understood?"

"Yes. Thank you."

Veierra drew a deep breath and exhaled. "Good. So then, perhaps we may actually owe *you* an apology, because the truth is, we have probably contributed to your mistaken concern about being a suspect in these crimes by conducting interviews and other interactions with you rather…aggressively in an effort to… Well, to put it plainly, Ms. Tate, we've been hoping to discourage you from continuing to stick your nose into our business. But when we discovered your friend's little bugging device in Inspector McMichaels's room the other evening, we finally admitted defeat—and decided to try other tactics."

"Wait, you knew all along?" I asked. "Who put that there, I mean?"

Her eyes narrowed just a bit. "Did Inspector McMichaels not already make that clear?"

"I thought he'd just figured it out because of what I said to—"

"Ms. Tate," McMichaels put in, "it took ten minutes to figure out where that thing had come from, and what it did and didn't mean. That wasn't your fault either. I was just putting things delicately in order to leave us all a little more wiggle room, though I think we're past needing it now."

"So, here's the bottom line," Veierra said, clearly beyond ready to move things along. "Since it seems that nothing's going to discourage you from poking your nose into these matters, we've brought you here to ask whether you'd be open to the possibility of working with us to assist, *formally*, in this investigation."

CHAPTER 18

For a moment, my mind went blank. Just completely blank. I knew what all those words the FBI agent had said meant…they just didn't have any meaning, put together like that.

Assist? In the *investigation?*

Me?

Veierra continued smoothly. "And just to be very clear, this invitation would not extend, in any way, to your friend Jennifer Darling. You would need to persuade us right now, convincingly, that you are capable of leaving her not merely *out* of any work you do with us, but completely unaware of your involvement in any way. You are entirely free to tell us no. If you do, we'll just have you sign an NDA, which stands for a non-disclosure agreement, and send you on your—"

"I know what that is," I said, still trying to get my mind in full gear again. "I just signed one the other day. But…are you saying…?" *Good grief. Were they asking me to become a* cop?

"What I'm saying, Ms. Tate, is that we could actually use some extra eyes on the ground at this point, and although we do have some concerns about your capacity for discretion, there are a number of other things about you that would be uniquely useful in this regard."

Discretion. There was that word again. "Like…what?"

"Well, you already happen to be pretty deeply embedded in close relationships with a number of the people we are actually investigating, for one—a fact that must never, and I mean *never for any reason*—be repeated to anyone outside of this meeting."

I shook my head. "It won't be, but… Never mind. It won't be. Is that all?"

"No, actually. There's also the surprising and useful combination of having been so quickly and widely accepted and liked in this usually insular community, and your utter lack of prior history here. And it's even useful that so many people assume, for various reasons, that you're an important suspect in this case, as that will make it much easier for us to communicate with you without arousing suspicion. If you agree to help us, we may even work to amplify that misunderstanding so that we can haul you in for questioning more frequently."

This is completely cookoo! I can't be… Except I just had to hear it all. "What exactly would you want me to do?"

"We would like your help as what is called a 'confidential informant,' meaning that you would just go on being you, doing exactly what you're already doing now, with all your normal friends and acquaintances—including Jennifer Darling. My earlier caveat was not meant to suggest that you should curtail your friendship with her in any way. In fact, the last thing we would want is for anything about you or your life to change in any detectable way. The only thing you'd be doing differently is keeping your eye out for information related to persons or topics we'd alert you to, and reporting occasionally on whatever you've heard or observed regarding those specific topics. You would never be required or expected to report anything about anyone else, or on any matter unrelated to the specific persons and subjects we had clearly asked you to watch for. In other words, you *wouldn't* be a general snitch for law enforcement, now or ever."

I cannot be a cop! Which I had no idea how to say to a room full of, basically, cops.

"Well?" McMichaels asked pleasantly, after the silence had begun to stretch a bit.

Veierra said, "You could help us keep others from being harmed or killed, Ms. Tate. You could help keep Marie Tolliver safe. Her expedited toxicology report has just come back—one of the reasons we must leave today—and she was definitely poisoned; possibly something worse than that. I can say nothing more about it, but I do not believe she is out of danger yet."

"Lisa…told me about the actors." *But I still cannot be a cop.*

"Yes. Lisa Cannon's troupe of actors are exactly the sort of people we could use your help with. I understand you've written a play they will be performing soon."

"Yes." *They know everything, don't they. Everybody thinks they're such bumblers. But they clearly aren't.* "But Lisa Cannon is one of my best friends here, and my employer. It was her I signed the NDA for the other day. And, I'm sorry, but no way could I spy on her. If that's what you're hoping, I can't do it."

Veierra shook her head. "She's not one of the people we want your help with. So that shouldn't be a problem."

Thank goodness. Did that mean Lisa wasn't on their suspect list either? I sure hoped so, but then again, it might just mean they have somebody else to spy on her.

Still…that wasn't the real problem, was it. What if I didn't agree to help them now and then Marie got murdered for real next time? Or if not Marie, then—well, anyone else? There had already been far too many bodies found around the island. And then of course I had the horrible vision of Jen, unable to stop sticking her nose into all of this, ending up being one of them.

"I… I'm sorry," I said, wiping away a sudden tear. "This is so unexpected. And so, well, complicated."

"Yes, we understand," Veierra said. "And, again, you're free to say no, but we do need an answer one way or the other before you leave this room. All our immediate to-do lists will be affected by your choice."

I did want to help. I really did. My new life on Orcas Island would be so much nicer without all the scary intrigue. And if I could help get things settled down…?

I glanced over at Sheriff Clarke. The guy who clearly thought, and not without good reason I will admit, that I had too big a mouth. If I said anything of what I was thinking right now, how much worse would my nice new Orcas life be?

McMichaels had always seemed like a nice enough fellow, from all I could tell, but…

"I know you're all in a hurry here," I finally said, "but would it be possible for me to talk about this privately with you, Agent Veierra?" I swallowed, trying not to glance at the two men there. "I mean, just the two of us? Only for a minute?"

Glances were exchanged around the table, then shrugs. The two men rose silently. McMichaels gave me a smile as they both left the room, closing the door behind them.

Agent Veierra gazed neutrally at me, waiting.

I was really going to do this, I thought with amazement. "I was raised as an adopted child," I began. Not two days after finally allowing myself to think about all this without shutting down, now I was going to tell someone else even this much of it—a *cop*, no less. Life was…so strange. "My birth mother was mentally ill." The words felt like they squeezed out of a tight little space in my throat. I felt a bit short of breath.

Veierra nodded. "We have already checked into your records and background, Ms. Tate. I am, of course, interested in anything you wish to tell me, but I know the basic facts of what happened with your parents, if you'd rather not…"

I looked down, nodding. Of course they knew. Of course they would have checked long before anything came to this. They knew everything.

Well, except maybe this: "My stepfather called the police to come restrain my mother lots of times before…what happened, and…" I looked up at Veierra, suddenly frozen, caught wordless between an urge to cry, and a fierce desire to scream my rage at people just like…

No, not like Veierra, actually. That was why I asked to talk to her about it. But just like Clarke, and who knew about McMichaels? Who would he have turned out to be in a similar situation? "They didn't help her," I said, pulling myself back together by sheer brute force. "They didn't want to. And when he finally…tipped his hand, and they came to take me away from him, they didn't want to help me either."

Veierra's face remained unchanged, except for the slightest tightening around her eyes and mouth. "I understand," she said. Just those two words. But underneath her perfectly professional restraint, I heard sorrow, and something more. Anger? I wasn't sure, but it was there, and I knew I'd made the right decision in picking Veierra to say this to.

"I…respect most of the officers I've met since coming here, including you. I've grown to like a few of them much more than I ever thought I could. But in general, Agent Veierra, I have a lot of anger at policemen, and…" I shook my head, and could feel my shoulders hunching, almost against my will. "I can't be a cop. Explain that to the others in whatever way you have to, but, I'd like it if there were a way to keep from insulting every law enforcement officer in this county."

Veierra drew a long breath, and let it out in a slow exhale. "I am…honored that you feel I can be trusted with this, Ms. Tate, but—"

"Cam. Please, if it's all right, can you just call me Cam? In here, at least?"

"Of course." Again, that ghost of a smile. "The first thing I need to say, Cam, is that no one has asked you to become a 'cop'. Nor will they; because that's not what you are, or will be, or will be seen as by anyone—least of all, cops themselves. No one's going to give you a badge, or a weapon, or any special training, or even a single privilege or power of authority that any other civilian citizen in this country doesn't already have as well. You're not going to hang out with any of us, or slap backs and tell jokes over a beer, or whatever else you may imagine cops do when they're alone together. No one would allow you to presume you were a cop just because you're helping us, even if you wanted them to. You will be just what it seems to me you have been trying to be all along: a local resident eager to help solve these mysteries and bring horrible people to justice, while protecting innocent people, including your friends. The only contact you would have at all with cops would be occasional briefings, which, as I said before, are likely to be only slightly more cordial than any of the times you've already been questioned. Nor will anyone in this community, or anywhere else, ever hear about or be given cause to guess your role in these matters. That's all guaranteed in great legal detail by the NDA you would be signing." She spread her hands. "*No one* is *ever* going to see you as a *cop*. Does that help at all?"

I was so busy trying to absorb everything she was saying, and figure out how I felt about it all, that I couldn't begin to figure out what to say to her.

"I will be sorry if you say no, Cam," she went on. "We're not going to find anyone else here nearly as well suited to these tasks as you are—and I'm not just talking about how conveniently you happen to be situated in this community right now."

I looked up at her. "What's so special about me? Besides my incredible talent for discretion, I mean."

Veierra smiled ruefully. "Is that really something you can't manage, Cam? Because all you need to do is say it is, and you're off the hook. No need to explain anything else to Clarke, or anyone."

"No. That's not the problem, actually. There are plenty of things about me that no one's ever known—or ever will. Not even you guys, who know every secret in the world." I was pretty sure about this now. If they'd known…it would have come out by now. "So you can trust me on that. And the last few days have been like a crash course for me in all the ways I've been an open book to everyone without ever guessing it. Believe me, that's going to change now, too, whether I do this thing with you guys or not."

"Good," she said. "And I believe you."

I smiled. "Thanks." But I just had to know. "So, what are these wonderful qualities in me that you won't find anywhere else?"

"Your character, Cam. Your unusual honesty—provided you can edit it some. Your equally unusual loyalty. Just here this morning you have tried to protect all sorts of people for things that weren't actually your problem, and from which they really needed no protection—apparently unconcerned for potential costs to yourself. And, frankly, your strength and humanity too."

I knew I was just staring at her, but she hardly blinked. "Strength? Me?"

"Oh yes," she said, with emphasis. "How many people who've been through traumas like the childhood you just discussed with me do you suppose prove able to set that down and become the kind of well-liked, deeply respected and appreciated person that so many very different people on this island seem to have embraced? Many of your friends here have real discomfort with each other, Cam, but they all think the world of you. We've interviewed quite a few of them, so I know. Moving from your beginnings all the way to who you are today took more strength than most people could imagine, I believe." She tilted her head, as if weighing some decision. "As did the favor you performed for Deputy Rankin yesterday morning."

I gaped at her, even if it would have been harder to believe by now that she *wouldn't* know.

"That was the right thing to do, Cam," she went on. "And a lot of people wouldn't have done it. Whatever you may suppose about Sheriff Clarke, he respected you for that. And I see no reason why you shouldn't know that it was he who more or less confirmed our interest in you for this task after that interview a few days back."

Ohhh. "Is this what that was about?"

Veierra nodded. "When he told us how you pretty much worked out the whole thing about Marie Tolliver's missing phone right in front of him—and then read him the riot act about being so transparent as well," Veierra's smile became very wide, almost a laugh, "even he had to admit that you seemed a natural at investigative deduction."

"Holy cow," I murmured. Then the obvious next question occurred to me. "Did Deputy Rankin know this? I mean about why I was really being brought in?"

Veierra shook her head. "No one here beneath Sheriff Clarke himself knows about this level of our investigation—including and especially Deputy Rankin. Way too much turbulence in those waters to risk letting him have any idea about our interest in you."

I was starting to get light-headed from so many revelations all at once. "Is that why he's being cut out of the loop on things? Because of me?" Just as I'd expected...except not for the reason I'd thought, not at all.

"Largely, though not entirely," she said. "Which is why even Deputy Sherman grudgingly respects what you did yesterday."

No, I wasn't buying that one. "Sherman? Nope, not her. That woman hates me, and I have no idea why!"

Veierra shrugged. "She doesn't, really. Well, I mean, yes, she does in a way, but only because of your association with Deputy Rankin. It's really him she can't stand. You're just collateral damage of a sort."

"Really..." Despite myself, I was curious. "But...I don't even have any association with—" I caught myself just before I could say *Kip* "—Deputy Rankin. Didn't I make that clear to everyone yesterday?"

Veierra just gave me a *Girl, puh-lease* look. "What you made quite clear is that you're aware and respectful of more than yourself."

Hm. "So, Sherman's gonna like me now? Good to have a little time to get used to the idea before she gets all smiley with me someday on the street."

She chuckled. "Cam, use some of that deductive ability we were just talking about here. Deputy Sherman is a woman in a man's profession—who really does want to be a cop. A top-flight, respected officer of the law. But while she does everything thoroughly, capably and carefully by the book, guys all around her, like Harris the womanizing gossip, not to mention Rankin who has violated all kinds of parameters about appropriate and professional behavior during the past year—these guys get pats on the head from colleagues and superiors while Sherman remains ignored and disliked. Yes, her own problematic personality has something to do with that, but it wouldn't if she were a man, would it. And Deputy Rankin is like the poster child for everything that triggers her. He likes you, Cam—no matter what he said yesterday—so Sherman doesn't. Is that really so surprising?"

"Wow," I said, taking that all in. "I never saw *any* of that." I smiled at her. "You ever thought about going into detective work?"

"I have, in fact." Just then, there was a quiet tap on the door. Veierra looked down at her watch. "And right now that work calls me away. I'm sorry, Cam, but we're out of time. What's it going to be? Yes or no? Will you help us—as nothing but a good-hearted citizen with really excellent reasons not to care much for cops?"

I bit my lower lip, wishing I could have more time.

"I don't mean to pressure you, Ms. Tate," Veierra said, suddenly all professional and formal again. "But the life you save could be Lisa Cannon's. Or Jen Darling's, or even your own. Whoever did this to Marie may well have reason to want any of them out of the way by now as well."

And at that moment, Paige Berry's voice came back to me. *Take the leaps that come. Take them all.* "Okay—I'll do it," I blurted, over the lump in my throat.

Veierra got up and opened the door. "Have you got it?" she asked McMichaels, standing there. He handed her a document—a lot thicker, I noticed, than the single page Lisa had had me sign. Veierra came back to set it down in front of me, along with a pen. "I do have to go, but when you've had a chance to read this over—"

"I don't need to," I said, picking up the pen. "I know you're not trying to trap me, and I'm doing this now—no matter what's written on all this paper. I won't understand half of it anyway. Just show me where to sign."

"I don't think... Are you sure?" Veierra asked. It was the first time she'd sounded even a tiny bit uncertain.

"Yes. Let's just do it."

"Okay. I guess it's only going to matter for half an hour anyway now." I wondered what she meant by that. Why only half an hour? But she was clearly in a very big hurry, so I let it go. She reached down and started turning pages, stopping at one near the bottom of the pile. "Here." I signed. She flipped to the last page. "And here, Ms. Tate."

I signed again.

"Thank you, Cam," Veierra said. "I appreciate this—personally."

I looked her in the eye and nodded. Feeling like I'd done the right thing.

"Now that this is done," she went on, "there's someone else you should meet. We've had another operative in the field for some time now, and you'll be working with him, sometimes very closely. He can fill you in on lots of other things you'll want to understand, I'm sure, and with the NDA taken care of, I just have time to walk you down the hall and introduce you, unless you need a moment first?"

"No, I'm fine." Someone *else* had been stalking around our lives in hiding all this time? Who in the world could it be? "Let's go."

Veierra handed the signed document to McMichaels as we walked out. "I'll meet you at the car in ten minutes," she told him. He nodded and walked away; Veierra led me in the other direction.

Several corners later, we came to yet another door in the labyrinth of the inner courthouse. Veierra gave a perfunctory knock before pushing the door open, waving me through ahead of her.

I walked into another conference room almost identical to the one we'd just left, and turned to see—

"*No!*" I gasped. "Oh, *no, no, NO!*"

"*Dah*ling! Welcome to the team!" JoJo Brixton, in all his cheerful outrageous glory, rose from his chair, his arms spread. As if he thought, what, I might run giggling up to hug him or some dang thing? "I'm so glad you said *yes!*" he went on, delight infusing his every word. "It will be such a relief to stop tiptoeing around things finally. And that sweater, by the way, is fabulous on you. Sets off your hair magnificently."

I whirled to face Veierra. "Is this…some kind of *joke? This is not possible!*"

She just looked past me, impassively, at JoJo. "Congratulations, Mr. Brixton. It looks like you've covered your unfortunate tracks quite well. You got lucky. Now try to learn something from your mistake." She wagged a finger at him. "No more freelancing."

"No ma'am." He seemed as close to chastened and respectful as I'd ever seen him. Even when he was apologizing to me. "I have learned that lesson all the way down."

"Good." Veierra turned back to me. "I really have to go now, but I imagine you two will have lots to discuss. When you're done, Ms. Tate, or just can't take any more of him, use this." She handed me a pager. "Sheriff Clarke will come and take you through the rest of your orientation." And then she was gone.

I turned back to JoJo, still too astonished for words. An entire cyclone of implications began to dawn on me.

"I told you I had reasons," he said soberly. "Very compelling ones."

<<<>>>

RECIPES

Lisa's Amazing Posole

Lisa didn't make this herself, but she knows who did.

Ingredients:
1 pound dry prepared hominy
8 tomatillos, husks removed
2 green bell peppers
2 seeded serrano peppers
2 small or 1 large yellow onions, quartered
8 cloves garlic, peeled
1 Tbsp. cumin
2 tsp. sugar
3 Tbsp. dry oregano
Juice of 2 lemons
2 Tbsp. olive oil
2-pound pork shoulder roast
96 ounces of chicken stock
sea salt and fresh cracked pepper to taste
If you have a jar of green salsa in your fridge, pull that out too

Toppings:
Sliced radishes, sliced avocado, shredded cabbage, sour cream, cotija cheese, chopped onions, etc.

Method:
Soak the hominy kernels for 6-10 hours. Strain and add to a large pot. Cover by two inches of water. Bring to a boil, then reduce to a gentle simmer until the hominy is chewy but not overdone (1-2 hours). Drain and set aside. (This can be done a day or two in advance.)
Roast the tomatillos, both peppers, onions, and garlic in a 400

degree oven for 20-25 minutes. Save the juices! Add the roasted veggies and their juices to a blender, along with the spices and the lemon juice; blend thoroughly, and set aside.

Season the pork with salt and pepper and put it in a large Dutch oven or other large heavy pot with the olive oil; brown on all sides. Add the blended veggie mix, chicken stock, and green salsa (if using); bring to a boil, then simmer very low, covered at least at first, for three hours or until the pork is absolutely falling apart. You should be able to push it apart (and off the bone, if any) with your cooking spoon. Then add the reserved hominy, let it get back up to temperature and cook for a little longer, thinking about itself.

Serve in soup bowls with the toppings of your choice. Naturally, this freezes wonderfully, and is even better after aging a few days.

Apricot Relish Used in Hipster Ex-Boyfriend's Pork Sandwiches

Ingredients:
1 small onion
3/4 cup dried Mediterranean apricots
1/2 tsp. large grain garlic salt
1 tsp. powdered yellow curry
1 Tbsp. dried thyme
2 Tbsp. chipotle infused olive oil
3 Tbsp. rosemary infused olive oil
4 Tbsp. Blenheim Apricot infused vinegar (split 2 & 2)
2 Tbsp. simple syrup infused with lemongrass & ginger
1 Tbsp. Sweet Heat BBQ sauce (any smoky sweet & spicy BBQ sauce will do)
2 Tbsp. sweet red pepper onion relish

Method:
Slice onion into paper thin shreds

Chop 1/3 of dried apricots into large chunks, and remaining 2/3 into finer pieces.

Sautee sliced onion and chopped apricots on medium low heat along with garlic salt, yellow curry, chipotle infused olive oil, and 2 Tbsp portion of apricot infused vinegar until onions are clarified and mixture has begun to brown.

Now add dried thyme, red pepper onion relish, and BBQ sauce and continue sautéing for two more minutes.

Finally, add rosemary infused olive oil, remaining apricot infused vinegar, and lemongrass/ginger simple syrup and stir just until whole mixture is back up to full temperature.

Then turn off heat entirely, mound contents in center of hot pan and let sit until pan has cooled.

Any unused portion may be refrigerated up to one week for later use.

Spread generously onto thick slices of crusty, fabulous bread, then load sandwich with roasted pork tenderloin slices—or any other meat of your choice.

House-made Limoncello

Courtesy of an Italian auntie, that's why it's in metric.

8 or 9 large lemons
1 liter pure grain alcohol (Everclear or similar)
350 grams white sugar
1 liter water

Peel the lemons of their zest only (no white part). Put the peels in the alcohol, cover, and let sit for a month. Dissolve the sugar in the water; when cool, strain the peels out of the alcohol, and add the lemon infusion to the water. Bottle in attractive little bottles and drink carefully. Serve very cold (it's best kept in the freezer).

Chili The Best Way

Canned chili with beans, your choice
Pre-grated cheddar cheese
Chopped onions (you need to chop these yourself)
Crackers (optional)

Heat and serve, does this really need explaining?

What To Do With Thirty-Three Gallons of Kale

If you have any ideas, please let Cam know.

ACKNOWLEDGMENTS

The still-imaginary Laura Gayle would like to yet again thank the very real authors Shannon Page and Karen G. Berry for bringing her to life, so that she could write yet another book.

Shannon and Karen would like to once again thank Sergeant Herb Crowe of the San Juan County Sheriff's Department, this time for sartorial advice specifically, as well as his ongoing general support and good cheer.

We would like to thank our husbands, Mark and Tony, for their love and help and support (and in Tony's case, ten hours of driving). Mark also went above and beyond, giving us editing and plot help, in addition to designing and executing the compelling cover.

Karen would like to thank Shannon and Mark for their week of generous, safe, and quiet hospitality, which made progress possible on this book and at least one other.

Thank you to the whole team at Book View Café for production help on this book, especially Sherwood Smith for her careful proofreading and Jennifer Stevenson for her lovely formatting of the ebook.

A million thanks to Jenny and Kelly and the rest of the team at Darvill's Bookstore for their AMAZING support. Thank you to Chaz Brenchley for posole guidance, and to Rancho Gordo for making such incredible hominy and including it in the quarterly bean box.

Shannon thanks her dear auntie Susan Dutton in Italy for the house-made limoncello recipe—in this book, and in her freezer.

And thank YOU, our dear readers, for continuing on this ride with us!

Photograph by Mark J. Ferrari

Laura Gayle is the nom de plume of two friends who love to collaborate.

Shannon Page was born on Halloween night and raised without television on a back-to-the-land commune in northern California. Her work has appeared in *Clarkesworld, Interzone, Fantasy, Black Static*, Tor.com, and many anthologies. Books include the contemporary fantasy series The Nightcraft Quartet; fiction collection *Eastlick and Other Stories*; personal essay collection *I Was a Trophy Wife*; hippie horror novel *Eel River*; cozy mystery series the Chameleon Chronicles, co-written with Karen G. Berry; and *Our Lady of the Islands*, co-written with the late Jay Lake, as well as a forthcoming sequel co-written with Mark J. Ferrari. Her many editing credits include the essay collection *The Usual Path to Publication* and the anthologies *Witches, Stitches & Bitches* and *Black-Eyed Peas on New Year's Day: An Anthology of Hope*. Shannon is a longtime yoga practitioner, has no tattoos (but she did recently get a television), and lives on lovely, remote Orcas Island, Washington, with her husband, author and illustrator Mark Ferrari. Visit her at www.shannonpage.net.

Karen G. Berry has lived in or near Portland, Oregon, for forty years, but remains solidly Midwestern in outlook and recipes, which is why you never find any of hers in the recipe sections of the Chameleon Chronicles. She has one wonderful husband, three wonderful daughters, two wonderful grandsons, and several thousand books. A marketing writer by day, Karen is a prize-winning poet and has published seven novels and one nonfiction book, *Shopping at the Used Man Store*. As a committed underachiever, Karen finds all of this fairly amazing. Visit her at www.karengberry.mywriting.network/.